DEATH & THE VIKING'S DAUGHTER

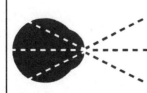

This Large Print Book carries the
Seal of Approval of N.A.V.H.

AN AUCTION BLOCK MYSTERY

Death & the Viking's Daughter

Loretta Ross

THORNDIKE PRESS
A part of Gale, a Cengage Company

GALE
A Cengage Company

Farmington Hills, Mich • San Francisco • New York • Waterville, Maine
Meriden, Conn • Mason, Ohio • Chicago

LIBRARY OF CONGRESS CIP DATA ON FILE.
CATALOGUING IN PUBLICATION FOR THIS BOOK
IS AVAILABLE FROM THE LIBRARY OF CONGRESS

ISBN-13: 978-1-4328-5102-6 (hardcover)

Published in 2018 by arrangement with Midnight Ink, an imprint of Llewellyn Publications, Woodbury, MN 55125, USA

Printed in the United States of America
1 2 3 4 5 6 7 22 21 20 19 18

This book is dedicated to the memory of my big brother, Jerry Dean Hicks, whose service in Vietnam inspired Death Bogart's service in Afghanistan. R.I.P. Semper fi.

ONE

"Now, there's a body in the rosebushes. Is that gonna be a problem?"

The stairway that climbed the south wall of the living room rose at a gentle incline. There was a floral-patterned carpet runner down the center of the hardwood steps and a sturdy bannister. The whole thing was beautifully proportioned, elegant without being pretentious.

Wren Morgan leaned on the newel post and studied Myrna Sandburg.

"You mean like an old grave? Like from the 1800s?"

"Oh no. We put him there in '92."

Myrna, Wren judged, was in her mid to upper seventies. Her white hair was cut in a fluffy bob and she wore pumpkin-colored polyester slacks and a pale gold sweater that appeared to have been crocheted by hand. She did not look like a homicidal maniac.

"Well, who was he?"

"Oh, I don't know. Just some drifter that was passing through. We never knew his name. We call him Bob. John Doe seems like such a cliché, don't you think?"

"Mrs. Sandburg, I don't understand."

"Well, it was because of the eminent domain, you see."

"Not really . . . Was the government trying to take your house?"

"They didn't actually try, per se. But at one time they were certainly talking about it. You know, this road out front, it doesn't really go anywhere now."

"Yes, I noticed that." It was one of the things Wren found attractive about the property. It was the last house on a two-lane blacktop. County maintenance on the road ended just past the driveway and the surface quickly deteriorated before disappearing under the lake. Anyone living there would have a decent road to drive on, but the traffic would be all but nonexistent.

They were only about four miles outside the East Bledsoe Ferry city limits, but it would be as quiet as living far out in the country. Thomas, her burly old tomcat, and Lucy, her three-legged hound, should be safe from traffic without having to be penned up in a small yard. Wren had a weakness for strays.

"Well," Myrna said, "back in the early nineties some of the county road board members started talking about putting the road back through. It would be massively expensive to take it back along the old route, though, because when the dam went up and Truman Lake came in it covered more than a mile of roadway. But a couple of them fellers got the bright idea that if they ran the road right through my living room and down the back of our land, they'd hit a narrow point on the lake and it wouldn't cost so much to build it. Well, we weren't having any of that. So we talked to a lawyer and he told us that if there was a cemetery on the property, the government couldn't take it. So we went to the coroner's office and asked if he had a body we could have, and he did."

"I see," Wren lied. She frowned, staring at the opposite wall. The room was an absolutely hideous shade of pink, but it could always be painted. "And they just had a body lying around that they let you have?"

"Pretty much, yeah. Of course, it was just bones by that point. Some hunters found him in the woods sometime in the mid-eighties. They couldn't tell the cause of death, but they figured it was probably from exposure. They never did identify him and no one came looking for him, so they said we might as well lay him to rest. So we put him in the rosebushes, with a nice little stone and everything."

"Okay, I understand. And did that get rid of the government?"

"It did. Well, that and they found out it was still going to cost a couple of hundred thousand dollars. They decided maybe they didn't need a back road shortcut to Toad Suck that bad after all. So, do you like the house?"

Wren took a minute to look around again before she answered. It was a sprawling combination of country farmhouse and Queen Anne Victorian. The rooms on the first floor were large and airy, with wood floors and high ceilings. There were four bedrooms, one of them tiny and tucked under the eaves, a wraparound porch, and a real turret. Most of all, the house just *felt* good. It had such a warm and welcoming atmosphere that even the knowledge of Bob's presence didn't put too much of a damper on Wren's enthusiasm.

"I do," she admitted. "Though it is a bit bigger than what we were looking for. I'll have to have my boyfr— I mean, my *fiancé* come out and look at it." She ran her fingers over the ring on her left hand, reminding herself that it was real.

"You aren't looking together?"

"We thought, to start out, we'd each go look at houses on our own, as our schedules allow. When we find one we think might work, we'll have the other check it out and go from there."

"But you're going to have him come look at this one?"

Wren smiled, understanding the older woman's eagerness.

"Yes, I am. I know you're anxious to sell. Won't it make you sad to leave, though?"

"Oh, it will. But time marches on. And it hasn't been the same since Brendan passed. I'm going to Chicago. My oldest son and his wife have built me a little cottage in their back yard, so I can live close but still have my privacy. I've never lived in a city before. It should be interesting. Always something to see or do." Myrna took a light jacket from a hook by the front door. "Come outside and let me show you the property."

Wren obediently followed her out. November had settled, melancholy and dismal, over the Missouri countryside. The year was flying by, Halloween a memory already and Thanksgiving just a couple of weeks away. The thermometer in her truck had read in the low forties when she arrived, so it was still too warm for the snow that was forecast. More likely, if the heavy gray clouds produced anything it would be a stinging, cold rain.

It had been a dry autumn and they could use the moisture. But it would still be depressing, as the fading daylight and falling temperatures always were.

The house faced west, where the narrow, winding ribbon of road led to the main highway to the north. East Bledsoe Ferry, where Wren had grown up and lived all her life, was to the northwest. To the southeast was nothing but woods and lake. A small herd of horses occupied a field across the road and the nearest neighbor was almost a mile away.

"It's peaceful," she observed.

"That it is. In the spring, of a morning, the woods fill up with songbirds and you can watch the sunrise over the lake from the east window in the turret. On summer nights there are thousands of tree frogs and crickets singing in the darkness, and owls, and whippoorwills."

"It sounds lovely."

Myrna led her around the house to the southern side yard. "There are sixteen different kinds of rosebush planted here. Oh, I wish you could see them in bloom! I always get such a showing from them. Bone meal. That's the secret. Lots of minerals."

There was a small, simple gray stele in the middle of the winter-bare canes. Myrna gave Wren a shrewd look.

"The kind you buy at the store," she added. "Not Bob's bones. Bob's in a box."

"Okay, great! Thanks for clearing that up."

They strolled on around the house. The yard was circled by field-fence, but it looked more decorative than something intended to keep anything out. On the back lawn there was a grape arbor and a clothesline. The gentle mound of a storm cellar rose in the southeast corner, and the northeast corner was obviously a vegetable garden, tilled and mulched now in preparation for the coming of spring.

Beyond the fence, the land sloped down to a wooded hollow.

"There's a creek that runs across, along there." Myrna pointed. "It empties into the lake. It's not big enough to fish or anything, but it's good for wading. The lake is shallow at the edge there and there's a sand beach, so you can swim if you don't mind a few fish and a little mud. The government has an easement all around the lake, so the property line actually stops fifty feet shy of the normal waterline."

"Any flooding?"

"A little, when there's really a lot of rain. At its highest, though, it's never gotten as high as the tree line."

They continued on, back to the front. Wren was silent, pensive.

"So, what do you think then?"

"I think it's nice," she said.

In fact, she thought it was too nice. She considered herself a simple woman with simple needs. This house and land seemed like more than she had a right to claim. It was too elegant. It was lovelier and more comfortable and more spacious than she deserved.

But it wasn't only about her anymore. She was looking for a home for Death. He'd had a rough time of it. He'd been wounded nearly to the death, left disabled and out of work. His parents had been killed in a car accident, his brother had been lost to him, seemingly forever, and he'd been betrayed and abandoned by his wife. Alone, in pain, homeless and penniless, he hadn't complained or given in to despair. He'd soldiered on and fought his way back.

If there was anyone in the world who had a right to a safe, comfortable home, it was Death. Wren wanted that for him, wanted it more than anything. And she could see them living here. She could imagine herself cooking in the big, light kitchen, the two of them hanging out in the living room on a lazy Sunday night. There was a small room downstairs that Death could use for a home office. In December they could hang Christmas lights from the gingerbread trim and put a lighted tree in the bay window.

She could see them relaxing on the lawn on a summer evening. Lanterns hanging from the trees and fireflies chasing among the horses in the field across the road. Cold beer and baseball on the radio in the twilight with Thomas lounging on the porch rail and Lucy in the side yard.

Digging up Bob.

"So you're going to have your young man come look at it?" Myrna asked again.

"Yes, I am. I have your number, I think. I'll have him call you and arrange a time."

"Well, I'll look forward to meeting him, then. What's his name?"

"Death Bogart."

"Deeth?"

"Yes. It's spelled like 'death' but pronounced 'deeth.' His mother was an English Lit professor. He's named after a detective in an old mystery series by Dorothy Sayers."

"Wow." Myrna blinked and tipped her

head to the side thoughtfully. "That makes Bob sound downright boring."

Death Bogart pulled his 2001 Jeep Grand Cherokee off the state highway and down onto a blacktop road that had seen better days. Off to his left, up against the edge of the autumn woods, stood a faded billboard, weathered to the point that it was barely legible:

OZARK HILLS SUPPER CLUB
Cold Creek Harbor — 4.1 miles
Members Only

The road wound north, through the trees, following the line of the lakeshore so that every now and then Death caught a glimpse of silver water through the branches. The edges of the road were ragged, with chunks of asphalt falling away onto the verge, and the surface was littered with potholes that would swallow a lesser vehicle. It was narrow and he hoped not to meet any cars coming the opposite direction. Both would have to drop their outer wheels off onto the soft edge to pass, and the hills and curves were dangerous.

At the end of the road was a rusted old bridge that hadn't been maintained, and it was barricaded and no longer safe to drive on. A gravel path led away to his right, toward the lake, and opened out into a pair of parking lots. The lot on the left, against the creek, contained a single car: a clean, newer-model sedan. From this parking lot, a wooden footbridge crossed the creek. A split-rail fence lined a path through a sparse stand of trees, and in the distance Death could see a collection of unpainted buildings, weathered dark gray. They looked like the outbuildings of an abandoned farm, but the path was neatly maintained and there was a flag flying above the largest building.

The lot to Death's right was crowded with a familiar collection of cars and trucks, many of them with the logo of Keystone and Sons, Auctioneers, on the side. They were clustered in front of a low, sprawling building with the Ozark Hills Supper Club logo fading away on the front. At the northwest corner of the building stood a massive metal pole, its yellowed white paint flecked with rust. It had a large bracket at the top, but the sign it had once held was long gone. Behind the main building, a small, tall building stood right up against the water's edge. A sign painted high up on the side read *Ozark Hills Supper and Yacht Club Boathouse.*

Death drove slowly past the collection of vehicles, but Wren's truck was not among them. Michael Keystone, just coming out of the building, waved to him. He was the youngest son of Sam Keystone, one of the twin brothers who owned the company. Death rolled down his window to talk.

"No Wren today?"

Wren had known the Keystone family since she was a child and had started working for them right out of college. She was an assistant auctioneer and an expert appraiser.

"She's supposed to be along in a bit," Michael said. "We thought she was with you? She said she was looking at a house."

"Yeah. We're not looking together right now. We both have an idea what we want so she's looking at some and I'm looking at some, and if either of us finds one that looks promising, then the other will go see it and see what they think."

"That makes sense. Well, she should be along anytime now. Why don't you wait for her? You can have my parking spot. I'm right up here by the door."

"Oh, I can park over there somewhere." Death's combat injuries had left him with a severely compromised lung capacity, a weakness that he hated to acknowledge. He

18

had a handicapped parking tag in his glove compartment, but stubbornness (his brother called it "idiot jarhead pride") kept it there.

Michael waved one hand dismissively. "You might as well take this spot. I have to leave anyway. The electric company was supposed to have the lights on for us, but apparently there's a line down somewhere. They can't tell us how long it'll be, so I'm going to go get a generator and some gas to run it."

"Need any help?"

"Maybe getting it started when we get back. We haven't used it for a couple of years, I don't think. Go on in and take a look around. This place is nuts. Just take a flashlight."

Death backed out of Michael's way, then maneuvered his Jeep into the vacant spot when the younger man was gone. He dug a flashlight from between the seats and climbed down, popping the collar of his denim jacket against a stiff breeze. Dead brown leaves chased each other across the gravel lot and a high-altitude wind sailed small black clouds along the underside of the silver-gray overcast.

The building had an air of faded grandeur that was out of place on the deserted lake-shore. The walkway across the front was paved with tan stones in an ornamental pattern and empty fountains flanked the double entrance door. Broken metal poles embedded in concrete outside the entrance suggested that a canopy had once covered the door.

The right-hand door stood ajar. Death pushed it open and ventured inside. There were no windows and he had to snap on his flashlight to find his way.

To his immediate right was an enclosed booth, like the ticket booth in a theater. A faded painted sign asked people to please show their membership cards and offered coat checks for fifty cents. Past the reception area a dark hallway ran left and right, parallel to the front of the building. In the circle of his flashlight, the hallways were papered with a garish, busy design. He ran his hand over it and found that the palm trees and tropical fruits were embossed. Fake potted palms stood in recesses every ten or fifteen feet and Death, stopping to examine one, was surprised to find they were made mostly of curled and rolled art paper.

He followed the right hallway until it divided into an enclosed stairwell and a smaller corridor that turned left and dead-ended beyond a single doorway. That door led into a small dining room with tiny windows and three other doors leading off of it. One door led to another long corridor that ended in a set of restrooms. One of the others led into a smaller dining room, and the other led into yet another corridor that seemed to have no outlet.

From this corridor Death could hear familiar voices, just faint enough that he couldn't make out what they were saying. It made no sense to him to have a hallway that led nowhere, and he paced up and down it three times trying to figure out what the point was. It was only when he noticed an anomaly in the beam of his flashlight that he realized there was a doorway right in front of him, camouflaged to look like part of the wall. The wall here was made of decorative paneling that mimicked the texture of a coconut and there was another wall of the same material some four feet inside the open door, so that you had to step into the wall, then turn left or right to enter the next room.

Shaking his head, Death went through and found the Keystone twins, not surprisingly, bickering with one another.

The original sons in Keystone and Sons, the twins were identical, but dressed and acted so differently that you'd never know it unless you were told. They were in their early sixties now, with their own sons and grandsons to help them run the business their father had started. Roy always wore overalls and a flannel work shirt, and Sam invariably dressed in a suit with a hat and a string tie.

Roy was standing precariously on a rickety table, his head bent sideways under the ceiling, trying to pry up a ceiling tile.

"It woulda been a stupid thing to do," he was saying.

"I'm not saying it wasn't, although they didn't know that yet, I suppose. But that's what they did. I'm sure of it. I remember reading it in the *Record* at the time."

"You remember a forty-five-year-old newspaper story?" Roy scoffed.

"I remember things," Sam countered. "That's what people with brains do. I don't expect you to understand, of course."

Death looked to the side, where Roy's wife Leona and Sam's wife Doris were seated on barstools, setting up a filing system in a portable case. The room was large, with a bar along one wall. Short screens and artificial plants divided the open space into cozy dining areas and a dance floor. "Do I want to ask what they're arguing about?"

The women smiled at him. It was Leona

who answered.

"Sam thinks this place was modeled after the Beverly Hills Supper Club."

"Ah. Should I know what that is?"

"Was. And not necessarily. It was before your time. It was a fancy nightclub in Cincinnati —"

"Kentucky," Sam corrected her. "It was across the river, in Southgate, Kentucky. But just outside Cincinnati."

"Right. Whatever. Anyway, it burned down in the late 1970s. It was a terrible fire. Well over a hundred people killed."

"And Roy's trying to climb into the ceiling because . . . ?"

"One of the things that made the Beverly Hills Supper Club fire so bad," Roy said, climbing down carefully, "and there were a lot of bad things about it, was that there were no firewalls. The floor plan was a maze, no clearly marked exits, and some of the exits were locked. The place was full of flammable materials, no smoke detectors, no fire alarms, and no sprinkler system."

"The wiring was a nightmare too," Sam said, "and there were way more people present than the building had the capacity for. This room, for example, corresponds to what was called the Cabaret Room in the original building. Now, the one in Southgate was larger — this place isn't an exact copy and the original was still being modified and added onto when this place was built in the early seventies. Anyway, the Cabaret Room in the original had a seating capacity of about 650, but the night of the fire there were more than a thousand people there."

"More than a thousand people," Death said, "trying to evacuate a burning building through that maze of corridors?"

Leona had her phone out, looking up the fire. "One hundred and sixty-six fatalities," she said. "The fire started in the drop ceiling of one of the rooms across the hall. Two employees found it just about a minute before 9:00 p.m. It was only smoldering until they opened the door and then, with the rush of oxygen, it flashed over. The building was rated for a total capacity of 1,500 people but there were an estimated 3,000 actually present. The fire department was called at 9:01 and arrived at 9:05. A busboy stopped the show in the Cabaret Room and began the evacuation at 9:06. The power failed at 9:10."

"We tend to forget how quickly tragedy can strike," Sam said.

"All but two of the bodies they pulled out of the ruins came from the Cabaret Room,"

Leona continued, studying her phone. "There were double doors opening into the corridor. Volunteer firefighters said they found the living and the dead there, all together, stacked like cordwood."

"All that," Roy said, "in spite of the fact that there were clear zoning and building laws that should have kept the Beverly Hills Supper Club from operating under those conditions."

"So why . . ." Death waved one hand around at the darkened room and the building in general. "I don't understand why someone would build a replica of a big, fancy nightclub out here in the middle of nowhere in the first place."

"You haven't met Claudio Bender," Doris said.

"He's an odd duck," Leona explained.

"Odd how?"

"Hmm. How do I describe him? He's this little old man with white hair, kind of looks like Santa might if he were thin and shaved. He has one of those mobility scooters he takes with him, and he rides that everywhere while his son follows him around doing whatever he says and not talking or anything."

"I'm afraid Mr. Bender is obsessed with material possessions," Sam said.

His brother snorted. "Ya think?" Roy turned to face Death directly. "He got in touch with us right after we contracted for this auction and told us that we need to check with him about everything in here before we sell it, to find out if it's something he wants to keep."

"Don't the owners of what you're selling do that sometimes?"

"Sometimes. But he's not the owner. He sold the place, lock, stock, and barrel, back in the early eighties."

"Ah. What did you tell him?"

"I told him no."

"The issue we have here," Leona said, "is that out here away from any municipal boundaries, there aren't really any zoning or building laws. Even though it's not an exact replica of the one that burned, you can tell by looking at it that this place is poorly designed when it comes to safety. We want to be sure to know all of the problems with it before we try to hold a public auction in the building. We also want to be able to give any prospective buyer a comprehensive list of issues that will need to be addressed, if we're going to auction off the property."

"I thought you had some big hotel chain that wanted to buy the land and raze the building?"

"There was a developer that showed interest, but I think he drifted off when the Vikings next door wouldn't sell."

Roy climbed back up on the table and smacked his palm against the ceiling tile. "Anybody got a hammer?"

Death froze suddenly and held up his hand. "Wait? Did you hear that?"

"Hear what?" Doris asked. "I didn't hear anything."

"I thought I heard someone yelling for help. There it is again. From outside, maybe. What's the quickest way out of here?"

"This way," Leona said, leading him to the back of the building as Roy climbed down and the others followed. Another camouflaged doorway led to another dark corridor that angled off to the left and ended in a glass door. Beyond the door lay a landscaped garden between the building and the lake, its stone paths and fountains and statuary overgrown with dead and dying weeds. The door was locked, but Leona had a master key on a key ring in her hand and she wrestled it open.

Once they were outside, the could clearly hear young voices, coming from the north, crying for help. They rounded the building in a group, Death's damaged lungs slowing him down and Roy Keystone outpacing all of them. The rest of the family was converging on teenaged Robin Keystone, who was crouching beside a huddled figure on the footbridge over the creek.

Death, ever the Marine gunnery sergeant, pushed through the crowd and took charge.

"Robin, what happened?"

"I don't know," he said. "I just happened to look over and see him. He was standing on the bridge, looking at the lake, and then he kind of staggered and fell. I think he had a heart attack. I don't think he's breathing."

TWO

"Okay, don't touch him. Has anyone called 911?"

"I did." Surprisingly, it was nine-year-old Matthew who answered, holding up a cell phone that Robin quickly reclaimed.

"Okay. Good job there." Death shooed them back and went to one knee beside the crumpled figure. It was an elderly man, he'd guess in his mid-seventies to early eighties. Contrary to Robin's panicked assessment, Death could see the man's chest rising and falling. He checked for a pulse and was rewarded with a faint, fluttering heartbeat. "Who is he?"

"One of the Vikings," Doris said. "Look at his clothes."

The man was wearing a thick blue tunic, tight at the top, that flared out at his waist and reached his knees. He had loose trousers on under it, with simple, leather ankle-length boots. A mustard-yellow cloak, trimmed in braid and fastened at his right shoulder with an ornamental brooch, covered him and pooled around him on the wooden bridge.

"Do you know his name, though?"

"No. I'm sorry. When we were here before we talked to a younger couple."

"Is he dead?"

"Matthew, hush!"

"He's not dead," Death reassured them, though he was concerned with the older man's lack of response. "He's got a bruise starting on his temple. I think he hit his head when he fell. I don't want to move him unless we have to. He could have other injuries from the fall and moving him could make them worse."

Sirens signified the approach of emergency vehicles, the sound growing louder and blending with its own echoes coming back from across the lake. The engine and search and rescue vehicles from the Cold Spring Volunteer Fire Department arrived first, with a sheriff's department cruiser coming right behind them.

Wren pulled in just after the deputy and nearly fell out of her truck in a panic.

"What happened? Is someone hurt? Oh my God! What happened?"

The Keystones drew back to admit the

first responders. Death explained what they knew to the EMT — it only took a few words — and then dragged himself to his feet and went to reassure her.

The younger members of the family were already explaining, in excited tones, what had happened.

"I'm the one who called 911," Matthew bragged.

"Yeah," one of his siblings said, "because he's got experience at that."

"Oh for crying out loud!" Matthew huffed out a breath that lifted a lock of hair from his forehead. "I only set the kitchen on fire one time. Get over it already!"

"Do you know who he is? Or anything about him?" Deputy Orlando Jackson interrupted their conversation. "Any idea what made him pass out?"

"Nope," Death said. "Robin saw him fall and started shouting."

"Is that his car?"

"Probably?" Death said. "It doesn't belong to any of us, and I'd think if there was anyone else on the other side of this bridge all the commotion would have gotten their attention by now."

Jackson nodded once and returned to his vehicle for a tool to open the sedan. On the bridge, the EMTs were working over the fallen man. Death put his arm around Wren and they wandered after Jackson, curious.

He used a slim-jim to pop the lock on the driver's door and stuck his head into the car. There was nothing under the visor, and he spent only a few seconds examining the contents of the glove compartment. Frustrated, he blew out a breath and then stuck his hand under the seat.

"Aha!" He pulled out his finds and laid them on the car seat. "Wallet, cell phone, crap!"

"Crap?" Wren was pale beneath her freckles and her red hair stood out bright around her head. Death knew that following the emergency vehicles to where her friends were had frightened her.

"He's got a medic alert bracelet! Cardiac." Jackson brushed past them and ran the bracelet over to the EMTs, then returned, talking into the radio pinned to his left shoulder. "I've called for a medevac helicopter. We're going to need to find it a place to land. If you've got a medic alert bracelet, why the hell aren't you wearing it?"

"It was an anachronism?" Wren shrugged when he glared at her. "Some of these reenactors take their roles very seriously. If he'd been doing it for very long, it was probably just second nature to remove anything that didn't belong to the era. Who is he?"

"Neils Larsen."

"Well, his name's authentic."

The fire department engine crew was already busy preparing a landing zone for the helicopter. They'd tied a bright red streamer to an antenna on the engine in order to determine wind direction and were using red auxiliary lights to mark out the corners of a large, square section of the open field that ran between the yacht club and the creek, down to the lake.

"Neils Larsen," Death said. "I know that name. I think he's the man whose daughter disappeared."

"What? When?" Jackson reached through the window of his cruiser and turned off the emergency lights. Across the parking lot, the fire-fighters were shutting down their own apparatus, turning off lights and closing the doors and windows and compartments. The Keystones were coming toward them in a group, urged on by a couple of young firefighters. Leona Keystone was busy counting heads, making sure her entire brood was accounted for.

"Back in the late seventies some time," Death said. "Roy Keystone mentioned it and I was curious so I looked up what I could find about it later. Her family lived in

Columbia, but she was last seen alive in Cincinnatti. She disappeared from a Renaissance festival when she was seventeen. Her dad was a guest at the yacht club the weekend she went missing and he said he saw her ghost on the shore. That's why, when they were looking for a place to build a Viking settlement, they chose that plot of land."

With all the sirens turned off, Death could hear the heartbeat sound of an approaching helicopter. An older firefighter waved his hands to get everyone's attention.

"Okay, folks, the medevac chopper is going to be coming in for a landing in just a couple of minutes. I need everyone, and I mean *everyone,* to stay back here, well out of the way. The rotors can come down as low as four feet off the ground and if one hits you in the head, it can kill you. The tail rotors spin so fast they're nearly invisible, and when the bird comes in to land the wind it kicks up is as strong as a hurricane. So stay back, stay together, and you're going to want to close your eyes as it lands so you don't get any dust or debris in them."

The roar of the approaching helicopter reached a crescendo as it came in and set down without incident. The windstorm it created tugged at Death's clothing and pushed against him like a physical shove.

He put his arms around Wren and pulled her against his chest, burying his face in her hair as dry leaves and small pieces of gravel skittered off across the parking area.

The pilot shut the aircraft down completely and waited until the rotors stopped turning before he opened the door for the flight crew. A tall, lanky paramedic got off first, ducked out from under the wide blades, and stopped when he'd cleared their path. He glanced around, anxious, until his gaze settled on Death. Then he caught his eye, nodded imperceptibly, and followed the nearest firefighter to the downed man.

Death sighed.

"Don't roll your eyes because we love you," Wren admonished.

Randy Bogart had been a firefighter and nationally accredited paramedic with the St. Louis Fire Department before he moved to East Bledsoe Ferry to be closer to his big brother. He now worked for the medevac service and served on the volunteer fire department.

"I'm not," Death defended himself. "But you two could not automatically assume that if someone's in trouble where I might be, that it must be me."

"Well," she hedged, "it's not without precedent . . ."

■ ■ ■ ■

When the helicopter had gone, the fire department returned to their headquarters. Deputy Jackson locked up Neils Larsen's sedan and headed back to his own office with Larsen's wallet and phone to try to locate and notify the man's next of kin. The Keystones dispersed to whatever tasks they'd been doing before the excitement and Wren and Death lingered beside the bridge to talk.

"I know we'd be trespassing," Death said, "but I think we should go take a walk around the Viking settlement. Mr. Larsen wasn't expecting to leave like he did. He could have left the place unlocked. There might be a fire going or windows left open. Surely they wouldn't get upset with us if we checked to make sure everything was safe and secure?"

"Do Viking settlements have locks?"

"I don't know." He offered her his arm. "Let's go see."

The creek at this spot was no more than six feet across. The reenactors had bridged that space by dropping a pair of thick tree trunks across the stream. Four uprights, two at each end, were driven into the bank to anchor the trunks, which had been roughly planed to make them more or less even. The walking surface was formed from rough-hewn planks — they still showed the marks of hand tools — lashed to the crossbeams. In lieu of handrails, heavy ropes were strung from the two uprights.

It looked solid and sturdy and didn't shift or vibrate under the weight of their joint passage.

"Did you have any luck with the house hunting?" Wren asked as they passed across the stream and followed a worn path through the early autumn trees.

"Not so's you'd notice. I looked at a beautiful, practically new ranch-style house with massive cracks in the foundation and a 'fixer-upper' between a railroad track and the feed elevator. Nothing enticing. Did you?"

She hesitated. He waited for her to find her words.

"There was this one house . . . It's probably bigger than we need, but —"

"You like it?"

"It feels nice. It's a kind of country Victorian, on six acres, just a few miles out of town on a dead-end highway."

"Sounds great." She was struck by the house, Death could tell, and trying not to push it too hard in case he decided he didn't like it. But honestly, he was ready to go along with anything that would make her happy.

"There's a body in the rosebushes," she ventured.

He looked down at her. "Of course there is."

"Huh?"

"I wouldn't expect you to find a house without a body in the rosebushes."

Wren stopped in the middle of the path, dropped his arm, and let him walk away from her. "Now just what is that supposed to mean?"

Death spared her a brief grin but his attention had been caught by what lay ahead. He nodded to the clearing they were approaching and reached back with his right hand. "Come look. I think we've wandered into Iron Age Europe."

The Viking reenactors' settlement consisted of half a dozen unpainted wooden buildings grouped around a large stone fire pit and surrounded by a split-rail fence. The largest building sat across the compound from the path and faced it. It was a big rectangle, set with the shorter side toward the fire pit and the long side parallel the lake shore. It looked like a big primitive barn, with no windows, a single door made from planks and fastened on with strips of leather for hinges, and a thatched roof that nearly touched the ground.

To its left was a smaller structure that looked like nothing so much as a life-sized manger from a Christmas nativity scene. It had its own fire pit, complete with bellows, and an anvil placed near the middle of the enclosure. The walls were lined with wooden benches and hung with an assortment of ironmongery.

"They even have a smithy," Death observed.

"Do you feel like we should whisper?" Wren whispered. "Because I feel like we should whisper."

Death didn't whisper but kept his voice down. "Why? Are you afraid the Viking ghosts are going to get you?"

"Well . . . yeah."

He chuckled and put his arm around her, drawing her close. "Don't worry. Viking ghosts won't bother you. I imagine they know a fierce warrior when they see one."

"And you're volunteering to be my big fierce warrior?"

"Actually, I meant you," he said. "But I suppose it could apply to both of us."

A gust of wind brought with it a sudden

series of loud knocks and bangs and they both jumped and clung together.

"Hello?" Death called. "Anyone here?"

Only silence answered him, and Wren laughed. "Yeah. We're real fierce. You know what that was?" She pointed to a large tree that overhung the smithy. "The wind knocked down a bunch of black walnuts and they rattled off the side of the smithy."

He stood a little straighter, squared his shoulders. "I knew that."

Hand-in-hand they went forth to explore the deserted stronghold. The rail fence had a simple gate, with leather hinges and a loop of rope to hold it closed. It was standing ajar and they slipped through one at a time without touching anything.

Besides the fire pit, the central clearing held several long tables lined with benches. At the edge of the space was a covered well. They stopped to peek inside, then proceeded to the big building.

"This must be the mead hall," Death said.

There were no windows, only a single door. It was a simple affair, secured with a small board slipped into a pair of wooden brackets. Death lifted it and they peered inside. The interior was dark, lit only by a pale shaft of dim gray light coming down from a smoke hole in the roof. There was another fire pit, more long tables flanked by benches, and shelves on the wall laden with plain ceramic dishes.

There was no sign of fire in the fire pit nor any scent of smoke, so Death refastened the door and they moved on. The smithy and two other simple structures yielded nothing of interest. None of the buildings had windows; all had thatched roofs and handmade furniture. A tiny shed that Death hadn't seen at first, tucked back in the edge of the trees, proved to be a privy.

He wrinkled his nose. "Have I ever mentioned how much I like the twenty-first century?"

"It does have its charms," Wren agreed.

A long, tall building on the beach contained the group's longboat, a vessel Death had heard about from Wren and the Keystones but had never seen himself. It was about twenty yards long, a simple, shallow-keeled boat with a wide bottom. There were oarlocks lined down both sides of the gunwales, and a tall mast, currently bare of its sail, disappeared up into the shadows of the boathouse ceiling.

"Do you think they've put it away for the winter?" Wren asked. "I've never seen it up close before. I thought it would have a dragon on the prow. I'm a little disappointed."

"We'll have to dock them a few points for style," Death agreed.

They closed the door and refastened it. There was only one building left, a small structure no more than eight feet by ten that sat with its back to the lake and its door standing open. Wren stuck her head in.

"Well, that's an anachronism," she said.

Just inside the door was a tall workbench with a three-legged stool beside it. Even in the dim light, a splash of purple shone on the bench.

"Did Vikings have spiral notebooks?" Death asked.

"Or ballpoint pens?" Wren agreed, nodding to the pen beside it. "It must be important for him to bring it here. He wasn't even wearing his medic alert bracelet."

The notebook was open, lying face-down on the bench, and Wren picked it up and turned it over.

Sweetest, softest, fleeting
Songbird, long I sought thee . . .

"He was writing about his daughter!" Wren realized. "I shouldn't be reading this," she said guiltily, laying it back down the way she'd found it.

They closed the door behind themselves

42

and headed back toward the path through the woods.

"Boy, it's a good thing we came over here and closed that door. Otherwise someone might come along and go wandering around their encampment while he's gone."

"You mean like we did," Death said.

"Right. But without our pure motives and good intentions."

"Of course."

They walked together in silence for a few moments.

"It's really sad," Wren said suddenly.

"The old man writing poems about his daughter?"

"She's been gone for all these years and still he comes out here where he feels close to her and sits all alone in that dark little room remembering."

"That's understandable." They'd reached the middle of the bridge now. Death stopped and gently turned Wren to face him, tipping her head up so he could look down into her eyes. "Don't ever get lost. I'd miss you forever."

Her eyes went soft and sentimental. She reached one hand up to cup his cheek and stood on tiptoe. He leaned down, closing his eyes as they drew together. He could feel the heat of her, and the gentle puff of her warm breath on his cheek, when his phone vibrated in his jacket pocket and his brother's ringtone killed the mood.

He kissed her quickly before answering. She was laughing at him as she walked ahead of him off the bridge and back into the twenty-first century. Death put his phone on speaker.

"Hey, what's up? Everything okay?"

"Looks like the old man's going to be okay," Randy said. "I asked him if I could let everyone know and he said that'd be all right. I think he's touched that so many people were worried about him."

"That's great! Do you know what happened? Or can you tell me?"

"Low blood sugar, probably. I get the feeling he hadn't eaten today. And he hit his head when he fell. That's not why he thinks he passed out, though." The younger Bogart's voice held a tantalizing tone that suggested he was holding back on something.

Death decided to play along with his brother. "Okay, why does he think he passed out?"

"He said he was in shock. He said he was just crossing the bridge to go to his car and get something for lunch when he looked up at the window in the sail loft of the yacht club's boathouse, and he saw her."

"Her? Stop playing mysterious, Randy. Who's 'her'?"

"His daughter's ghost."

THREE

"Our best bet, don't you think, is to sort all this silverware into sets and sell it that way?"

Death had left to see a man about a case and Wren and Leona Keystone were in the yacht club's enormous industrial kitchen sorting the contents for auction.

"Dishes, too," Leona agreed. "And I know just the people for a job like that." The Keystone matriarch stepped to the nearest door — a simple, uncamouflaged service entrance — and blew three sharp blasts on a police whistle she wore on a chain around her neck.

"You've got kids here?" Wren asked, curious. It was a weekday and normally they'd be in school this time of day.

"Just my fourth graders," Leona said. "It's a teachers' work day. Didn't you see them during all the excitement?"

"I guess I didn't notice. I —"

"Only had eyes for your young man?" the

older woman teased. "I can understand that. If I were a few years younger, I might have eyes for your young man myself."

"Hey now!"

The door burst open and nine-year-old cousins Matthew and Mercy Keystone charged in. At first glance they did not look like cousins. Matthew was fair and freckled, with red-gold hair and cornflower blue eyes. Mercy was a mixed-race child, a beautiful little girl with dark skin and eyes and shining black curls. But they were built alike, both long and lean and tall for their ages. And both were quick and bright, though Mercy tended more toward being clever, whereas Matthew tended more toward getting into mischief.

"You called us, Grandma?" Mercy asked.

"I didn't do it," Matthew said immediately. "And if I did, she made me."

"Park your bottoms on a couple of chairs. I've got a job for you." Leona set them up at the table with gray plastic bus tubs full of assorted silverware and a box of thick rubber bands and explained what she wanted them to do. "Just put four knives, four forks, and four spoons in a bundle and put a rubber band around it."

"What if there's leftovers?"

"We'll figure that out when we get there."

Wren and Leona set up at the other end of the table with a mountain of china, a simple white pattern with a blue band around the rim, and the four of them set to work. This was the drudge part of preparing for an auction — sorting and organizing mundane things into manageable lots.

"Did you have any luck with the house hunting this morning?" Leona asked.

"Well . . . maybe." Wren shifted a little. "I saw one place. It's bigger than we were looking for, and really, it's nicer than I'd thought we could get. But I think we could swing it, if Death likes it. And I'd really like to give him a nice home. He deserves the best I can give him."

Leona smiled down at the stack of plates she was taping together with packing tape. "So do you, dear."

Wren shrugged and blushed, smiling a little.

"So tell me about it. Where is it? Would I know it?"

"It's out at the end of CC, just before it ends at the lake. A lady named Myrna Sandburg lives there now."

"Oh, yes! The old Duvall place. That was back before you were born though. That is a nice house." She stacked a couple of more sets of plates. "There's a body buried in the

48

rosebushes, you know."

"A body?" Matthew perked up. "What kind of body?"

"A dead one, presumably," Wren told him dryly.

"It was a man who died in the woods sometime in the eighties, probably," Leona explained. "They never found out who he was so the Sandburgs took his body to lay him to rest on their property."

"That's cool!" Matthew said. "Can we get a dead guy and bury him in our yard?"

"I'm gonna say no to that one."

"Do you think the house is haunted then?" Mercy asked.

"Well, I don't know," Wren said. "I guess if we do move in there, we'll find out." She leaned forward over the table and lowered her voice conspiratorially. "Do you know where there *is* supposed to be a ghost, though?"

"No! Where?"

"Right out there in that little building down by the lake. The old boathouse? The old man on the bridge told Randy that the reason he passed out was because he saw a ghost in the window of the sail loft."

The two children went suddenly still, their gazes skittering away. Leona's grandma-radar went off.

"What did you do?" she demanded.

"Nothing!" Matthew replied. "Nothing at all!"

But Mercy's lower lip was trembling and her dark eyes were wide and filling with tears. "We didn't mean any harm," she whispered.

By the time Death hit downtown Kansas City, the worst of the noon rush hour had passed. He found a space in a parking garage next to Barnes and Noble and strolled across Country Club Plaza to the Mercer building, a classy, thirty-plus-story office block with an expensive restaurant on the ground floor and a street musician out front using an amplifier that probably could have qualified as a sonic weapon.

The elevator let him off on the eighteenth floor, into an elegant reception area with plush gold carpeting, dark, cherrywood furniture, and oriental red-and-gold wallpaper. It occurred to him that the last time he'd been in a building this nice he'd been in Afghanistan and it had been on fire.

The receptionist was a small, spare woman in her mid-sixties, with a cap of silver hair and the dark eyes and strong features of a Native American. She looked up at his approach and he stopped in front her of desk with a smile.

"Death Bogart to see Mr. Appelbaum?" He did not offer her his card because he didn't actually know why he was there, and he didn't know if she was aware, or should be made aware, that he was a private investigator. That question was quickly resolved when she touched an intercom button and said, "Frank, your young detective is here."

"Oh, good. Send him in."

The woman smiled at Death and directed him toward a door off to his left, with a marbled glass light and a bronze nameplate. He thanked her and went to meet his newest prospective client.

Frank Appelbaum was a portly middle-aged man who wore his white hair in a conservative crew cut. His eyes were bright and blue, and when he came around his desk to meet Death his handshake was firm but not fierce.

"Mr. Bogart. I've heard good things about you. It's a pleasure to meet you.

"The pleasure is mine, sir."

The office was large. A pair of windows looked out over downtown Kansas City and let in plenty of gray light from the overcast day, but the room still had a crowded, cozy feeling. It felt like how Death imagined the study in an old British manor house would

51

feel. The color scheme here had switched from red and gold to blue and gold. Dark wood bookshelves crowded with old volumes and art objects almost hid the royal blue wallpaper, and the carpet was a rich indigo.

Appelbaum directed Death's attention to the side of the room, where a large easel held a life-sized painting of a woman. She was dressed in an elaborate gown and armor. A conical helmet capped her head. A spear and shield completed the outfit and she stood with her chin raised, looking defiantly at the viewer.

"Do you appreciate art, Mr. Bogart?"

"That's a broad topic. I like some art. This is a nice piece."

"Thank you. The subject in this portrait is my great-great-grandmother. She was a minor opera singer in the first decade of the twentieth century. More well-known in her own time than in ours, I'm afraid. Fame rarely lasts, I think."

"That can be a good thing." Death studied the picture, wondering if this was going somewhere or if they were simply making small talk. Perhaps Appelbaum needed time to work up to the subject at hand.

"Her name was Miriam Appelbaum, but she used the stage name Mimi Blossom. She performed mostly at small venues in the Midwest. There was a time when almost every little town had an opera house, before opera gave way to vaudeville and that in turn gave way to the cinema. She did have one period of brilliant success, though, when she traveled across Europe with a company performing Wagner. Her greatest triumph was as Brynhildr in the Ring Cycle. They appeared before the heads of state," Appelbaum announced pompously, then half laughed at himself and lifted one shoulder.

"Minor heads of state, anyway," he continued. "Deputy ministers and assistant secretaries and illegitimate third cousins of royalty. That sort of thing. At any rate, Mimi was proud of them and of herself. I only knew her briefly, when I was young and she was quite old. She'd sit in her wheelchair in the nursing home with her gaze distant and her eyes shining and sing snatches of arias in a quavering voice. This portrait is one she had commissioned when she returned to the States. It's by Volkmer. Have you heard of him?"

"No, I'm not familiar with that artist. I'm sorry."

"Don't be. He's mostly known regionally. He's generally considered to be technically adept but hardly groundbreaking. More a craftsman than an artist, if you follow me. Still, he had some lovely work and there are a few collectors who quite like him." Appelbaum gave Death a bright, rueful smile. "And now you're wondering if I brought you all this way to ramble on about dead opera singers and obscure artists."

"It's always interesting to learn new things," Death said, "but I will admit that I'm curious."

Appelbaum nodded. He waved Death to a chair and went back around his desk to claim his own seat.

"About twenty minutes southwest of here there's a private museum, the Warner Museum of Frontier Arts. Have you heard of it?"

"No, I'm afraid not."

"It's in Lee's Summit. There was an upscale men's college there in the twenties. It went under after the stock market crashed. The main building was this lovely, Italianate mansion. It was in danger of being torn down before the museum owners rescued it. They bought it and refurbished it to hold their collection." Appelbaum folded his hands on the desk and leaned forward. "The Warner family have been friends of my family for generations. In

1967 my grandfather allowed them to take Mimi's portrait on a long-term loan arrangement. The agreement was that they could display the piece indefinitely, but that anytime a member of the family wanted it back, the museum would return it. Chase Warner, the current museum director and one of my contemporaries, contacted me about two months ago regarding the painting. He wanted to know if it would be okay to allow an art history student to study it using modern technology as part of her doctoral thesis. She wanted to do things like x-ray the painting to look for information about the painting techniques, pigments used, things of that nature."

Appelbaum took a folder from a drawer in his desk and paused a moment, looking down at it pensively but not opening it right away. Finally he sighed, tapped it with his forefinger, and went on.

"When they x-rayed the painting, what they found was another painting underneath."

"But that's not really unexpected, is it?" Death knew he might seem like a big dumb jarhead, but his mother had been an academic and his parents and grandparents had seen to it that he and Randy were exposed to a wide range of cultural experiences.

"No. No it's not. In fact, it would be remarkable if there wasn't anything under the painting. Artists frequently do studies of the work they're painting before they get to the final version. And they're often poor — 'starving artist' is a saying for a reason. Canvas is expensive and it's not unusual for an artist to paint over an earlier work. The reason this painting is cause for comment is because of the nature of the painting under this one. They aren't just able to detect the painting under the painting. Scientists can use the information they find to identify the specific pigments used, and in what combination, and they can actually produce a computer image of the underlying painting."

He slid a sheet of paper out of the folder and pushed it across the desk toward Death.

Death studied it. "A cityscape?"

"Chicago, to be precise." Appelbaum leaned forward and tapped one finger on the picture, pointing out a tall, slender rectangle rising above the other buildings on the right side of the painting. "This building is the Aon Center." He sat back and looked Death in the eye. "Construction on it began in 1970 and it was completed in '74."

Death pushed the paper away and sat back

so he could look at Appelbaum directly. "The painting of your great-great-grandmother is a forgery."

"It has to be. And it's a forgery that was done at some point after my family lent the painting to the Warners."

"Forgive me for asking this," Death said, "but from what you've told me, the original portrait doesn't seem like a particularly valuable piece of artwork, in monetary terms."

"It's not. It's worth a few hundred dollars maybe. Mostly it has sentimental value." He clasped his hands on the desk and leaned forward. "The Warner family are our friends. Their museum has very good security. The painting was stolen and replaced with a forgery while it was in their possession. I need to know how this happened. I need to know why."

Death had never intended to become a private investigator. When he joined the Marines, he'd been choosing a career. If that fell through for some reason, his next choice would have been to either follow in his father's footsteps and go into a career into law enforcement or follow his grandfather and brother into the fire service.

Life, as he had learned, is not interested

in your intentions.

The walk back to the parking garage hadn't been too bad, but then he decided to climb four flights of concrete steps rather than take the elevator. By the time he was sitting behind the wheel of his Jeep, he was lightheaded and had spots in front of his eyes.

He took a few minutes to just sit there and catch his breath. Then, since he wasn't in any hurry, he pulled out his phone and called to check in with Wren. She answered on the second ring and the sound of her voice, as always, made him smile.

"Hi, sweetheart. What's up?" she asked.

"Just calling to check in with my beautiful bride-to-be."

She laughed across the phone line. "I didn't know the Blarney Stone was in Kansas City."

"No blarney," he assured her. "I'm totally sincere. Hey, listen. Have you ever heard of the Warner Museum of Frontier Art?"

"Hmm." Death could picture her thinking about it, closing one eye and wrinkling her nose. "Maybe? I'm thinking they have a buyer who occasionally comes to our auctions, if we have something out of the ordinary. Doris would know." Doris was the company's art expert. "Why?"

"I'm headed that way before I come home. It's connected to a new case I have." He gave her a brief rundown on the case of the counterfeit lady (and laughed at himself as he thought of the title, like Watson writing up Sherlock Holmes' newest adventure).

"Okay, that's weird. Why would anyone go to the trouble to forge a painting that wasn't that valuable?"

"I don't know. I was hoping you'd have ideas."

Wren started to answer him, then paused to speak to someone at her end. Death heard her say "no thanks, I'm fine." In the background he could hear footsteps on a bare floor and the unmistakable sound of police band radios.

"Where are you?" he asked.

"I'm at the sheriff's office."

"Ah." He frowned at his phone. "Do you need bail money?"

"Not yet?"

"Seriously, what happened? Is anything wrong?"

"It's fine. It's just, you remember that ghost that Mr. Larsen said he saw in the old boathouse? His daughter's ghost?"

"Yeah."

"Well, what he saw was Matthew Keystone. He and Mercy were messing around in the boathouse, up in the sail loft, exploring. It was used for storage and there's a ton of junk up there — sails and rope and life jackets and oars and fishing tackle. You name it. Against the south wall there's a row of lockers. They all have combination locks on them and darling Matthew knows how to get them open without the combination."

"That boy's going to be either a cop or a robber when he grows up," Death said.

"Isn't that the truth?"

"So what did they find? Because I'm still not hearing anything that sounds like 'police station' to me."

"A bundle of clothes stuffed into one of the lockers, way back in a corner. It looks like one of the costumes the Viking re-enactors wear. There's an overdress and a pinafore-type thing, and a kind of a headpiece with a scarf to cover the hair. Matthew put the headpiece on and was prancing around pretending to be Miss America. He must have gotten in front of the window and, with his red-gold hair and fair coloring, Mr. Larsen mistook him for his daughter."

"Okay, but . . . ?"

"I'm at the sheriff's office because I brought in the dress and pinafore. They're pretty badly rotted, but they were rolled up and hidden inside a small canvas sail and that probably protected them some. But they're absolutely caked with some kind of rusty brown stain. I could be wrong, but I think it's blood. I don't think Mr. Larsen saw his daughter's ghost at the yacht club the day she disappeared — I think he saw *her.* I think this was probably her costume, and I think it was absolutely drenched in blood."

FOUR

Wren was just saying goodbye to Death when deputies Orly Jackson and Tommy Thomas came back into the room together.

"What I'm saying is that there are protocols for a reason!" Tommy waved his arms at Orly like he was trying to attract the attention of a lazy bull. "If we expect to do good police work, we have to follow the protocols. And not just when it's convenient. We have to follow the protocols all the time!"

Orly was eating something out of a Kansas City Chiefs mug and he spoke with his mouth full. "Blah blah blah. Blah blah blah blah."

"What's wrong?" Wren asked.

"He's psycho," Orly said.

Thomas turned to her, aggrieved. "He used my forensic slow cooker to make noodles."

"I'm hungry," Orly defended himself.

"Some of us have been working all day."

Wren blinked. "You have a forensic slow cooker?"

"It's for boiling bones clean when we find partly skeletized remains. You know? Human remains that are mostly decayed but still have some flesh on them. First we take samples of the remaining tissue, then we have to boil the bones to get the skin and maggots and whatnot off of them, so we can study them for clues and maybe get an artist to do a facial reconstruction on the skull. That sort of thing."

"Gah." Wren moved a little farther from him, disgusted. "Do you get a lot of partly skeletized human remains?"

"None yet," Orly said. "But he's hoping."

"I'm trying to be prepared. Once something has happened, it's too late to be ready for it. And it doesn't help when this wannabe chef comes in and uses my equipment to cook with."

"Jeez! I didn't hurt anything. And I'll wash the slow cooker."

"Like that's gonna help. There will still be traces of your cooking. What happens when I have to send a sample to the FBI and they want to know why the victim has chicken DNA?"

Orly put his spoon back in his mug and

set it down so he could talk with his hands. "One," he said, "if you can't clean it well enough to get rid of traces like that, you can't use it more than once anyway, because the DNA of every previous victim will show up with each new victim. Assuming you ever get more than one victim to work on. And two, you said you take samples before you boil the bones, so there wouldn't be chicken DNA in your samples anyway."

They both looked to Wren, as if she were some kind of judge in their debate.

"I'm still not sure why you have a forensic slow cooker," she said.

"Salvy let him get it last year," Orly said. Salvy was Casey Salvadore, the much-beloved local sheriff. "It was on sale for, like, three dollars on Black Friday."

"It's a valuable piece of laboratory equipment," Thomas insisted.

"Like the blender and the paint mixer?"

Wren made a face at Orly. "It is kind of gross that you're cooking in something that's used to boil maggoty dead bodies."

"Theoretically used to boil maggoty dead bodies," Orly corrected her. "It's not like it's ever actually been used."

"Not on a human," Thomas said, "but I found this roadkill possum . . ."

Orly gave Thomas a look of horror. His

eyes grew wide. He slapped a hand over his mouth and ran out of the room.

"That was mean." Wren peered at the young deputy, studying his face. "You're lying," she decided.

"Maybe I am and maybe I'm not. He'll never know."

Wren sighed and shook her head. "What about the clothes?" she asked. "Could you find out anything? Was it really blood or not?"

"It was blood. There's this chemical we use, luminol? It reacts with the iron in blood and glows under a black light. I tested it on a corner of the dress and it lit up like a Christmas tree. Now, this only tells me that it is blood. It doesn't tell me if it's human. I've sent samples to the state crime lab. We'll have to see what they find out. You say there was a missing girl who could have been wearing this outfit?"

"The Viking's daughter. I don't remember her name, if I've heard it."

"Viking?"

"The Viking reenactor. The old man who passed out at the yacht club today. Mr. Larsen."

"Well, I looked through our internal files on missing persons and couldn't find anything. Do you know when she was reported missing?"

"Back in the late seventies, I think."

"Ah. Those records might not be in the computer database yet. I'll ask the sheriff about it when he gets back. Anything criminal that happened in Rives County, ever, he knows about it."

"Salvy's not here right now?"

"No, he's at a luncheon the Chamber of Commerce is holding. They're giving him an award for protecting their businesses. Salvy's in a league of his own when it comes to catching guys trying to steal."

The early 1900s was a time of great optimism in the United States. The Age of Industry had arrived and anything seemed possible.

Death thought about what was to come: the Great Depression, two world wars, Korea, Vietnam . . . Many things born in that bright dawn had not survived.

One of those things was the Ruskin Heights Seminary, an ambitious men's college intended to groom and educate the young gentlemen who would one day lead society. The seminary had collapsed shortly after the stock market did in '29, but its gorgeous Italianate main building had survived and found new life as a home for the Warner Museum of Frontier Art.

Death stood in the lobby, reading a brochure he'd taken from a stand inside the door:

In the 1800s, as America surged west, hardy and resourceful pioneers made use of whatever they had at hand to make their lives both easier and brighter. American folk art came into its own, with hand-carved bowls and utensils, rustic toys and tools, and textile arts such as quilting and needlework that remain popular even today.

What is less well-known is that frontiersmen and women also placed a premium on the traditional fine arts. Burgeoning communities prided themselves on their level of civilization. Museums and opera houses were widespread. Every little town had at least one glee club, and small town businessmen and their wives formed poetry clubs and literary societies. Painters and sculptors and poets and musicians joined the trek west and left us with art and images that have, even now, the power to stir the human soul.

The Warner Museum of Frontier Art was founded with a grant from the Abigail Warner Foundation. Its purpose is to collect, study, and celebrate all forms of art created west of the Mississippi between the end of the Civil War in 1865 and the Great Depression in 1929. We invite you to stroll through the house and grounds. Study our collections of painting, sculpture, folk and textile arts, and depictions of frontier architecture. Enjoy a quiet afternoon in the formal gardens or join us in the ballroom to listen to some of the Midwest's finest musicians perform. Follow us online for concert and special event schedules.

Heels clicking on the marble floor drew Death's attention. He looked up to find a bright-faced young woman in a sleeveless yellow dress coming toward him with a smile. Death smiled back, not quite as energetically.

"Hi! I'm Lila. Would you like me to show you around?"

"Hello, Lila. Do you work here?"

"Yes, I'm interning here as part of my master's degree in film history."

"Film history? At a frontier museum?"

"Sure. The first motion picture cameras were invented in the 1890s. New Jersey was originally the center of the American film industry, but Thomas Edison and his associates held patents on all the cameras and film and processes used. That gave them almost complete control over the industry, so independent filmmakers went out to California so they could —"

"Break the law without getting caught?"

Lila gifted him with a sunny smile. "Yeah. And the good filming weather helped too."

Death smiled back. "I'm Death Bogart. I have an appointment with Dr. Warner."

Lila's smile fell away and she looked like she was going to be ill. "Oh, right. I'll take you to his office."

"Thank you."

She took three steps, stopped, and turned back.

"I swear we don't know how that painting got switched," she said. "We can't understand how it was even possible. Do you know where it was hanging?"

"No."

"Come on. I'll show you."

The lobby they were in was enormous, with marble floors and dark wood display cases. The ceiling two stories above was pressed and painted tin. A double row of windows along the front wall let in plenty of natural light and the walls were white with gold trim. The most prominent feature was a massive, curving staircase that rose to a central landing before dividing to swoop off to the left and right and meet the second-floor gallery at either end. The treads were of dark wood with a white and gold stair runner and the balustrades looked like nothing so much as broad bands of gilded lace.

Death followed Lila up the left-hand flight of steps. At the head of each flight, an elaborately framed portrait hung. The portraits were placed about six feet off the floor, in plain sight of anyone who happened to be passing through the lobby or the gallery or climbing the stairs. The one in front of Death was a severe-looking woman whose eyes seemed to follow him as he moved.

Below the painting there was a glass case filled with china and an assortment of ceramic figurines.

"This is Leland Warner's mother. Dr. Warner had us move his great-great-grandparents up here after we let the other paintings go for study. We had to wrap and store every single item in the glass case, then move the glass case, and then it took three men and two ladders to lift the painting down. It took the entire day."

"It certainly doesn't seem like it would have been easy to switch the picture," Death agreed. "You were here when they took it down?"

"Yeah."

"What happened after they took it down? Was it stored somewhere? Who was here, and who knew where it was going and what was going to happen to it?"

"Nothing happened after we took it down. It didn't go into storage. Cecily Myers was here with a pair of technicians from Eiler Laboratory. She's the grad student who's doing her thesis on Hans Volkmer. Eiler Labs is who did the x-rays and other tests on it. They signed for the paintings and took them right then."

"And they took both paintings for study? They were both by Volkmer?"

"Yes. The other was an unknown actor portraying Hamlet in a University of Missouri theater production circa 1905. And I know what you're going to ask, and no, they found nothing to suggest that the Hamlet picture was replaced as well."

"Mr. Bogart."

Dr. Chase Warner spoke Death's name but didn't turn to look at him. He was standing in his office facing out the window. Warner was a stocky man, a little under average height, and he stood ramrod-straight with his hands clasped behind his back.

"Sir."

"I swear to you, as God is my witness, that I did not have anything to do with forging that painting."

"I'm neither judge nor jury, Dr. Warner," Death said. "I'm just a gumshoe trying to figure out what's going on."

Warner turned then and quirked up one eyebrow. He allowed himself a slight smile. "A gumshoe, eh? How very 1940s of you."

Death grinned. "Please. Come tell me what you know." He adjusted an imaginary fedora. "I'd like to get home. I've got a hot date with a cold whisky and a warm dame."

That drew a laugh from the other man. He came over and sat behind his desk, and Death took a visitor's chair and leaned forward with his arms on the wood surface.

"This museum has had that portrait for a long time," Death said. "How long have you been the director?"

"Since '87," Warner replied. "October 23, 1987. I took over when my mother became too ill for the position. She'd been running the museum since my father was killed in a traffic accident in '70. Before him, it was my paternal grandfather. He died, in fact, in this very chair."

"So it's always been a family affair?"

"Yes. My great-grandfather, Leland, originally established the collection. He had a younger sister, Abigail, who died of cholera while she was still in her teens. She was a great lover of music and the arts and he started the collection in her memory and as a way to give his mother something to distract her from her grief. In the beginning it was just a few rooms in the family mansion."

"The family mansion," Death said with a light chuckle, shaking his head. "You say that like it's normal."

"Well, it is normal for us. My great-great-grandfather immigrated here from Germany, well, Prussia, in the 1890s. He worked for a while at a winery in the Missouri River Valley, saved his money, and eventually opened a series of general stores, at first along the river where the paddle wheelers put in. When the railroads came through, he found out ahead of time what the routes were going to be, bought up land in advance, and expanded his businesses. He was a shrewd businessman. He figured out where people were going to be and what they were going to need and then he just planted himself in their path with his merchandise. Made a fortune."

Death nodded. "And who was director of

the museum when you first took possession of the painting? The, um, forged one, I mean."

"It's known as 'the Ring Portrait'," Warner offered helpfully. "Because she's in costume for the Ring Cycle."

"Right. The Ring Portrait. Who was director of the museum then? Your father?"

"That's right."

"Where was it originally displayed, if you know?"

"Yes, above the left-hand flight of the grand staircase. It's always been there. Until recently, that entire hall was given over to theater mementos. The glass case was filled with props and small framed photographs of famous actors. There were half a dozen easels in the upper hallway displaying a selection of playbills. The ballroom, where we stage musical recitals and performances of nineteenth- and early twentieth-century plays, is at that end of the balcony."

"When did you remove those things?"

"At the same time we took the paintings down for Ms. Myers and the technicians. Honestly, we only intended it to be a temporary change. Since the paintings were going to be gone for a time, we thought we'd replace the theater display with more, shall we say, generic pieces. It's giving us a chance to clean them and do some basic conservancy."

Death leaned back, steepled his fingers over his midriff, and thought.

"What about security?" he asked.

"We have security, of course."

"Internal? I mean, do the guards work directly for you or do you contract with a security company?"

"It's a security company, Armstrong Security. They provide two to four guards during our regular hours, depending on what kind of crowd we're expecting. Two on weekday mornings, for example, but four on weekends and holidays. We also have a state-of-the-art security system and they monitor it from their headquarters in real time. And we hire off-duty police officers for extra security if there's an event going on after hours."

Death sighed. "Right now there's just too big a window of opportunity. We know the forgery was made sometime after 1970. Probably after '74. It could have been switched with the original at any point since then, so there's more than four decades we have to account for."

"What can you do?" Warner sounded hopeless. Lost. "I can't believe this happened. This is a nightmare."

"The real painting isn't that valuable, cor-rect?" Death asked.

"That's not the point. It was in our care and we let something happen to it. Someone I've considered a friend my whole life entrusted me with a family heirloom. And now it's gone. And I can't even tell him how or when or why."

FIVE

Gianni's Pizza was a staple in East Bledsoe Ferry. It had been around since Wren was in grade school, a tiny, family-owned pizzeria in a dark concrete-block building that still had a faded, 1950s dairy logo on the side.

Wren pushed open the heavy wooden door and ducked inside, waiting for her eyes to adjust from bright sunlight to deep gloom. Gianni's had only two windows and both were stained glass. When she could see again, she helped herself to a seat at a booth along the front wall. It was nearing the dinner hour and the restaurant was already half full.

The head waitress came over and, without asking, set a glass of soda down by Wren's elbow. "Just you tonight?"

"Death'll be here. He's on his way back from the city, though. He might be a bit."

"Okay, we'll hold off until he gets here.

Let me know if you need anything."

The waitress left and Wren pulled out her phone, but before she could pull up the game she'd been playing it buzzed in her hand and the screen flashed *Mom.*

Suddenly, Wren had butterflies in her stomach. She took a deep breath and ran her thumb across the answer icon.

"Mom? Hi! Did you get my message?"

Wren's parents, after her father retired from the Department of Conservation, had shocked their family by selling their house and buying a camper. They were spending their leisure years traveling the country with no set itinerary. Her mom made dolls and stuffed animals by hand that she sold at craft fairs. Her dad had become a champion at pitching horseshoes.

"You did send a message!" Her mother sounded jubilant. "I thought there was a message but I couldn't figure out how to listen to it."

"So . . . you didn't hear it?"

"It wanted my password. Do I have a password?"

"I don't know. Don't you know?"

"Wrennie, you know I don't know how this contraption works. I'm doing good to use it for a phone, let alone do anything else with it. What was your message? Is everything okay?"

"Yeah. Yeah, everything's great. Um . . ." Wren swallowed hard. "You remember me telling you about Death? Death Bogart?"

"Oh, yes. The young man you've been sweet on. A Marine, right?"

"Right. Well, a former Marine."

"What about him?"

"Well, how would you like to have him for a son-in-law?"

Her mother was silent for so long, Wren thought perhaps they'd lost the connection. "Mom? Are you still there?"

"I'm here. Are you saying you want to marry him?"

"I'm saying I'm going to marry him. He proposed and I said yes."

"You're moving awfully fast, don't you think?"

"No faster than the situation warrants."

"Wren Elizabeth . . ." Her mother hesitated. "I don't want to be a wet blanket, but you haven't even known each other for a year now, have you?"

Wren slid around in the booth and turned sideways so she could put her feet up on the bench seat and her back to the window. "I know we're moving fast. But I also know that it's the right thing to do. Wait until you meet him. When you meet him, you'll understand."

"Well, we'll just have to head back that way so we can do that. Daddy and I were talking about coming home for Thanksgiving anyway. We'll go ahead and start that way now. Though I hope you're not rushing into a wedding *quite* so fast! When are you planning on doing this, if you don't mind my asking?"

"We haven't set a date yet. We're thinking maybe in the spring." Wren steeled herself and forged ahead. "We're going to sell my house and look for something bigger, a place to start a family."

A few beats of silence.

"Really?" her mother finally said, voice flat.

"Really." There was more to it than wanting to start a family, actually. Death's time in the service had left him with issues beyond the physical. When they first met, Wren had tried to wake him from a nightmare and he'd reacted violently. Because of that, Death didn't feel that he could sleep in the same room with her. Even though she'd promised not to repeat the mistake, anytime he tried to sleep next to her he had nightmares about accidentally killing her. They were looking for a house large enough for each of them to have their own room, until the time came when he would be able to stay with her all night.

She wasn't going to try to explain that to her mother over the phone right now, though.

"And whose idea was it to sell your house and look for a bigger one?" her mom asked. "I wonder what your godmother would think?" Wren's house had been a bequest from her mother's favorite aunt.

"I think Nan would understand," Wren replied. "She'd love Death too, and so will you when you meet him."

"And what kind of house are you looking for?"

"We haven't really decided yet. We just started looking. I did find one house I really like, but Death hasn't had a chance to see it yet."

"There, in town?

"Just a little southeast of town, on CC. A lady named Myrna Sandburg is living there now."

"Oh, of course. I know Myrna. That's the old Duvall place. Frannie Duvall's father gave them the land when they got married and Ned built her that house. Just after the First World War, I believe. The cellar is left over from an 1830s log cabin that was there before. That is a nice house."

Wren slumped in her seat a little, relieved that her mother had finally found something to approve of. "Yes, it's lovely, isn't it?"

"Yes, it is . . . You know there's a body in the rosebushes, right?"

"My gosh! It looks like the Brady Bunch exploded in here!"

On Saturday morning, with the rest of Keystone and Sons occupied with auctioning off the equipment from a closed restaurant, Wren returned to the yacht club with Robin Keystone along to lend a hand. They had entered a large dining room on the north side of the building. A three-sided bar occupied the central area, while garishly colored tables and chairs sat in alcoves created by various room dividers and collections of artificial plants. Macramé hangers held more artificial plants, and there were shelves with an eclectic assortment of conversation pieces. The walls were covered with bold paintings and wall hangings; there was an emphasis on bright colors and geometric designs. Small, oddly shaped lamps with orange- and raspberry-colored plastic shades provided lighting.

Though she wouldn't say as much to Robin, this place gave Wren the heebie-jeebies. After listening to Sam and Roy talk about the Beverly Hills Supper Club, she'd researched the place. They hadn't been exaggerating when they said Claudio Bender had built his nightclub as a copy of that one. Not only did it imitate the crazy floor plan of its doomed predecessor, but the decorations were modelled after the original too.

After reading accounts of the deadly fire at the Beverly Hills club that had claimed 165 lives, Wren could walk through the Ozark Hills Supper Club and pick out where the fire had started, envision how the furnishings and decor had fed the flames, and imagine the terror of all the victims lost in the maze-like building, trapped in the dark and heat. She imagined this was how a ghost would feel, walking through the memory of the place she'd died.

"It's called kitsch," she said, pushing her own unease away. "We'll list it as an impressive assortment of mid-1970s kitsch."

"Kitch? Like kitchen?"

"Kitsch." Wren spelled it for him. "It's basically the 'oh my god, that's horrible! I love it!' school of collecting."

Robin gave her the side-eye and she laughed.

"Don't knock it. There are a lot of people who like this kind of stuff. I have a friend in Kansas who makes her living dealing in kitsch."

"Hello? Is anyone here? Is someone here? Hello?"

A strange voice sounded from the direction of the entryway. Wren and Robin exchanged a glance and moved together toward the door.

The man who stood just inside the entrance was a stranger to Wren. He was tall and thin with blond hair fading to white and pale blue eyes behind thick glasses. He wore a heavy wool coat, and Wren read nerves in his taut posture and the way he kept his hands in his coat pockets and his elbows tucked against his sides.

She moved forward, instinctively putting herself between Robin and an unknown man even though she got no bad vibes from him.

"Hi, can I help you?"

"Hi. Yeah. Um, are you the Keystones?"

"I'm Wren Morgan. I work for the Keystones. They're not here right now." She could feel Robin glaring at her as she said it, but she wasn't letting him take over this conversation until she knew who the man was and what he wanted. "Can I help you?"

"Hi." He stepped forward and offered her his hand. "I'm Jacob Larsen. From Arnhold."

"Arnold?"

"The Viking settlement next door? It's called Arnhold. It means 'stronghold of the wolf.'"

"I see. Larsen . . . Are you related to the gentleman who was taken ill yesterday?"

"Yes, he's my father. That's why I wanted to stop by. To thank you for helping him."

"That's no problem. I'm just glad we were here to help. Is he going to be okay?"

"He should be, yes. They're keeping him in the hospital for a couple of days, to try to pinpoint exactly what happened, but they don't think it was anything serious." Jacob Larsen shuffled his feet on the carpet, gazing at the floor and looking like a child facing his principal. "There was something else I wanted to talk to you about."

Wren glanced back at Robin again and he met her gaze with raised eyebrows. She had a feeling she knew where this was going.

"The clothes?" she asked. "The dress and other things the kids found up in the sail loft?"

"Yeah, that. The, uh, ghost my father thought he saw. That was just a little girl playing dress-up?"

Robin snickered and Wren shushed him with a glance.

"A little boy, actually. He was just fooling

around."

"Matt's a bit rambunctious," Robin put in, defending his cousin, "but he's not a bad kid."

"Oh, no. I'm sure he's not. The sheriff said you seemed to think that the clothes had something to do with my sister's disappearance."

Wren chose her words carefully. "We did wonder if that was a possibility. From what we heard, your father said he saw her on the lakeshore here at the time she disappeared, and she was wearing clothing like that."

"He thought he saw her," Larsen said. He shifted uncomfortably. "It's highly unlikely he actually did. How much do you know about her and about what happened when she went missing?"

"Not a lot," Wren admitted. "I'd be interested to hear about it, if you want to tell me. If you don't, of course, I understand."

"Oh, no. I'd love to tell you. My family tells this story, still, to anyone who'll listen. After all these years we're still hoping to find someone who can help us find out what happened to her. It's a bit of a long story, though."

"Then there's no need to tell it standing here in the hall." She'd noticed he looked stiff and sore, as if standing was hurting him. "Would you like to come into the other room and have a seat?"

"Yes, thank you. I'd like that very much."

They returned to the dining room and helped themselves to seats at a small, round table. Wren introduced Robin and he apologized for the appearance of the room.

"It's okay," Larsen told him. "I remember when things like this were in style. You should see the clothes that went with them. And God help me if my daughters ever find my high school yearbooks. I had an honest-to-God Afro my senior year."

"Your sister," Wren began. "I'm sorry, I can't recall her name."

"Ingrid. Her name was Ingrid."

"Ingrid. That's pretty. It was back in the seventies when she disappeared, wasn't it?"

"Yes, in '78. She was seventeen."

"I'm so sorry. What happened?"

"It was the end of July, the summer between her junior and senior years in high school. I was in my first year at the University of Missouri, but my family lived in Columbia, so I still lived at home. Ingrid was planning on coming to Mizzou as well. She was mad about the Viking stuff. She did volunteer work with the MU museum — my dad arranged that — and she wanted to be an archaeologist. Of course, this was before the Viking Reenactors got together and built Arnhold. I think of her every time we come down. She'd have loved this place. She belonged to the local chapter of the Society for Creative Anachronism, though. Through them, she got a chance to be a performer in a traveling Renaissance faire. On Independence Day, she left for Chicago with the SCA president and his wife. That was the last time we saw her."

"What happened?"

He shrugged. "We don't know. The last weekend in July, one of the other professors Dad worked with invited him to go boating down here. The man who owned the yacht club then was a history buff and his favorite history was anything to do with northern Europe."

"Claudio Bender," Wren said.

"Yes, that's right. Have you met him?"

"No, I haven't had the pleasure."

Jacob Larsen laughed a little.

"What?" Wren asked.

"Sorry. It's just that people don't generally describe meeting Bender as a pleasure. I mean, he can be very generous for a good cause if it strikes his fancy. But he expects to be treated like royalty in return. Literally. He and his son come down to Arnhold sometimes and we have to treat them like a visiting chieftain and his court."

"You have to?"

"We coddle them for monetary purposes," Jacob said ruefully. "We're sluts that way. A lot of our members are connected with various colleges or museums. The Benders are obsessed with their own history. A lot of times it's possible to sweet-talk them into backing research or education or conservation projects, so we try to stay on their good side. That's what Dad was doing here in '78, in fact."

"Sweet-talking the Benders into backing something for the university?"

"A summer dig in a bog in Belgium. It was a joint venture with a private museum back east. The chair of the department brought Dad along to push the Viking angle on the dig. They were talking Vikings all weekend, so it's a safe bet that Dad had Vikings on the brain to begin with. That Sunday afternoon he was on a sailboat with some other men about twenty yards offshore when he thought he saw a woman in full Viking costume standing just inside the trees."

"Just a woman?" Wren asked. "Not Ingrid?"

"Not right then. He only got a quick

glimpse of her as he was turning his head. By the time it registered what he'd seen and he looked back again, she was gone. They scanned the shore with binoculars, but there was no sign of anyone. A couple of days later, someone from the Ren faire called and asked us if Ingrid had come home." Jacob paused. "A group of performers were camping on the fairgrounds in Cincinnati and it seems my sister never made it back to her tent that Saturday night, and she never turned up to perform on Sunday. Dad reported her disappearance to the police. Because she was a minor, they started investigating immediately, and Mom and Dad and I drove up there and searched too. We never found any sign of her, nor anyone who admitted to having any idea of what happened."

"Who was the last person to see her?"

"We don't even know. She was roaming freely through the faire, in character as a Viking maiden, directing people to the shops and performances, posing for pictures and answering questions. Even then, right after it happened, it was impossible to pinpoint exactly when she disappeared. The police thought she simply ran away. To be honest, that's what Mom and I thought too, though we always hoped that someday she'd come home. She'd had a rough junior year and I know she wasn't looking forward to going back to school in the fall. And I thought then, and think even more so now, that we could have been more supportive of her. But Dad, she was his baby girl. He just couldn't accept that she'd ever leave him. As time went on, he convinced himself that she'd been killed and that she'd visited him in spirit. After all these years, it's still something my parents never speak of. Neither of them can handle the other one's point of view."

"You say she had a rough junior year," Wren said. "Why is that?"

Larsen looked down, his mouth tight around the corners and an unhappy glint in his eye. He ran a hand through his thinning hair.

"Ingrid got cornered at a party." He made it sound like an admission. "She was a cheerleader and a bunch of kids were out in somebody's field having a bonfire to celebrate winning some football game. One of the players got her alone in a wooded area and got fresh. Pinned her to a tree and was kissing her. Got handsy. She punched him in the throat and got away and left. But she wasn't willing to leave well enough alone. She reported it to the police and to school officials. Wanted something done to punish him. But he was a football player. That carried a lot of weight back then. Everyone told her that boys will be boys, and that a girl who goes to those kinds of parties should expect that. Nothing ever happened to him. But Ingrid got thrown off the cheerleading squad and she was ostracized as a troublemaker."

"That's horrible!" Wren was aghast.

Larsen lifted his shoulders, unhappy. "That's the way it was."

"That doesn't make it right."

They sat for a long moment in silence while a wind off the lake whistled around the building and dust motes danced in a beam of light from the room's single high window. It was Robin who finally spoke again.

"So you don't think she could have come here?"

"No. How would she get here? And why would she want to? She had no way of even knowing Dad was down here." He sighed and shook his head. "Tell me about this costume you found. I went by the sheriff's department but they'd already sent it to the state crime lab, so they couldn't let me see it. Do you remember what it looked like?"

"Well," Wren said, "there was a simple

dress that was probably white or cream-colored. It was hard to tell what color it was originally. It had yellowed badly, but I don't believe it was nearly that yellow when it was new. And then there was a dark blue over-dress, kind of like a pinafore. And a circlet with a veil attached that I took to be a headpiece."

"And the dress was stained?" Larsen persisted.

"It was absolutely caked with blood," Wren said, her voice soft with regret. "There were holes rotted in the fabric because of it, but there was still enough that you could see what the garments had originally been."

Larsen thought about it for a moment, then nodded to himself. "You know," he said, "I think you probably did find evidence of a crime, but not the one you're thinking of."

"Oh?"

"We're reenactors. We wear the clothes and use the tools and follow the customs of our ancestors who lived twelve hundred years ago. Everyone in the group takes it seriously to some extent. You have to, just to justify the expense and time commitment. But some take it more seriously than others. One thing that was a common part of life in the 800s that we seldom do now, certainly not in the same manner, was hunting. Norsemen and women hunted their food, dressed out the kills, butchered them and prepared the meat."

"You think someone was hunting."

"Probably, yes. Now, I don't know that for a fact, nor who it would have been. Though I can think of a couple of likely candidates over the years."

"But why would they hide the bloody clothes?" Robin asked.

"Because they were hunting out of season," Wren said drily. "Or without a license."

"Or both." Larsen nodded. "Anyway, we'll know eventually, after the crime lab runs the tests on the blood."

"I wonder how long it will take to hear back," Wren said.

"The deputy I talked to said three to six months."

Six

Death drove slowly past the Sandburg house, taking in the autumn-bare lilacs massed in front of the wraparound veranda, the turret rising over the treetops, and the broad lawn neatly manicured under a coating of red oak leaves. The road got bumpy as soon as he passed the driveway and he divided his attention between steering and studying the house, trying to get a feel for it before he went to look at it up close.

The rosebushes were concentrated in the side yard. Some of them climbed trellises and there was a wooden arch covered with thorny canes and a wrought-iron bench to one side. He could just make out the stone in the middle.

He passed the yard, looking for a place to turn around, and was surprised to find a beat-up old pickup parked off to his right in a short, unkempt driveway just beyond the edge of the pasture. A familiar figure was sitting on the tailgate.

Death parked in the middle of the road and went over to talk. "What are you doing out here?" he asked.

East Bledsoe Ferry Police Chief Duncan Reynolds was out of uniform, dressed comfortably in faded overalls and a flannel shirt with holes at the elbows. He held up a cigar box in his right hand.

"I'm holding the box," he explained.

Death went over closer. A sheet of paper lay on the tailgate next to him, covered with the outlines of leaves and natural objects. Before he could speak, the weeds rustled and a small, towheaded boy came out of the woods carrying an acorn like it was a holy object.

Death dropped down to one knee. "Hey, Mason! What have you got?"

The child, without speaking, held the acorn out for his inspection, then pulled it back against his shoulder as if he thought Death might try to steal it.

"I see. Is Grandpa helping you with your schoolwork?"

Mason nodded.

"Whatcha got, Tiger?" Reynolds asked.

Mason went up to him and stood on tiptoe to lay the acorn on the sheet.

"Okay, which one is that?"

The child found the outline of an acorn and his grandfather nodded gravely. "Good job. Mark it off, now."

Mason used a purple crayon to cross out the acorn and dropped the actual acorn in the cigar box his grandfather was holding.

"What are you going to look for now?" Reynolds asked.

Mason pointed to one of the outlines and Death looked over his little shoulder.

"That's an elm leaf," he offered helpfully. "There's probably one —"

Mason gave him a dirty look. "I can do it."

Death stepped back and raised his hands in surrender. "Okay. Sorry. I'll stay out of your way."

"Ah ah!" Reynolds said. "What do you say?"

"I can do it!" Mason insisted.

"I know you can. But Mr. Bogart offered to help you. What do you say?"

The little boy frowned up at Death fiercely, scrunched up his face, and said, "No thank you anyway."

"We're going to work on that delivery," his grandfather said. "Go on, get your next leaf."

Mason scampered away into the edge of the woods again and Death laughed.

"He's independent. That's not a bad thing."

"He's contrary," Reynolds said. "He's just like his mother was at that age." He laughed. "Grandchildren are a grandparent's revenge on their own kids, you know? Every time Debbie calls me to freak out over some mischief he's gotten into, I just laugh and laugh."

Death smiled, but he was hit with a wave of sadness as it was driven home to him, not for the first time, that any children he had would never know their grandparents.

At least, not their grandparents on his side.

"Chief," he said, "can I ask you something?"

"Sure." Reynolds nodded at the truck. "Pull up a hunk of metal and tell me your troubles."

Death took a seat at the other end of the tailgate. "Do you know Wren's parents?"

"Not well. I've met them. Wren's dad was a conservation agent, which I'm sure you know. I think he and Salvy are pretty good friends. And I think my wife knows her mom, but I don't really. Why?"

"Just curious." Death kicked his feet in the air and looked down at the dirt below him. He sighed. "She told her mom that we're engaged. They're on their way back here to meet me."

"Ah." Reynolds grinned. "Nervous?"

"A little. I don't think her mom's too happy with the idea."

"Well, Wren's her baby. Her being grown up doesn't change that. You'll understand that someday."

"Yeah, I know, but . . ."

"But what?"

"What if they hate me?"

"What if they love you?"

"That would be nice."

"Look," the chief said, "you love Wren, right?"

"Of course."

"Well, they raised her. They get a lot of the credit for the person she turned out to be. You've just got to give them a chance."

"That's not the question. The question is, will they give me a chance?"

"I kind of think Wren will insist on that, don't you?"

Mason coming back with another leaf interrupted them. Death waited patiently while the boy marked it off on his sheet, deposited it in the box, and picked out something else to search for. When he'd vanished back into the edge of the trees, Reynolds turned to him.

"You didn't come out here looking for me to hold your hand. What are you doing out this way?"

Death tipped his head back toward the Sandburg house. "House hunting. Wren likes that place. She wanted me to take a look."

They didn't have a clear view of the house from there, just a chunk of the corner visible through the trees. Reynolds studied what he could see of it.

"Nice place. I could see you two living out here. Is it in your price range, if you don't mind my asking?"

"I think we could swing it," Death said. "We were crunching the numbers last night. With both our incomes, it should be within reach. Especially if we can find a buyer for the house where she lives now."

The chief nodded. "If you like it, go for it." He shifted on the tailgate, yawned, and stretched. "Oh, by the way, did you know there's a body in the rosebushes?"

When he'd called, Death had arranged to meet Myrna Sandburg at three o'clock. He crossed the porch and knocked at two minutes to the hour. While he waited, he studied the porch. The flooring was sturdy under his feet and the railing looked sound,

100

though he noticed a couple of rails that would need to be replaced. The veranda seemed to be made for a porch swing. There was no actual swing in sight, but he found a pair of hooks on the ceiling that were obviously there to hang one from.

Brisk, light footsteps sounded inside the house and a little old white-haired lady opened the door and studied him.

"I don't know you," she announced.

He blinked. "I'm Death Bogart. We spoke on the phone?"

"Oh, I know who you are. But I don't know you. My momma always said that if you let strange men in the house they'll ravish you. Are you planning to ravish me?"

"Uh, no ma'am."

"Well, why should I let you in then?"

Death gaped at her, open-mouthed, and she cackled suddenly. "Look at you! You're blushing! And you've got dimples. Now that's just adorable. I can see why that little girl thinks you're a keeper." She opened the door farther and stepped back. "Come on in and take a look around."

He stepped past her into a short hallway. There was a beautiful stairway rising on his right, and on his left the room opened out into a spacious living room that was the most hideous shade of pink he'd ever seen.

"You don't like the color," Myrna said, watching his face. "I know it. Doesn't anybody seem to like the color but me."

"It's certainly . . . intense," Death said, trying to be diplomatic.

"The realtor said it's the color of a chapped baby's butt. He wanted me to paint it. Wasn't no sense in that, I said. I had no way of knowing who might buy it or what color they like. I might have painted it a color you hated even worse."

"That's certainly possible," Death conceded politely, though privately he thought it unlikely.

"That don't mean you can't paint it. Paint's not that expensive. Just imagine it a color you like."

He smiled at her, charmed in spite of himself, but she already had her back to him and was moving away through a doorway that had no door.

"Come in here and look at the kitchen and dining room. Dining room's got a lighted built-in china hutch and all the cupboards in the kitchen are real hard-wood."

Forty-five minutes later, Death and Myrna stood in the side yard looking up at the house. She'd shown him the inside from top to bottom. He'd peeked into the tiny, dusty

attic, peered into the crawl space underneath, examined the plumbing and wiring
and heating and air conditioning, and
walked around the outside of the house
checking the stone-and-concrete foundation
for stress fractures.

"What do you do for water?" he asked.

"Private well." Myrna indicated a squat
structure made of concrete blocks. "Deep
well convertible jet pump. You could trade it
out for an in-ground pump if you like. I like
the above-ground model. It's easier to work
on or replace if something goes wrong, and
in-ground pumps have a bad habit of getting hit by lightning."

"Really?" Death asked. "Even though
they're way down in the ground?"

"Because they're way down in the
ground," Myrna explained. "The wires leading down to them act as a ground. Lightning
will follow it right down and blow up your
pump. With a jet pump, the pump and all
the wiring are on the surface, so it's not
tempting fate that way. With a really deep
well, you'd probably need a submersible,
but the water table isn't that far down here.
This well only goes down seventy feet or
so."

Death looked around the yard and his
gaze fell on the tombstone. "What about

Bob?" he asked whimsically.

"Oh, he's not nearly seventy feet down. More like six. Probably more like four, actually."

Death laughed. "Do you think he'll mind having someone new to share the property with?"

"Oh, he's never been any trouble. We sacrifice a virgin to him once every seven years and he leaves us right alone."

Death shook his head and went on around to the front of the building. He was more winded than he'd care to admit and he helped himself to a seat on the porch steps.

"I still don't understand about Bob," he said. "Someone found a body in the woods and you wanted to bury someone so the coroner's office just gave him to you?"

"It isn't quite as simple as that," Myrna said. She seated herself beside him. "Deer hunters found him in the woods in 1985. In the fall, during bow season. He was lying at the bottom of a steep slope, covered up with a heavy covering of leaves and dirt. Not like he'd been buried, but just like he died there and got covered up naturally over the years. The only reason they found him was because a big rainstorm had washed a gully down the side of the ravine and his arm bone was sticking out. From the amount of leaves and crap on him, the cops think he'd been there for at least two or three years by that point."

"But they tried to find out who he was and what happened to him?"

"Well, sure. But it ain't as easy as it sounds."

"No, I know it's not. It just kind of throws me that they let you bury him without knowing who he was."

"What were they supposed to do? Leave him in a drawer at the morgue forever?"

"I guess not."

"They didn't just give up on him," Myrna said. "It's still an open case. A cold case, sure. But still. They've got his DNA on file and they check it against missing persons, and they even had a guy do a facial reconstruction with his skull to try to see what he looked like."

"Now that I'd like to see."

"Talk to the sheriff's department. They still have the original model of his head and they can tell you everything they know about him. Who knows? Maybe you can figure out where he came from. You are a detective, right?"

"That I am."

"And you like the house." She grinned up at him. "You do, don't you?"

He grinned back. "I do. I really do."

"So what do you think?"

"I think I need to talk to my fiancée."

"How did the restaurant sale go?" Wren asked.

"Pretty well, if you don't count the fist fight."

Wren stopped setting the table in Roy and Leona's big dining room and turned to look through into the kitchen, to where Leona was sliding a roast out of the oven. "Fist fight? Between whom? And why?"

"A couple of customers. They both wanted the industrial bread mixer. We had to call the police. They ended up pressing charges against each other and both got arrested."

"Who bought the mixer?"

"Another guy entirely. Young man opening a bakery up in the city."

Wren shook her head. "People. Honestly."

With the Keystone men off attending a bachelor party, Wren and Death had been invited to join Doris and Leona for dinner and a movie. Death now helped Leona transfer the roast to a serving platter, Wren finished setting the table, and they ferried the food from the kitchen to the dining room and sat down to eat. Given their huge family, the Keystones' dining table was designed for at least a dozen people, even without extra leaves. The four of them clustered around one end, passed the food around, and chatted while they ate.

"What have you two been up to?" Doris asked. "Is there anything exciting going on? You know us old women like to live vicariously through you."

Death and Wren exchanged a glance and a smile.

"We're going to make an offer on the Sandburg place," Wren said. "Wish us luck."

"Oh, that's a beautiful house," Doris said. "You know there's a body in the side yard?"

"Yeah. We know."

"That's old news," Leona told her sister-in-law. "Wren and I already discussed that. What else is new? Death, what have you been up to?"

"I have a new case, up in the city. It's kind of odd."

"What kind of odd? I love odd," Leona said.

"That's why she married Roy," Doris teased.

"I'm not denying that."

Death grinned at their exchange. "The kind of odd that involves a painting in a museum being replaced by a forgery, but no one knows when or how. And it wasn't a valuable painting, so no one knows why, either."

"Really?" Doris perked up, interested. "What painting? And what museum, if you can tell me?"

"There was an article about it in the Kansas City paper, so I don't suppose it's a secret. The museum is the Warner Museum of Frontier Art, and the painting in question is called the Ring Portrait by an artist named Volkmer."

"Oh, I'm familiar with Volkmer," Doris said immediately. "I don't know that specific painting, but I know the artist. You're right, his work isn't considered that valuable in monetary terms."

"Why do you say it like that?" Wren asked. "In monetary terms? Are there other terms?"

Doris set down her fork and dabbed at the corner of her mouth with a napkin. "Volkmer was probably a better artist than he's given credit for," she said. "In a time when painting and the arts tended to be seen as lofty and pure and idealistic, he treated his work as a business. He took commissions from anyone who could afford to pay him and he painted the paintings his subjects wanted. Very workmanlike, though he showed flashes of what might have been brilliance from time to time. Critics of the period thought very little of him, but because he painted people the way they wanted to be depicted, a lot of his paintings were highly prized by the subjects. A Volkmer that doesn't have a high dollar tag attached might still be something that someone was very sentimental over."

"So I should look at who might have wanted the painting for sentimental reasons but didn't have the legal right to actually own it?" Death asked.

"That's what I would do. You know, though, it's funny . . ."

"What's funny?" Leona prompted.

"Well, since we sell artwork sometimes, I always get notices when things have been stolen from museums and private collectors. This is probably the third time this year I've heard about something that wasn't particularly valuable being replaced by a forgery."

"Could there be a connection?" Wren wondered. "Maybe someone who's good at forgery is doing it just because they can."

"Do you remember what the other things were?" Death asked.

"Not off the top of my head, no. But I keep those notices in a special file on my computer. It's in the cloud, so I should be able to get to it from my phone." She rose to go get her phone out of her purse.

"I don't want to interrupt your dinner," Death objected.

"Nonsense. I'm curious myself now."

Doris got her phone and sat for several minutes flipping between screens before she glanced up. "Here it is. There were two earlier this year and one from a couple of years ago. I don't think they could be connected though."

"Why do you say that?"

"None of the other three are paintings. One was a thirteenth-century clay pot from a peat bog in Belgium."

"That wasn't valuable?" Wren asked.

"Not terribly. It wasn't intact, for one thing. It had been glued back together from mostly original fragments, but it was really just broken pottery. Not that the museum wanted to lose it, of course."

"What else?"

"It was discovered missing in July. From the Brandburg House, a history museum in Pittsburgh. They digitized their catalog and put a lot of pictures online, and a student in California noticed that the fracture lines on newer pictures of the pot didn't match the fracture lines on older pictures. In February, a museum at a small, private college in

Maryland discovered that a collection of seventeenth-century Prussian coins had been replaced with forgeries. But the one two years ago was the strangest one of all. The strangest one I've ever heard of, in fact."

"You're drawing out the suspense deliberately," Leona said accusingly. "Spill already."

"Have you ever heard of an angel crown?" Doris asked. "They're also known as 'death crowns.' "

The others shook their heads.

"It's something from back when feather pillows were commonplace. Sometimes people would find a nest or crown-like arrangement of feathers inside a feather pillow. In some places, especially in the south, like Appalachia, the crowns were supposed to mean that the person who'd owned that pillow had gone to heaven. If they were found in the pillow of someone who was still alive, it was seen as a death omen, although some people believed you could defeat the omen if you broke apart the crown."

"And someone forged one of these things?" Death asked. "Really?"

"Apparently. A family named Eichenwald owned an angel crown that had belonged to their great-great-grandmother, the family matriarch, who had been the first to immigrate here from Germany in the 1890s. They lent it to a local history museum, where it was put on display as part of an exhibit on local superstitions. When the museum returned it, one of the kids complained that it didn't smell the same. They started examining it and it was a fake made from acrylic feathers and sewn together with transparent thread."

Seven

Most people were off work on Saturdays and Sundays, which made the weekend the best time for Keystone and Sons to hold auctions. Days off for the company tended to be on Tuesdays and Wednesdays, unless there was a specific reason to hold a sale on those days. So it was that Tuesday morning found Wren in her kitchen, pulling dishes out of the many cabinets and cupboards and trying to decide what to move and what to get rid of. It was ridiculous. If she could pack this much stuff into a little one-bedroom bungalow, what might disappear into the cupboards and closets of the Sandburg place?

She had been attending auctions since she was a girl, and working for the Keystones since getting a part-time job helping Leona with the books when she was sixteen. For all those years, Wren had tended to pick up random odds and ends if they took her fancy and the price didn't climb too high.

She had a *lot* of dishes.

She also had a lot of knickknacks and collectibles. They sat on her windowsills, crowded around the corners of the china hutch, took up space on high shelves, and perched atop the cabinets. Looking around at everything, it was hard not to despair at the sheer amount of work that moving would entail. Even for someone who broke down estates and organized auctions for a living, it was a daunting task.

Wren sat at the kitchen table, studying the room and noting all the odds and ends that she'd acquired, put on display, and then more or less forgotten. As her eyes roamed over her collection, she noticed a ceramic figurine she hadn't really looked at in years. It was a little girl playing dress-up. She wore droopy blue jeans, a red shirt, and a bridal veil, and she was holding a fancy gown up in front of herself.

That's me, Wren thought. I've had it all these years and never knew that before. Oh! I wonder if I have a Death somewhere.

She rose to fetch the piece and set it aside somewhere safe. As she carried it back to the table, she tipped it up and looked at the bottom. It had someone's initials — too faded to read now — scratched into the bottom along with the date *7-18-78.* It occurred to Wren that this was very near the date when Ingrid Larsen disappeared, and, as she set about sorting and organizing the contents of her kitchen, her thoughts were with the missing girl.

When lunchtime rolled around, she stopped to make a sandwich. Then she got out her laptop and searched "Ingrid Larsen Missing." The first thing that came up was a page on the website for the National Center for Missing and Exploited Children. She clicked on it and studied the screen.

It didn't give too much information she didn't already have. There was a basic list of Ingrid's personal information — her name, date of birth, a physical description, a record of where and when she'd last been seen, and the notation that she'd be nearly sixty now.

There were also pictures, two of them. The first was a standard school picture, a head-shot showing a teenage girl looking straight at the camera and smiling faintly. She wore a scoop-neck blouse in a busy red-orange print, and her long blond hair was parted in the middle and hung down straight to frame a thin, oval face. The second picture was a computer-generated image, age progressed to middle age.

She looked like a nice girl, Wren thought. She seemed a little sad in the school picture, but that could have been Wren's own imagination painting emotions onto the picture, since she knew that Ingrid hadn't been happy that last year.

Wren clicked back to the search page and scrolled. Ingrid's family also maintained a website and blog dedicated to searching for her. Wren followed the link and found more pictures.

The school picture was there, and the age-progressed image. But there were also half a dozen spontaneous snapshots. Ingrid looked happier in these, for the most part: posing with another girl her age, sitting with what was probably her family around a Christmas tree, and smiling next to a display case in a museum. The last picture showed her in the Ren faire costume she'd been wearing when she disappeared.

The photograph was in color. Ingrid wore a long, off-white shift topped with a voluminous blue overdress. Primitive brooches held keys and pouches and crude tools. Her hair was bound in a braid on top of her head and a circlet held a veil that draped down her back.

Wren closed the window, signed off on the computer, and closed it gently. Her

116

heart was troubled.

She couldn't be certain, but the clothes Ingrid was wearing when she disappeared looked very much like the blood-stained garments the children had found hidden in the boathouse by the lake.

Emily Morgan looked up from her sewing as her husband flipped on his turn signal and eased off the road and into a gas station on the highway just outside of East Bledsoe Ferry.

"We're stopping now? We're almost there."

"Unless you want to run out of gas in her yard," Edgar said mildly. "We're sitting on empty."

"I suppose if we must, we must."

He swung the pickup/camper combo deftly into the nearest row. "It won't take but a minute," he reassured her. "We can just use the pay-at-the-pump."

Emily made a face. "You know I don't trust those machines. What if it messes up and takes too much money out? Or doesn't show that we paid for our gas? Do you want to take a chance on being chased down and arrested for stealing gas?"

It wasn't a new argument. Edgar just shook his head.

"You go on and pump the gas," Emily

said. "I'll just run in and pay for it."

Setting her project down — she was making sheep out of woolly socks — she climbed down from the cab and crossed to the building. There was a line at the register and she stepped to the back of it, looking around at the interior of the business and noting that nothing had really changed in the year she'd been away. Then she turned her attention to the counter and did a double take.

Eric Farrington was standing at the front of the line with a stunningly beautiful woman and a sweet-faced toddler. Having known Eric all his life, Emily frowned to herself. "That can't be normal," she thought. Farrington was a troublemaker, a local jail guard who had his job only because his uncle was the mayor.

Eric was digging in his wallet and complaining loudly. "I just don't see why I'm the one who's always gotta pay for everything."

"I'm sorry," his companion said. "I told you, I'm broke right now."

"You're always broke."

"I have a kid. Kids are expensive. And it's not like his father has ever paid me a dime of child support."

"And why do you stand for that? There are people and . . . agencies . . . and . . .

118

things that handle that. Garnish his wages. Throw his ass in jail."

"I've tried, okay. But he's a slippery bastard. It's not as easy as you seem to think."

"Whatever." With an annoyed huff, Farrington snatched his change off the counter and charged out of the store. The woman sighed and glared after him, but picked up her baby and followed.

Emily watched them through the window as they got into Eric's car and drove away. The voice of the cashier drew her attention back inside.

"Mrs. Morgan! You're back!"

She turned around. The girl working the cash register was an old friend's daughter. "Oh, hello, dear. Yes, we're just here for a visit."

"Well, it's great to see you. Are you having fun?"

"Oh, yes. It's a lot of fun." She pointed out the window, toward where Eric had been parked. "I think I've missed a lot here, though. Who was that young woman with Eric Farrington just now?"

The cashier's eyes lit up. "You don't know?"

"No. Know what?"

"That's Madeline Braun. She's Death Bogart's ex-wife!"

Emily's eyes narrowed and her mouth tightened. "Oh really?"

Death had been to Columbia many times but he'd never before ventured onto the campus of the University of Missouri. He parked in visitors' parking and made his way past Ellis Library, an odd conglomeration of new glass and steel and old stonework, and crossed a curving road. All the buildings on the opposite side of the road sat with their backs to him. He followed a paved path between two of them and came out on Francis Quadrangle, the heart of the university.

Once upon a time he'd marched for miles with a full pack and thought nothing of it. Now a stroll across an autumn campus taxed his reserves. He took his time, pausing now and again to look around and let his breathing recover from the exertion. The quad was a big, grassy rectangle distinguished by the presence of six massive Ionic columns, all that remained of the university's original building. A few students clustered around them, leaning against them or sitting on the chest-high bases. One young woman sat alone in the dry grass with her back to the westernmost column and her head bent over a book. A young man had climbed up to stand on another, looming over his group of friends. It was a windy, mostly overcast day. Dead brown oak leaves skittered along the sidewalk and pale gold light shone down on old marble and yellowing grass.

Death stood at the south end of the quad, with Jesse Hall, the main building, at his back. The school of journalism anchored the northeast corner and Peace Park opened from the southeast corner. While he was checking the campus map on his phone, the space around him suddenly filled with young bodies, and just as quickly it emptied again — students leaving one class and hurrying to the next.

Wren had been a student here a few years back. Death smiled to himself, picturing her as a younger woman caught up in the bustle. Her red hair must have shone in the crowd. He knew she'd had a fondness then for glitter gel pens and teddy bears, and in his mind's eye she was always laughing.

According to the map, the building he wanted was on his right. But when he reached it and climbed the steps, it was closed. Not just locked, but shut down and dark, with an empty air that suggested an abandoned building. He checked the name on the front — Pickard Hall. The information in his quick Google search had said that this was where he was supposed to be, but obviously that was wrong.

He returned to the sidewalk and snagged a passerby.

"Excuse me, but I'm looking for the Museum of Art and Archaeology. I thought it was in this building. Do you know . . . ?"

The student, a reed-thin young man with thick glasses and a heavy-looking backpack, shrugged. "Nah, man. That building's empty. They moved everything out of there three years ago. It's, like, radioactive or something."

"It's what?"

"That's what they said."

Death blinked, bemused. "Um, okay. Well, do you know where the museum is now?"

"I think they moved the department next door." He indicated the building Death had just walked past. "You could try there."

Death thanked him and did as he suggested. The building in question was named Swallow Hall. It was another old brick and stone affair, recently remodeled, and the sign by the door verified that it was now home to the department of Art History and Archaeology. When he went inside, though, there was no sign of any museum.

He looked around for a few minutes and eventually found a sixty-something professor with his office door open. The man sat at an overflowing desk, poring over a stack of small blue booklets with a red ink pen. His office was crowded with bookshelves filled equally with books and fragments of pottery. The nameplate by his door read *Dr. Bailey.*

Death tapped on the doorframe

The professor looked up. "I'm still grading the Byzantine exam."

"Yes, sir. I'm sorry to disturb you. I'm not one of your students. I was just hoping to ask you a question."

"Shoot."

"What happened to the museum? I was supposed to meet someone in the cast gallery, but the building is closed. A kid outside said something about radiation?"

Dr. Bailey lay his pen down and sat back. "Ah, yes. Unfortunately, we've been displaced from our old home. They discovered the building was contaminated with traces of radiation."

"How did that happen?"

"Back in the early 1900s, Pickard Hall was used by the science department. They were doing experiments with radium before they realized it was dangerous. Just recently, they discovered the building still had traces of radiation. Less than the federal maximum allowed, but we still had to move. Our museum and the Anthropology Museum are out at Mizzou North now."

"Mizzou North?"

"A former cancer hospital. And, yes, I see the irony. Take Providence to Business Loop 70 and turn left. It'll be on your right."

Death thanked him and had turned to go when a missing person poster on the side wall caught his eye. He nodded toward it, a question forming on his lips, but Bailey spoke before he did.

"A former colleague's daughter. They never found her, I'm afraid."

"You don't think they still might?"

Bailey shrugged. "I suppose anything's possible, but it's been almost forty years."

"Right. I think I met her father the other day," Death said.

"Neils Larsen? Really? Where'd you see him at?"

"Down by Truman Lake. There's this Viking kind of village —"

"Arnhold. Sure. You a reenactor?"

Death grinned. "No. My fiancée was working at the yacht club next door."

"Oh, good Lord. Is someone trying to make a go of that place again?"

"No, it's being sold off. Wren's an auction-eer. You're familiar with the yacht club? Are you a reenactor?"

"No, though I've been out to Arnhold a time or two. I've been to the yacht club a time or two as well. When it was open, back in the day. Back then pretty much everyone in the department got dragged out there sooner or later."

"Really?" Death eased himself into a visitor's chair. "How's that?"

"Guy who owned it is a history buff, for a given value of the term history buff. That is, he's interested in anything that glorifies his personal history. His family came from northern Europe. You tell him he's probably descended from noble Viking warriors and you'll be his new best friend. Tell him Iron Age Switzerland saw people practicing hu-man sacrifice and he'll never speak to you again."

"And would that be a bad thing?"

Bailey laughed. "From a personal perspec-tive, no. But from a professional one, yes. See, the thing is he's loaded. Seriously. Guy practically owns his own mint. And with the proper amounts of flattery and persuasion he can sometimes be convinced to part with a little of it for a good cause. So whenever the head of the department was trying to find funding for a new expedition or a piece of equipment or something, he'd round up whoever he thought could sway Bender and drag them down to the yacht club for a weekend."

"Bender?"

"Yeah, Claudio Bender. And his son, Henry, who is my age and still follows him around like a shadow, catering to his every whim."

Death laughed, then glanced at his watch and rose. "It was nice meeting you. I'd better go find that museum. I'm going to be late. Thanks for the info."

"No problem."

He started to leave, then turned back with an afterthought. "By the way, um. How bad is that radiation? It's just, my fiancée minored in art history when she was here, so . . ."

"Oh, it's not too bad," Bailey said.

"Oh good."

"I mean, you might have glow-in-the-dark kids, but hey! At least you'll save a fortune on nightlights."

Two blocks shy of Wren's house, Edgar eased his truck over to the side of the road and put it in park. He turned off the engine and slid around in his seat to face his wife.

"What are you going to say?" he asked.

Emily was still fuming. If anything, she was angrier now than she had been when she first returned to the truck.

"I'll just smile and say, 'Hello, dear. So where's this lousy, scumbag of a deadbeat father you think you're going to marry?' "

Edgar made a show of considering it. "Do you think that might not go over too well?" he ventured at last.

"Well, what do you suggest I say?"

"I don't think you'd ought to say anything."

She glared at him. "What? But —"

He held up one big hand and tipped his head. "Don't you think we might not know the whole story here?"

Emily sighed and slumped in her seat, pouting.

"Wren's not an idiot," Edgar continued. "She's not going to involve herself with the sort of man who'd let his child go hungry."

"So maybe she doesn't know."

"Doesn't know? That he has an ex-wife with a toddler? An ex-wife who's running around town with Eric Farrington? This is East Bledsoe Ferry. I doubt there's anyone in the county who doesn't know."

"Well, then . . ." his wife trailed off uncertainly.

"I'm just saying that if you go off half-cocked, it isn't going to do anything but start a fight."

"So, what? I'm supposed to just act happy that our daughter's planning to marry this lowlife scumbag?"

"We only have one side of the story here."

"But his ex-wife said —"

"And she might be lying. We don't know her and we don't know what's going on. You know, and I never thought I'd be saying this, but Eric Farrington was right. There are people who track down deadbeat dads and laws to put them in jail. Doesn't it seem odd to you that if Death really is neglecting to pay child support, he hasn't been arrested? It's not like he's hiding. This is a small town," Edgar said again. "I just think we need to wait and see what we can find out."

Emily thought about it for a minute. "So I should go in and say, 'Hi, honey. So tell me all about Death. Like, why isn't he paying any damned child support?' "

"Yeah, because that wouldn't start a fight at all."

"What? I'm not allowed to ask?"

"If you assume the worst, you're not only insulting her boyfriend, you're insulting her judgment. Trust me. I've been dealing with you Morgan women for a long time. This is not a good plan."

Emily sulked some more. "She could have been honest with me about it. Whatever it is."

"How wasn't she honest? She told you Death had been married before, didn't she?"

"Married, yes. But she never said a word about him having a baby."

"The whole two times you've talked on the phone?"

"She could have called more."

"Uh huh. And how many of those voice messages from her are still sitting on the phone waiting for someone to listen to them."

She made a face at him. "You don't know how to retrieve them either."

He chuckled, a rumbling sound deep in his chest. "That's not the point."

Emily sighed. "Okay, fine. What do you think we should do?"

"I think we should play it close to the vest. Take some time to get to know the boy and try to find out what's going on."

"If he turns out to be a con artist —"

"It'll hurt Wren. A lot. If that happens, I don't want her to feel she can't come to us. I don't want to alienate her. So no accusations, no lectures, no gotcha moments. Okay?"

Emily was silent for over a minute, looking away out the truck window.

"Em?"

"Okay, fine. I'll do it. But don't expect me to like it."

"No ma'am."

EIGHT

"Okay, so Rolly, Eldon, Tristan, and Cory are starting college next year, right?"

Wren sat in her living room with her feet up on the coffee table and a notebook in her lap. She was surrounded by stacks of dishes, glassware, pots and pans, and random kitchen utensils. Behind her, in the kitchen, the cupboards were empty for probably the first time in decades.

"Yes, that's right," Leona said over the phone. "Why?"

"I was wondering about their living arrangements. Are any of them getting their first apartments?"

"No, I believe they're all going to live in the dorms, at least for the first year."

"Dang."

"Again, why?"

Wren sighed. "I've just got a lot of stuff and I was thinking I could pass some of it on to help them get set up on their own."

131

"I see. You know, we could always sell it," Leona suggested. "Put it in the weekly consignment auction."

On Friday evenings the local auctioneers took turns running a consignment auction in one of the barns on the county fairgrounds. It kept the building in use throughout the year, and a portion of the proceeds each week went toward supporting the local food bank.

"Yeah, but I don't really want to sell them," Wren said. "I mean, I shouldn't be attached to all of this stuff, but . . ."

"But you are."

"Yeah. Does Mercy have a hope chest? I've got some nice things set aside she could have for her hope chest. We could let her pick out what she wants. And why do only girls get hope chests? Boys need dishes and linens and things too."

"That's a good idea. And if the point is to set them up for having their own home, they should have some basic tools, too. For girls and boys both."

"Right! Like a hammer and some nails and screwdrivers."

"Pliers," Leona agreed. "A utility knife. A flashlight."

"So can we make this happen?"

"Let me look into it," Leona said. "We're

not in a dire hurry here, are we? You're not ready to move just yet and those dishes aren't going to explode if we don't instantly find them a new home."

"No. They're just sitting all around my living room looking breakable." Wren looked forlornly at the stacks of plates and bowls and the precarious towers of cups.

Leona laughed. "Well, don't break them. I'll talk to the kids' parents. I'm sure we can find a hope chest for Mercy. I don't think she has one yet. And I don't see why we can't get them for the boys too. Have you thought about offering Randy any? He's looking for a house, right?"

"Yeah, but he's already got a whole household full of stuff in St. Louis. He finds a house, he just moves whatever he wants from there."

"Oh, of course. Well, hang in there. We'll get it figured out."

"Thanks."

The two women said their goodbyes and hung up. Wren was just sitting there, thinking about nothing very much at all, when Lucy started barking joyfully in the front yard. Wren went to see what the commotion was about and saw her parents' camper parking behind her truck in the driveway.

She ran outside and down the steps and

met them in the yard. Wren's mom was a short, plump woman whose dark hair and eyes and tan complexion stood as evidence of her Native American ancestry. She had a cheerful demeanor and a perpetual smile that hid an iron will. She was smaller than Wren, and when Wren hugged her, her cheek pressed against her mother's hair.

Her father, on the other hand, was a big, blue-eyed man with strawberry-blond hair turning white. The top of her head barely reached his chest, and when he enveloped her in his arms she felt like a child again, safe and content.

"I wasn't expecting you so soon. Where were you when I talked to you last? Did you have a good trip?"

"We were in Knoxville," her dad said. Her mother had started for the house and they followed with their arms still around one another. "We'd have been here sooner, but there's a lot of roadwork going on. Nashville was pretty much one big bottleneck and there was a detour in southern Illinois that took us miles out of our way."

Wren's mother reached the door, pulled it open, and stopped. She was looking at the piles of dishes and things all over the living room, and her eyes narrowed and her mouth tightened in disapproval.

"So. You really do think you're moving, then."

The parking lot at Mizzou North was nearly empty, and Death was able to find a close spot without using the much-hated handicapped tag he kept shoved out of sight in his glove compartment. He had been running early when he got to the main campus; now he was slightly late for his appointment. He'd phoned his contact and gotten no answer, but left a message on her voicemail and hoped she would be waiting for him.

He was meeting Cecily Myers, the art history grad student whose thesis on Volkmer had led to the discovery that the Ring Portrait in the Warner Museum was forged. Meeting in public had been her idea, and it was she who'd suggested they rendezvous in the cast gallery of the art history museum, in front of a statue called *Laocoön and His Sons*.

The former hospital looked like a hospital. Death, who'd had his share of unpleasant experiences in hospitals around the world, entered with a sense of dread settled into the pit of his stomach. Inside, it was obvious that someone had spent money and considerable effort on trying to make it not look like a hospital.

They hadn't met with a great deal of success.

He followed the signs in the lobby and rode up on the elevator, convinced in the back of his mind that when the door opened he would find himself in a functioning ward, with doctors and nurses and the soft hospital sounds of heart monitors and ventilators. It occurred to him, for one wildly irrational moment, to be afraid that none of this was real. That he was still in an induced coma back in Germany and that when he woke up he'd find that Wren and all the rest of his life was only a fever dream.

The doors slid open. It still felt like a hospital up here, but it was empty of life. He again followed the signs, down a hall and past empty rooms and a deserted nurses' station, and finally went through a door and into a museum. At last there were people, moving quietly among the exhibits.

The museum space had been completely remodeled and did feel like a museum, though even here there was an odd dynamic. Death walked slowly through the exhibits, taking them in as he made his way to the cast gallery.

Wren had told him about the cast gallery. When she was a student, she and a friend had made a habit of sitting on the floor in a corner to study. Her friend had always been sorely tempted to push Apollo over but had resisted the urge. Death knew that the museum's collection of plaster casts dated back to the early 1900s, and that they were an important and valuable collection in their own right.

Copies, Death thought. Someone had wanted something they couldn't have so they made a copy instead. Basically, it was the same thing his mystery thief had done, only his thief took it one step further and traded out his copy for the real thing.

He found Laocoön without any difficulties. He and his sons were busy being devoured by serpents in front of an enormous window. The sculpting was impressive, even if the subject matter was more than a little bit gruesome and creepy. Death looked around, and a young woman with fluorescent pink hair abandoned a headless statue of winged Nike and approached him.

"Mr. Bogart?"

"Yes. You must be Ms. Myers."

"Call me Cecily, please."

"Hi, Cecily. I'm Death."

"It's nice to meet you. I hope you don't mind meeting me here. It's just that I don't know you."

Death smiled at her reassuringly. "Not at

all. I approve, in fact. I handle a lot of missing persons cases. I can't tell you how many of them could have been avoided if only someone had exercised a healthy dose of paranoia." He nodded at the museum around them. "What do you think of the new location?"

She lifted thin shoulders in a shrug. "Well, it's not radioactive, so that's a good thing. It's not nearly ideal. I mean, some people like that it's more accessible to the city and to people going through on I-70. And there's more parking. But it's a lot harder for students to get out here. And students are the ones who need it."

"It feels weird," Death confided. "I think it's because the exhibits are all so old but everything else seems so new."

"Yeah. They had to get all-new display cases and things. They didn't know how badly the old ones were contaminated."

"But at least there's more room here, right?" Death said, thinking of all the empty floors above and below them. "If the museum acquires more stuff it will be able to display it."

Cecily laughed. "Yeah, you'd think so. Would you believe that only about three percent of the museum's holdings are currently on display?"

"Seriously? Three percent?"

"Yup. And the Anthropology Museum only has room for one percent of their collections."

"What is done with the rest of it?"

"It's kept in storage, studied, used for classes."

"Wow." Death looked around, found a bench, and led the way to it. Standing was beginning to take its toll on him. "So tell me about Volkmer."

Cecily bypassed the bench and took a seat on the floor to his left with her back against the wall.

"Hans Volkmer was a first-generation American   his parents came from Germany in the 1840s. He was a portrait artist who traveled the western half of the US from 1878 until his death in a steamship explosion in 1912. He worked like a traveling photographer. He'd set up a studio in a corner of a saloon or general store and paint portraits on commission. He'd let people watch him paint. Back then, on the frontier, that counted as a form of entertainment. He'd pay the store or saloon owner a small commission and the novelty of him being there painting attracted a crowd, so it drove business for the store and helped him get more commissions."

"Sounds like a pretty shrewd business-man."

"Oh, he was. He didn't get much credit for it, though. Other artists and critics considered him a hack and he was pretty widely looked down on. Only now are we realizing that not only was he a good businessman, he was actually a pretty good artist too."

Death nodded. "And what's your angle with your thesis? I'm wondering what led to the decision to have the Ring Portrait x-rayed and so forth."

Cecily smiled. "Oh, that wasn't really me, so much. I was just invited to join the project, since Volkmer is my specialty and I probably know more about him than anyone else alive." It wasn't a boast, the way she said it, but simply a statement of fact. "That was for a part of a documentary that's being made for public broadcasting."

"About Volkmer?"

"About transportation routes and how art supplies like pigments and metals and such were shipped across country. About how the availability or lack of materials affected art on the frontier."

"I see. And whose project is that?"

"There's a film class over at Central Missouri, in Warrensburg, that's making the

140

documentary. The whole thing is underwritten by a grant from the Nordstern Foundation."

"Okay," Death said, "one more question. Can you tell me what happened when they took the paintings down and transported them to the lab? You were there, right?"

"Yes, I was there. Nothing happened, really. Nothing out of the ordinary. The museum had to move a bunch of other stuff that was in a cabinet below the portrait. They were still packing up the last of it when we got there and we had to wait for about half an hour. Then they took the two portraits down and the lab technicians that were there helped pack them in special shipping crates. They loaded them into the back of the van they were driving and we took them to the lab."

"Did you ride with the paintings?"

"No, I had my own car. I drove behind them."

"And they went directly to the lab?"

"Yes, and we took the portraits in and they x-rayed them right then and there." Cecily pulled her phone out and glanced at it. "Was there anything else? I'm sorry, but I have a class I need to get to. I'm the teacher so if I'm late they'll all think they're getting a day off."

Death thanked her for her time and watched her walk away. When she was gone, he rose and returned to Laocoön, snapped a picture, and sent it to Wren. Then he called her.

"Hello?"

Her voice sounded a little bit off, but not terribly so. He didn't even think about it before he started talking.

"Sweetheart, I have bad news."

"Oh?"

"Yeah. I just tried to visit the museum in Pickard Hall, and the University has the building closed because of, are you ready for this? Radiation contamination. And it's been contaminated since the early 1900s. I figure that explains why you're so bright. But don't worry, honey. As soon as I get home, I'll strip-search you for radioactive isotopes."

There was a long silence.

"Wren?"

"I'm sorry. Wren's outside showing her dad the last of the garden."

A frisson of horror ran through Death. "Who — ?" His voice failed him. He cleared his throat and tried again. "Who — ?"

"This is Wren's mom. I saw her phone ringing and thought I should answer it. You must be Death."

Death took a deep breath. His hands shook and his heart was in his boots.

"Yes, ma'am," he said. "Yes, I am. Just at this minute I kinda wish I wasn't, though. You and Wren really sound a lot alike."

"Well, she is my daughter. What are you doing in Columbia?"

"I was meeting a girl. Not a girl! A woman. But not a woman! I mean, not because she's a woman. A client. Wait. Not a client. A witness. Sort of a witness." He made himself stop and take a deep breath. His chest felt tight and he didn't know if it was because of his damaged lungs or if he was having a future mother-in-law induced panic attack.

"Well," Wren's mom said, "I think Wren is expecting you for dinner. Are you going to be here or do you have further plans with this woman who's not a woman?"

"I'll be there, ma'am! I'm just ready to head back right now."

"Okay then. Now, you drive carefully. Wren's father is really looking forward to meeting you."

"And I'm looking forward to meeting both of you," he said. "Um, will you tell Wren I called?"

"Oh, yes. I'll tell her everything."

Death said goodbye and ended the call, then stood there for a long minute looking down at his phone.

"I am so dead," he said to himself.

NINE

Wren's driveway was full, with a pickup/camper and a sheriff's car. Death pulled his Jeep in behind the sheriff, along the front fence, and steeled himself and went in search of his bride-to-be and future in-laws.

He'd stopped on the way to pick up two bouquets of flowers, one for Wren and one for her mother, though he was a bit put out at the woman for answering Wren's phone and not identifying herself. Since being annoyed wouldn't make his future life any smoother, he resolved to at least try to make a good second impression.

He knocked, even though he was accustomed to coming and going as if he lived there, but when no one answered he went on in. The living room was dotted with stacks of dishware, which told him what Wren had been doing all day. The house, however, was empty. He went through the kitchen (surreal with the cupboards stand-

145

ing open and bare) and followed the sound of voices and a sporadic clanging to the back yard.

Wren and her mother were nowhere in sight, but Sheriff Salvadore and a man Death recognized from pictures as Wren's father were playing horseshoes. The sheriff was pitching while Edgar Morgan lounged in an Adirondack chair with a beer at his elbow and Wren's dog, Lucy, at his feet. Death watched while Salvy threw a ringer and a near ringer. "Five points. That brings me to nineteen." He turned to the house. "Are you going to lurk in the door all day or you want to come out and say hi?"

Death lay the flowers he was carrying on the counter, pushed the screen door open, and trotted down the steps. Wren's father rose up to meet him.

Wren had never mentioned that her dad was a giant. Death was a big man himself, but his future father-in-law had two or three inches even on him. And it wasn't just height. He was built like an oak, with broad shoulders, and his hands, when he offered Death a handshake, were huge.

"So you're Death," he said. His voice was a deep rumble, soft and surprisingly mild. "Come sit down and tell me a little bit about yourself."

146

Death took a seat near the other two men. Before Edgar could join him, Salvy reminded him that it was his turn. Edgar took up the two blue horseshoes, stepped to the line, and casually sailed them at the stake, one after the other. He threw them like Frisbees, with a flick of his wrist, and they both caught the stake and spun around it before coming to rest.

"Six points. Twenty-one and I win."

Salvy gave Edgar a baleful glare and Wren's dad chuckled — a deep, rich sound.

"Don't feel sorry for him," he told Death. "He can run circles around me on a ball diamond." He fished in a cooler by his chair and offered Death a beer. "So you're a Marine? What made you decide to join the Corps?" he asked as he reclaimed his seat. Wren's big tomcat, Thomas, jumped into Edgar's lap and made himself comfortable.

Death sank a little into his chair and ducked his head. He wasn't comfortable talking about himself but he understood the questions. If someone was planning to marry his daughter, he'd want to know all about the guy too.

"My dad was a cop," he said. "Grandad was a firefighter, and my little brother was already set to be a paramedic. My mom taught English lit and ran a volunteer

147

literacy program and my grandmother was one of the country's first female DAs. Our family was always strong in our belief in public service. I wanted to do that too, but I also wanted to go my own way. Try something new. I liked the Marines because of the traditions of honor and loyalty, and I thought it'd give me a chance to see the world."

"What happened?"

Death laughed a short, unhappy laugh and took a drink of beer. "I got blown up in Afghanistan." He didn't like telling this. It felt too much like admitting to weakness, too much like a flaw. But Edgar was bound to hear it somewhere and he figured it was better coming from him than from someone else. "I'm okay now, mostly. But my lung capacity was compromised. I was given a medical discharge. And now law enforcement and the fire service are out of the question too because I can't pass the physical."

"So now he's a bad-ass bounty hunter," Salvy offered. He was out of uniform but drinking tea. He saluted them with the glass.

Death laughed again, a little more real this time. "Part-time bounty hunter," he said, correcting him. "Mostly I'm a private detective."

"How do you make a living at that, if you don't mind my asking?"

"I do a lot of industrial espionage type of work. Figuring out what employees are stealing from their companies, who's trying to smuggle trade secrets to whom, finding holes in a corporation's internal security protocols. I also get a lot of missing persons cases and I have a decent success rate with those, though it's still nowhere near high enough given the stakes involved. And once in a while I get something that pays really well."

"Like finding a cache of missing jewels or two," Salvy offered.

Death had the feeling the sheriff was helping him out. "That does not hurt," he admitted with a grin. He looked around. "So where are the ladies?"

"Grocery shopping," Edgar said. "Mom wants to bake a Depression cake and Wren was out of raisins." He tipped his head. "Maybe that's them now."

Death hadn't heard a car drive up but now he listened to a single car door slam. The three men watched the kitchen door expectantly and (on Death's part) with some trepidation, but it was neither Wren nor her mother who appeared.

Randy Bogart was still in his medevac

uniform. He was moving quickly and his eyes lit up when he saw Death.

"Hey! What's going on? Where's Wren? Why are there dishes all over the house? Where's Wren? I got something to tell you guys!"

"Wren's out shopping with her mom," Death said. "Mr. Morgan, this is my kid brother, Randy. Randy, this is Wren's father, Mr. Morgan."

"Oh, hey!" Randy bounced down the steps and leaned down to shake Edgar's hand. "Wow, you're huge." He smacked the back of his hand against Death's shoulder. "Better not step out of line, dude. He's bigger than you are."

Death buried his face in his hands. "I apologize for my brother. I don't know why he's acting like a hyperactive kangaroo. Randy, have you been in the sugar again?"

"I found out something," Randy repeated. "You're not gonna believe this! When's Wren coming back? I wanted to tell both of you."

"In a little bit. We don't know. Tell us now and you can tell her when she gets back."

"Okay, but you have to let me tell her. No telling her yourself and hogging the glory."

"I promise. Now what is it?"

"Sit down."

"We are sitting down."

"Oh, right. Okay, then, hold on to your chairs. That house that you and she are planning to buy?"

"Yeah?"

"There's a body buried in the *rosebushes*!"

There was a long, awkward silence. Death made his voice as gentle as he could. "We already know that."

Randy's face fell. "What? No you don't! How would you know that?"

"The lady that lives there told Wren the first time she looked at it. Wren told me."

"How come no one told me?"

"We've hardly seen you, with all the crazy hours you've been working."

"Randy's an air medic with the helicopter service," Salvy explained to Edgar. "They're shorthanded right now and he's been pulling a lot of overtime."

Randy pulled over another chair and dropped into it, dejected. "Did you know?" he asked the two older men.

" 'Fraid so," Edgar said.

"How'd you find out?"

"We remember when it happened." Edgar turned to Salvy. "You ever figure out anything about that guy?"

"Nothing yet. My deputies still work it as

a cold case any chance they get, though with funding cuts and staffing shortages there's not a lot of time for things that aren't currently urgent. But we have his profile up everywhere we can get it and once every couple of years or so someone will think they recognize him. So far none of those leads have panned out, but I suppose it's progress of a sort. Maybe now, if his grave is going to be owned by a private detective, some progress can really be made."

All three of the other men turned to look at Death.

"I'd certainly be interested in looking into it. I was wondering earlier what you knew about it. Mrs. Sandburg said you had someone do a facial reconstruction?"

"We did," Salvy replied. "It's online at our department website and on several other sites that specialize in locating missing persons and identifying John and Jane Does. Or you can come by the station and see the actual sculpture in person. We had to make a reverse mold from the skull, then cast a polyresin replica and send it to an artist back on the East Coast. It's very lifelike. How close it is to how he actually looked, of course, remains to be seen."

"When did they find him?" Edgar asked. "During bow season, I know. Bow hunters found him. Was it '84?"

"Eighty-five, I believe."

"Of course. The year the Royals won their first World Series."

Growing up in St. Louis, Death was used to his dad and the other men relating things to what the Cardinals had done or to which football team they'd had at the time. It felt like a familiar measure of time, and it warmed him a bit to see Wren's dad doing the same thing.

"Where was he?" Death asked. "I know he was in the woods somewhere, but that covers a lot of territory."

"It does," Salvy agreed. "They found him out by the lake, over near Thibeaux Bend."

Death traced a map of the area in his mind. Truman Lake was a big, sprawling body of water with dozens of different arms and inlets. Its shoreline was longer than the coast of California.

"Thibeaux Bend — isn't that out by Cold Creek Harbor? Where the old yacht club is that the Keystones are getting ready for auction."

"Other side of the lake," Edgar said. "You're not wrong, they're probably less than a mile apart. But most of that mile is water."

"Oh, I see. Was anything found with him?

153

Clothing or change or anything? If he was hunting when he died there should have been a rifle or bow or something, right?"

"Fragments of a belt, I believe," Salvy said. "And one boot with the foot bones still inside. The remains had been out in the weather a long time and suffered significant predation. The bones were scattered and we — I say 'we,' but of course I was just a schoolboy at the time — we didn't begin to recover the entire skeleton."

"They did a forensic analysis of the remains, though. Right?"

"Of course. They went to the state crime lab. There's a full write-up in his file. We know he was a young adult, probably eighteen to twenty-five, 5'10", medium build. He was probably Caucasian, but they weren't able to tell definitively. The teeth they found showed no signs of any dental work and suggested Northern European ancestry, but they didn't find all of them."

"And there was no sign of what might have killed him?"

"Nothing at all. The pathologist thought he might have died of exposure. One of his leg bones was broken, but they couldn't tell if it happened before death, while he was dying, or afterward. It had been, ah, chewed on, I'm afraid. But if it happened while he was alive, it's possible he fell down the hill and broke his leg and then lay there and died waiting to be found."

"What a horrible way to go," Randy said.

Death tipped his head as a familiar sound reached his ears. It was the rumble of Wren's pickup. "There's the girls," he said. Two car doors slammed and again the men in the back yard watched the screen door expectantly.

Wren came through first, picking up the flowers Death had abandoned. "Look! Someone brought flowers! I bet I know who!"

Death stood to greet her and got an armful of redhead. He kissed her chastely on top of the head, mindful of the fact that her parents were watching, then took the flowers and presented one bouquet to her and one to her mother.

"Sweetheart. Ma'am, I hope you like alstroemerias."

Wren's mom beamed at him, a glint of something he hoped was humor in her eye. "They're lovely. Thank you." She looked around and cocked her head. "No Geiger counter?" she asked innocently.

Death felt his face grow hot.

"Here, Wrennie," her mom continued. "Give me your flowers and I'll go find vases for them. I think I saw a couple in the living room. On the floor."

She disappeared into the house and Wren leaned down to hug her dad, then saw Randy and hugged him too.

"Randy! You're here! I'm so glad. I've missed you, working all those hours. Did Death tell you our news?"

"I don't know. What news?"

"We found a house we want to buy! And there's a *body* buried in the *rosebushes*!"

"Odd bit of synchronicity," Wren said. A muffled shout and a series of thumps and bangs came from overhead. She paused and glanced up. "Are they going to fall through the ceiling?"

"I hope not," Leona said mildly. "Though I'd lay odds that if one of them were to, it'd be Roy."

"No bet there. What are they doing?"

"They're still worried about the possibility of a fire. If it's cold on the day we hold the sale, it would make sense to hold it inside. But the Beverly Hills Supper Club fire was horrendous. We want to keep the customers warm. We do not want to kill them."

"I understand, but I still don't get what

they're doing crawling around in the ceiling."

"Part of the reason that fire spread so fast was because there were no firewalls. So the guys have got some sheets of nonflammable insulation and they're making partitions."

"Oh. Cool."

"So what were you saying about synchronicity?"

Wren lifted four chairs upside down on a small round table and used chalk to mark a 7 on the bottom of each, to match the 7 in the middle of the table. They were sorting the furniture now and moving it into long rows to make it easy to go through and auction off. A few more days work on the main building and they'd be ready to move on to the boathouse. Leona had the sale penciled in for Sunday of the week after next, the weekend before Thanksgiving.

"Death was up in Columbia on Tuesday to meet someone about his investigation into that missing picture. Well, he wound up talking to one of the art and archaeology professors and the man had a missing persons poster for Ingrid Larsen on his wall."

"Well, isn't that something?" Leona was doing even numbers. She put together another set of table and chairs and labeled them with an eight. "Of course, her dad was a professor there, wasn't he? So I suppose it's not that strange."

"Yeah. Death said the professor knew Dr. Larsen. He knew all about this place, too. He's been to the Viking village, and he's also been here, to the club. He told Death basically the same thing that Jacob Larsen told me — that the guy who owned it was a wealthy history buff and the department chair would bring the professors down to try to sweet-talk him into donating money for their different projects and things."

"Bender?"

"You know him?"

"I don't know him. I've met him a time or two. You know, he tried to buy this place back? Must have changed his mind after he sold it. But he wanted the Vikings' land too and they wouldn't sell, so he gave it up. I gather he had some grand idea about opening a fancy resort hotel."

Wren snorted. "Why would he think that was a good idea? For that matter, why did he think a yacht club was a good idea? I mean, we're kind of out in the middle of nowhere here."

Leona laughed. She put three chairs up on the next table, but simply slid the fourth one out and sat down in it. "Unbridled optimism. There was a lot of that around here then."

Wren took a chair of her own. "I don't understand."

"Back in the sixties and early seventies, things were pretty bleak around here, economy-wise. There had been a few things to keep people working over the years — Warsaw had a button factory, until they drove the river mussels to extinction. East Bledsoe Ferry had a couple of fireworks factories until one of them blew up and killed several people. Coal and Lewis Station had coal mines that collapsed. Clinton had a white sulfur spring that was a tourist attraction until the hotel burned down, and a thriving mail-order baby chick business until everyone moved into the cities after the Second World War. By the time 1970 rolled around, there wasn't very much going on. And then they built the dam and started talking about all the tourism and industry it was going to bring. A lot of people were walking around with dollar signs in their eyes."

"I see a lot of failed businesses and buildings sitting empty," Wren agreed.

"Yup. Everybody and his brother was opening some kind of store or venture, determined to get rich. Boat storage, campgrounds, restaurants, bars, flea markets, souvenir shops, bait shops. You name it. Some of them stuck, but a lot of them didn't. For one thing, it took years for the reservoir to fill and back up along the tributaries to create the lake. People with businesses along the fringe went broke before they could strike it rich. This place was probably doomed from the start. When it opened, as I recall, there wasn't a lot of lake here yet. The channel was shallow, and there were drowned trees everywhere they didn't specifically clear them."

"So when did it go under, do you know?"

"That I couldn't say. Early eighties, maybe? My youngest brother graduated in '82 and I know it was closed by then because he and his class rented the place for an after-graduation party. I remember helping raise money for it."

There was a loud bang and Wren and Leona both jumped and looked up, thinking the twins had broken through the ceiling. But it was Robin, slamming the door open as he rushed in from where he'd been working in a garden shed out on the edge of the property.

"You guys!" he said. "Come quick. You gotta come see this!"

A ceiling tile slid to the side and Roy stuck

his head through upside down. "What's all the commotion?"

"Grandpa Roy! Grandpa Sam! Come look at this!"

"What is it?"

"Just come look!"

"Well, go get our ladder. It's in the other room."

Robin ran to fetch the ladder and the two men came down bickering amiably.

"Nice luck," Sam said dryly. "Now you don't have to admit that you walled us off away from the other opening."

"I didn't wall us off. You were as much responsible as I was."

Wren and Leona were waiting for them at the door. "What are we looking at?" Leona asked Robin.

"Come over this way, down by the lake."

The back door of the yacht club opened into the overgrown formal garden, with paved, symmetrical walkways and a dry fountain in the center collecting weeds and dirt. They followed the paths through it, then crossed a field and came to a stop on the shore.

"Well!" Wren said. "Will you look at that?"

It was a beautiful fall day, with the water reflecting back a cloudless sky and the reversed image of all the blazing red and orange and gold trees at the lake's edge. Sailing across the blue expanse, like a dream image or a phantom from the distant past, was the Viking longboat under full sail. Canvas billowed over it and half a dozen young men, stripped to the waist, manned the oars, adding to the boat's speed.

"I feel like we should be running to hide all our valuables and take up arms," Sam said.

"Really?" his brother asked. "I feel like I should be standing in the middle of the boat, telling them to row faster so we can conquer the world."

"I think it's beautiful," Leona said, "but I'm glad I live in this century and not that one."

Wren could only nod and wish that Death was there to see this with her.

TEN

"Why does someone forge something?" When the door between his office and the tiny apartment behind it opened, Death spoke without looking up.

"Bleaargh."

He looked up.

"Good grief, Randy! You gonna make it?"

"Oh yeah."

Randy scrubbed a hand through his already tousled hair and stumbled toward the coffee maker. He wore a loose robe over a T-shirt and a pair of boxer shorts and there was a mark on his left cheek from a fold in his pillow.

He poured a cup of coffee, took a sip, then hugged it like a teddy bear. "What time is it?"

Death glanced at the wall clock. "About three o'clock."

"A.m. or p.m.?"

"P.m., doofus. It's light outside."

"Oh, yeah." He wandered over and dropped into the chair across from Death. "Still Thursday?"

"Last time I checked."

"Oh. Good."

Death sat back in his own seat and dropped the pencil he was holding. "Man, you gotta stop working so many hours. All work and no play makes Jack a dull zombie."

"Ha. Ha." Randy cuddled his coffee close. "Rhianna's vacation ended yesterday and Jay's back as soon as he gets cleared by a doctor."

"Good. What happened to Jay again?"

"Fell off his kid's hoverboard. Presumably after saying, 'Hold my beer and watch this.' What were you blithering about? Forgery? Forging stuff? What?"

"Forging things," Death explained. "I asked you why someone forges something."

Randy shrugged. "Because it's the best way to shape the metal?"

"Not that kind of forging. Forging! Forgeries. Fake paintings and such."

"Oh. I dunno. Because you want to steal the original, I guess?"

"But that doesn't make any sense," Death objected. "Not by itself. If you steal something, you only have to take it without getting caught. But if you replace it with a

164

forgery, you have to, one, get a forged copy — and where do you do that? And two, you have to sneak the copy into wherever the original is kept. Three, you have to switch them. And, four, you still have to take the original out without getting caught."

"Do we have any cinnamon rolls?"

"Over there in the cupboard," Death said, pointing back into the apartment. Randy went to get one and Death kept talking. "Now, with most art forgeries, the point isn't to replace an existing painting or whatever, but to convince the experts that you've found an unknown one, or one that's lost, and get them to pay you a lot of money. But obviously that doesn't apply in this case."

"What case?" Randy demanded. "What are you even talking about?"

"Boy, are you cranky when you sleep too long! I'm talking about the case I'm working on. I have a new case." Death grinned. "The Case of the Counterfeit Lady."

"Did you hit your head again?"

"No. Listen!" He explained to his brother about the missing portrait. "So whoever took it had to not only remove the original, which would have been nearly impossible, but they had to replace it with a copy without getting caught."

Randy stuffed the last bite of cinnamon roll into his mouth and spoke around it. "What do you think happened? Why do you think someone forges something?"

"I think someone forges something because they want to steal the original and they believe replacing it will help keep them from getting caught."

"That makes sense," Randy said. He thought about it. "Okay, no. Actually it doesn't. I mean, yeah it does, but, duh. Obviously if you're gonna steal something you don't want to get caught. Are you just grasping at straws here?"

"No, really. I have a theory."

"Okay, shoot."

"The person or persons who replaced the painting with the forgery needed to replace it rather than simply steal it, because otherwise it would be obvious who had taken it as soon as it was discovered missing."

"Are you following you? Because I'm not following you."

"Drink more coffee. I think I figured out when and how the paintings were switched."

"When? And how?"

"In all the years that portrait was at the museum, it remained in the same location, on the wall above the stairs. In full view of anyone in the area, and with a glass case full of breakables under it."

"Are you sure of that? I mean, yeah, the museum people said that. But do you have any way of verifying it?"

"Wow. You're suspicious when you're sleepy."

"One of us has to pretend we have a brain. Answer my question."

"Yes, I have verified it. Frank Appelbaum, the painting's owner, who has no reason whatsoever to lie, backed the museum's statement. I also found a variety of old pictures from events and things that have taken place there and every one that shows that patch of wall above the staircase shows the painting there."

"Okay. I'll accept that. Go on."

"Thank you," Death said dryly. "Now, security could have done it, if there were two or more guards in on it and they planned it out in advance. But the Warner Museum has used the same security company forever. Their guards are all bonded and thoroughly investigated before being hired. Also, the security company has contracts with a bunch of public and private buildings, and they assign the individual guards at random just before their shifts start. They literally draw numbers to see where they're going to be working on any given night."

"So they couldn't plan a heist." Randy stopped and grinned. "We're talking about people planning a heist!"

Death sighed. "Could you send your inner child back to bed for a while and concentrate here?"

"Spoilsport. Fine! I'm serious. This is my serious face." Randy leaned on the desk and glared at his brother balefully. "Tell me what you figured out."

Looking at him, Death couldn't help but laugh.

"What I figured out," he said, "is that there's only been one time — so far as I've been able to ascertain — when it would've been not only possible but easy to switch the paintings."

"And that time was . . . ?"

"When they took it down to x-ray it."

Randy blinked, sat up, and frowned at him. "But there'd have been no opportunity. I thought you said the lab techs packed it into a shipping crate and put it directly into the back of their van. And then took it from there directly to the lab to start testing it?"

"That's what I said all right."

"Oooh." Randy nodded but his tone was skeptical. "You think the lab techs stole it?"

"It's the best explanation I can think of.

Say they already have the copy packed in an identical shipping carton in the back of the van. They slide the real portrait in next to it. When they reach the lab, they just pull out the copy instead."

"But when they x-ray it . . ."

"They're just the impartial scientists who discovered it was a forgery. Who would ever suspect them of being involved in the theft?"

"You mean besides a crazy jarhead?" Randy crossed his arms and slouched in his chair. "I don't know, man."

"Don't know? Don't know? What do you mean you don't know?"

"I mean, yeah. That would work and I can see it happening if this were a story. But for real life, it just seems a little farfetched. What I mean is, why are a couple of lab technicians going to want an obscure and not very valuable painting?"

"Yeah, I know. I figure they probably were just the hired help. Someone bribed them or blackmailed them or something. Whoever that was, they're the one we really want."

"But who could it have been?"

"That I don't know." Death sighed. "Cecily Myers is a possibility. Hans Volkmer is important to her and it would have to be a thrill to have one of his paintings, even if she could never show it to anyone."

169

"Where's a grad student going to get the money to bribe someone to steal something for her? And where did she get the forgery? Did she paint it herself?"

"I don't know. But she might not have had to pay them. Not in money, anyway."

"Ah. How sordid. And do you have any actual evidence for this, or . . . ?"

"No," Death admitted. "And I don't really think that's what happened anyway."

"No?"

"No. You see, when I was discussing this with Doris Keystone, she told me about three other instances in the past two years where some not-terribly-valuable collectible was replaced with a copy. She didn't think those cases were related to this one because none of the other items were paintings."

"But you think they are?"

"Someone replacing a worthless collectible with a copy is weird. The same weird thing happens four times in the space of two years, there has to be a connection."

"So what are you going to do now?"

"I'm going to look at the other three cases. I'm going to look for a common denominator."

"I haven't seen you around these parts for a while."

Edgar Morgan looked up from the paperback he was reading. It was still early — not yet six a.m. — and the diner was nearly empty. East Bledsoe Ferry Police Chief Duncan Reynolds was standing beside his table.

Edgar greeted him with a smile. "Pull up a chair."

"Thanks. I can't stay long." Duncan dragged a chair over and lowered himself into it. "You're meeting Salvy?"

"Yup. Doing a little fishing. Gonna take his boat out one last time before the weather gets too cold. I'm sure you'd be welcome to join us."

"Wish I could. I can't stay long. I just stopped to tell you Salvy's running a little late. He caught a drunk driver on his way over here and he's got to do the paperwork and hand him off to the chief deputy."

"I'm in no hurry," Edgar said. He brandished his novel. "I've got Louis L'Amour to keep me company."

"Where's the missus?"

"Still asleep. I had to sneak out on tiptoe this morning so I wouldn't wake up my girls."

Reynolds grinned at the mental image of the huge man walking on tiptoe. "So how's the vagabond lifestyle treating you? Do you like it as much as you thought you would?"

"It's good," Edgar said. "It's really good. It's had its ups and downs, of course. Got lost in the Appalachians during a thunderstorm. I'd prefer to never do that again."

"You think you'll ever settle down again?"

"I think we might. We've been talking about it. Maybe just a winter base. A little place to hole up during the cold months, then come spring we'll go wandering again. It would be nice to have a place to come home to."

The waitress came by with a refill for Edgar's coffee. Reynolds declined her offer of a cup and waited until she'd walked away. He drummed his fingers on the table and asked the question he was really wondering.

"So what do you think of your future son-in-law?"

Edgar shrugged, carefully noncommittal. "Don't really know enough to think anything yet. What do you think? Is there anything you think you need to tell me about him?"

Reynolds considered the question. "I think," he said slowly, "that there are an awful lot of things you *should* know about him. But it's not really my place to tell you, and I don't want to talk about him behind his back. Wren will tell you what you need to know, maybe. A lot of what needs to be said are probably things he won't say. But give him a chance. Take the time to really get to know him before you make up your mind. He's worth the investment."

He saw Salvy pull up outside the window and rose to leave. He turned back, though, before he'd taken three steps.

"I will tell you one thing. I think an awful lot of that young man."

Edgar gave him an impish grin. "So does my daughter, or so it seems."

Reynolds grinned back. "That she does," he agreed. "That she does."

The auction barn at the Rives County Fairgrounds had been designed by people who knew barns. For the ten days of the fair every July, the loft held animal feed and extra bedding and the main floor was divided into rows of pens with portable rails. For the rest of the year, the loft held the portable rails and the main floor of the barn served as a venue for 4-H meetings, community dances, an occasional wedding, and the weekly consignment auctions.

It was Keystone and Sons' week to host the consignment auction and the whole company was there to help. Leona and Doris were making a record of who brought in which item. Sam and Roy, with a couple of their older sons, were trying to figure out a bug in the speaker system, and Wren was helping some of the younger men set up tables and find a place for everything. There was already a good crowd on hand and it promised to be a fun and profitable auction.

Wren was wrestling a large air compressor into place when a little old man on a red motorized scooter nearly ran her over. He was slight, with pale blue eyes and blond hair turning white. He wore beige slacks and a light pink button-down and looked like somebody's kindly grandfather.

She jumped back. "Hey!"

"Stay out of the way," the old man said, unrepentant.

"Don't run over people," she returned.

"I won't if they stay out of my way." He wheeled his scooter back around so that he was facing her. "Listen, are you the company that's handling the auction out at Cold Creek Harbor?"

"The old yacht club? Yes, we're doing that sale."

"Supper club," he said.

"I'm sorry?"

"It wasn't a yacht club. It was a supper club. There's a difference. Get it right."

"Oh, I'm sorry. I was under the impression that they had boats there."

"Of course we did."

"Okaaay . . ."

"A supper club on a body of water can have boats, you know. That doesn't make them a yacht club."

"But don't yacht clubs also have restaurants a lot of the time?"

"Well, certainly.

"So what's the difference between them?"

"A supper club is classier, obviously."

"Okay, well . . . glad we've cleared that up. If you'll excuse me?"

Wren turned back to her work but the old man wasn't finished yet. "Listen, I need to talk to you."

"Sure. What about?"

"Do you know who I am?"

"No, sorry. Oh my God! Are you having amnesia?" Wren knew he hadn't meant it like that, but she'd always wanted to respond to that question that way.

"Of course not. Don't be foolish. My name is Claudio Bender. I used to own that supper club. I was the one who had it built, in fact."

"Oh, that's very interesting. It's nice to meet you." Wren offered him her hand but Bender didn't take it, and for a long minute she stood there with it stuck out in front of her before dropping it. "Okay, never mind."

"Listen," he said again. "I need to talk to you."

"I'm right here."

"When I owned that building, I lost a red-gold ring in the shape of an eagle. I need to know if you've found it."

"Not so far as I know," she said. "We'll certainly keep an eye out for it. But of course, if we find it, you'll have to talk to the current owner about getting it back."

"But it's my ring."

"It *was* your ring. You sold the building with all contents, so technically you don't own it anymore."

"Weren't you paying attention? I'm Claudio Bender."

"And I'm very happy for you. But I still can't give you something we've been entrusted to auction off without the express consent of the person we're conducting the auction for. But, hey! If it goes on the block, you're more than welcome to bid."

"You're a foolish girl. I'm going to talk to your superior."

"You just go right ahead."

He started to roll away and Wren thought of something. "Hey," she called after him. "Can I ask you something?"

Claudio turned back, annoyed. "I suppose so."

"Do you remember the afternoon in 1978 when one of your guests thought he saw his daughter's ghost?"

Claudio wheeled his scooter around and came back to her.

"How do you know about that? Have you been being nosy? You should stay out of things that don't concern you. It's rude. It doesn't matter anyway. He didn't see anything. There was nothing there. I suspect the man was drunk. These academics never can hold their liquor, you know."

"So you didn't see anything?"

"Not a thing. We sent my son to search the woods, as I recall. He didn't even find anything to suggest anyone had even been there."

"But Dr. Larsen's daughter disappeared that weekend. Doesn't that strike you as a little odd?"

"I suppose. But I really don't see how it has anything to do with us. And I don't know why you want to waste my time talking about something that happened before you were born when you won't even promise to give me my ring back."

"I'm just curious."

"An unattractive trait in young women.

You'll never catch a man that way."

"I already have a man. And the reason I'm curious is because Ingrid Larsen disappeared from a Renaissance festival where she was acting the part of a Viking maiden. And last week, two of the Keystone children found a Viking maiden's costume hidden in one of the lockers in the boathouse loft."

"That's ridiculous. Where is it? I want to see it."

"I turned it over to the sheriff's office. They've sent it to the state crime lab for testing."

"Why on earth would you do a thing like that?"

"Because," Wren said, "the skirt and the pinafore were caked with blood."

ELEVEN

Emily Morgan stopped on the sidewalk and studied the entryway. On the north side of the East Bledsoe Ferry town square, next to the Renbeau Bros. Department Store, stood a plain wooden door with a glass window. The sign on the window read, in neat lettering, *Bogart Investigations.* Beneath the name there was a phone number, and that was all.

Through the door she could see a steep staircase climbing up to the apartments above the department store. There was a small rectangular mailbox beside the door and on the wall inside there was a row of coat hooks, two of them occupied. She tried the door and it opened, jangling a little bell overhead. Emily huffed in a quick breath and let it out again, and then began to climb toward her future son-in-law's office.

Emily had done this whole "engaged" thing with Wren before. Just after her daughter graduated from college, she'd announced that she was marrying her high school sweetheart, a charming young man named Cameron Michaels, of whom Emily was very fond.

Cameron was a reporter for the local newspaper. He was neat, tidy, polite, an immaculate dresser, and had professed a dedication to abstaining from premarital sex, of which Emily had whole-heartedly approved. Unfortunately, it turned out that all his best attributes existed because he was, in fact, gay. Shortly before the wedding the burden of this secret became too much for him. The rehearsal dinner was dramatic and memorable, and the wedding, of course, never happened.

While Wren had been supportive of Cameron and they remained close friends, she'd also been deeply shaken by the fiasco and it had taken her some time to jump back into the dating scene. Her mother, of course, had hoped that she'd pull herself together and get on with her life, but she'd never expected Wren to get engaged again to the first charming rogue who came along.

A charming rogue who had yet to make the slightest mention of his son by another woman.

"Death Bogart," she muttered under her

breath. "Sounds like a character on a soap opera. I bet that isn't even his real name."

The steps ended in another door. This one was standing open, and Emily went into the office beyond. Death's brother Randy was there, dressed in sweats. Long and lean, he stood with one leg up on a corner of the desk, tying a running shoe. He saw her and his face lit with an open, easy smile.

"Hey, Mrs. M! What are you doing here?"

"Oh, I just thought I'd come down and see where you boys work. So this is your office, is it?"

"Uh, yeah. Well, it's Death's office. Also his apartment, through that door. I'm just staying with him until I find a place of my own."

"You don't work together?"

"No, ma'am. This is Death's business. I'm an air medic with the medevac air ambulance service."

"Oh." She was impressed in spite of herself. "But you don't have your own apartment?"

"Not just yet," he said. "I just moved here from St. Louis a couple of months ago." He finished lacing up his shoe and tying it and turned to pound on the interior door that led to Death's apartment.

"Hey! Are you decent? Wren's mom is here."

There was a flurry of footsteps and then Death yanked the door open and stuck his head out. He had a toothbrush sticking out of the corner of his mouth. His short hair was wet and there were traces of shaving cream on his face. He tried to speak, realized he had a toothbrush in his mouth, and made a face while holding up his index finger in a "just a minute" gesture.

He disappeared, and when he reappeared a moment later he was wiping his face with a towel. He tossed it over his shoulder and addressed her anxiously.

"Hi. Good morning. Um, is anything wrong?"

"No, of course not. Why should anything be wrong?"

"I just . . . I don't know. I wasn't expecting you."

"She just wanted to see where you work," Randy said. "For a given value of work, that is."

Death glared at his brother. "Ixnay on the artasserysmay."

"I see you're both versed in cryptography," Emily said dryly. Both boys had the grace to look abashed.

"Hey, come on in," Death said. "Help

yourself to a seat. Would you like some coffee?" He crossed to a coffeemaker on a side counter, picked up the empty carafe, and turned it upside down as if that would somehow make coffee magically appear.

"You didn't start the coffee?" he asked his brother. "Why didn't you start the coffee?"

"I didn't want any coffee. I'm going running. Why don't you start the coffee? It's not hard. All you have to do is put coffee in that little basket and then pour water into the top."

"I know how to make coffee."

"Well then, why don't you do it instead of standing there grousing about it?"

"You know, I've had puppies that act like you two," Emily told them.

The brothers stood stock still for a moment and just looked at her. Then Death waved the empty carafe.

"I'm just gonna start some coffee," he said.

Emily crossed to the desk and Randy hurried to pull a chair around and hold it for her. She rewarded him with a bright smile as Death came back from his apartment with a full container of water. He poured it into the top of the coffee maker, put the empty pot on the pad underneath, and turned to lean against the counter and face her while it brewed behind him.

"So," Randy asked her, "are you all alone? Where's Mr. Morgan today?"

"Oh, he left early to go fishing with the sheriff again. They're old friends, you know."

"So I've heard," Death said. "I don't know him well, but from what I've heard, Salvy seems like a great guy."

"Yes, he's a doll."

Emily looked past Death through the door into his apartment. Given the size of the building and the size of the office, it couldn't be very big.

"This isn't a very spacious place for two young men," she observed. "Don't you ever have visitors? Friends? Family maybe?"

"Randy is my family," Death said. "Randy and Wren."

"Really? You don't have anyone else at all?"

"No ma'am."

The conversation petered out and the three of them waited out a long, awkward silence. Finally, Death glanced over his shoulder and noticed that the ready light had come on on the coffeemaker. As he turned toward it, Emily spoke again.

"A little weak, don't you think?"

He'd forgotten to put any coffee in the basket.

Death thunked his elbow down on the counter and dropped his head into his hand. "I swear I'm not usually this incompetent," he said. "The truth is, I'm nervous because I want to impress you."

"Well, your goal is admirable."

He took a coffee filter from a drawer in the counter and scooped coffee from a nearby canister before pouring the water back through.

"So what *do* you do here all day, besides attempting to make coffee?"

Randy grinned at her, amused. Death grimaced.

"I'm a private investigator. I, uh, investigate. Privately. Umm . . . right now, for example, I'm working on a case involving a forged painting. I'm getting ready to leave, in fact, because I have an appointment with the director of the museum where it was housed."

"Really? I love museums. Which one?"

"Are you familiar with the Warner Museum of Frontier Art?"

"Oh, yes. I haven't been there in years. I'd love to go back again."

"Well, why don't you ride up there with him?" Randy suggested. "It'd give you a chance to get to know one another, and then you could look around the museum while he has his meeting."

"Randy," Death said. He looked dismayed. "She just got to town after traveling for months. I doubt she wants to go driving to the city again so soon."

"Oh, no. That's fine," Emily said. "A drive that short hardly even counts as traveling for me anymore. I'd love to go. If you wouldn't mind the company, that is."

"No, not at all," Death told her. "I'd love the company." He favored her with a smile, charming and flustered.

One thing was certain. Emily could see exactly why her daughter was attracted to him.

"Show me where you found the Viking clothes," Wren said.

With winter just around the corner, the auction season was winding down. Keystone and Sons had just one sale on the books that Saturday morning, and it was only a small auction to clear away the excess belongings of a septuagenarian who'd moved to Florida. The goods consisted almost entirely of unremarkable furniture, run-of-the-mill appliances, kitchen utensils, and random bedding. If it wasn't hands-down the most boring auction of the year, it would certainly be in the running for the title.

Mercy Keystone had begged not to go to it, but her mother, a nurse practitioner, was working that day. With her father occupied in helping to set up and call the auction, Mercy had to go somewhere. So, after promising to be good, crossing her heart, and pinky-swearing, she was allowed to accompany Wren and Robin back out to the yacht club to work toward getting it ready for the upcoming sale.

"It was in here," Mercy said now. "In the top of the boathouse."

She led the way into the small, dark building.

The first floor of the boathouse consisted of walkways around two slips for boats to come in off the lake. Wren entered cautiously, testing the strength of the floor and calling out to Mercy to be careful when the girl ran in and dashed fearlessly down the narrow wooden path. The slips had been dug out to allow even sailboats with a fairly deep draught to enter, but there hadn't been a lot of rain in the last month. There was a drop of at least a yard to the surface of the water, and Wren could see the bottom.

The walls of the boathouse were hung with coiled ropes and nets and oars, and there was a small rowboat in a cradle on the back wall. The two slips were surrounded by a waist-high wooden railing and at the back of the slip on the left, facing the lake, a section of that railing extended up, forming a ladder to the loft overhead.

Wren followed Mercy up the ladder. The loft was light and airy, with large windows overlooking the lake to the east and the yacht club and parking lots to the west. She hadn't climbed up to look at the spot last week because she'd been in too much of a hurry to get the bloody clothes to the sheriff's office. Now that she had the time, she looked around with interest.

On three sides, the walls were lined with all manner of things. There was a great deal of cast-off furniture, some of it broken; a life-sized mechanical Santa in a gold suit; a roulette wheel; and dozens upon dozens of boxes, bags, crates, and other containers. Wren opened one at random and found it full of Christmas lights. The milk crate next to it was completely full of hula dolls.

"We're going to have to get all this stuff down for the auction," she said. "We'll wait until everyone's here and form a bucket brigade."

The south wall was covered with lockers. When the kids had described them, Wren had pictured them as gray metal affairs like the ones they'd had in high school. But these were wooden compartments, each about two feet square and three feet deep. They had brass handles and fancy brass combination locks that of course had not slowed Matthew Keystone down in the least.

About half of them stood open. Wren nodded at them. "Your cousin do that?"

Mercy shrugged. "He said you'd only have to open them eventually anyway."

"He was probably right," Wren admitted

"Don't worry. I won't tell him."

They grinned at one another, and then Mercy led the way to the southwest corner of the loft. "This is where we found the clothes."

The locker Mercy indicated was no different, so far as Wren could see, from any of the other lockers around it. She peered inside but it was completely empty now. The sail that the clothes had been wrapped in still lay on the floor nearby, the canvas marked with the same rusty bloodstains as the costume it had hidden for who knew how long.

"Are you warm enough? Are you too warm? Please feel free to adjust the heater if you'd like."

Death had been less nervous under fire.

"No, I'm fine."

Emily Morgan sat in his passenger seat with her back straight and her head held high and her purse on her lap, the handle clasped in both her hands. She was a short woman. The seat belt crossed her ample bosom and ran under her chin, so that it looked like it was trying to hang her, but he couldn't think of any way to fix it.

"Would you like a pillow?" he offered.

She gave him a questioning, sideways look.

"The seat belt," he explained, gesturing at his own neck. "It looks uncomfortable. I thought maybe a pillow . . ." His voice trailed off uncertainly.

"Do you have a pillow?"

"Well . . . no."

She smiled. He couldn't decide if it was friendly or predatory. "I'm fine, thank you," she said. "Tell me more about this forgery."

"Oh, right. The forgery. Well, it's a painting by an artist named Hans Volkmer. A portrait of an early-nineteenth-century opera singer dressed as a character from Wagner's Ring Cycle. Have you heard of the Ring Cycle?"

"Yes. I've seen it performed."

"Oh. Uh, great. Well, this was a portrait of an actress who was in that. By Volkmer. Have you ever heard of Volkmer?"

"No, I can't say that I have."

"He was an artist. A painter. A portrait painter."

"That would explain why he was painting portraits."

"Right." Death sighed inwardly. He was fairly certain that by this point his future mother-in-law had decided he was an idiot. "Anyway, the subject of this portrait left it to her heirs and they lent it to the Museum of Frontier Art." For what seemed like the twentieth time, he launched into the story of the forged painting. Wren's mother listened attentively, not interrupting him to ask questions, and the explanation lasted until they were pulling into the museum parking lot.

"So what are we doing here today?" Emily Morgan asked.

"I have a theory about how and when the paintings were switched," he said. "It's occurred to me that there might be security video that would allow me to confirm or discount that theory."

Death led the way to the building and held the door for her. Once inside the museum, she stopped to admire the grand staircase. "Look at the graceful flow of those bannisters."

"I know," he agreed. "Like a waterfall of

gold lace. It looks like it was tatted rather than built, don't you think?"

He caught her giving him an odd look. "What?"

"I can't believe you know the word 'tatted'," she said.

"Well, hey. I'm not a complete barbarian. Unless you like barbarians. In which case I'll try harder." He glanced at his watch. "I need to get to my meeting with the museum director. Will you be okay on your own?"

"I think I can manage a short time without a keeper. Shall we meet somewhere when you're finished?"

"I can just come find you, if you like. It's not that big a place."

"All right then. Have fun. I'll see you in a little while."

Death made his way to Warner's office, the knots in his shoulders loosening. Warner was waiting for him. He asked him to come right in and got right to the point.

"You've found something?"

"I have a theory," Death said. "I'm hoping that you can help me test it. When Eiler Labs came and got the paintings to run tests on them, where was their vehicle parked?"

"In the garage," Warner said. "You enter it from a separate lot at the back of the building, and it connects directly to the work areas of the museum via freight elevator."

"And are there any security cameras in that area?"

"Yes, of course. Why?"

"Just a hunch. Could I see the footage from when the paintings were being loaded?"

"Sure. We'll have to go over to the security room. I'll have one of the guards meet us. They understand the machines better than I do."

Warner led Death out of his office and down a corridor to a small room tucked out of the way in a corner of the building. En route, they passed a room labeled *Textile Arts* and Death heard a pair of familiar voices come from within.

"Mr. Bogart is adorable. He seems really sweet, too. Is he your son?"

"No, dear. He's my daughter's fiancé."

"Oh."

Death sighed and followed Warner into the security room.

The guard, a petite blonde woman, was there before them. She was sitting in front of a desktop computer with a large screen that showed at least two dozen different camera feeds and covered both inside and outside the building. She was searching through the time stamps on a shot of the garage.

"I think this is the one you want," she said. "It's got the clearest shot of the van the lab used."

"Can we see the back of the van?" Death asked.

"Yep, should be able to."

She hit play and Death and Warner leaned in behind her to watch the video. The freight elevator in one corner of the screen opened and a small knot of people got out. Death picked out Lila and Cecily Myers and even Warner. There were also two men in lab coats, one of them pushing a two-wheeler with the crated paintings, and three other men, one of them in a security uniform.

"What are we looking for?" Warner asked.

"I want to see the inside of the van."

One of the techs unlocked the doors and swung them open, and they had a three-quarter view of the interior.

"Lot of junk in there," Warner commented. "I expected a lab to be a lot neater."

"You'd think, wouldn't you?" Death agreed.

The paintings were each in their own packing crate. These were made of thin wood and about three feet wide by four feet high and perhaps eight inches deep. Each of them had a label in the upper right corner.

"Can you focus in on the labels?" Death asked. "Is there any possibility of seeing them clearly enough to read them?"

"Sure." The guard manipulated her computer, freezing the screen and bringing the two labels up in side-by-side windows. Each had the name of the painting, the name of the artist, the name and address of the Warner Museum, and a serial number. Death noted which was the Ring Portrait, then nodded at the guard to continue the video. He watched as the techs slid first one packing crate and then the other into the van. The Ring Portrait went in first, then the Hamlet.

The crates were stood upright next to one another, beside another wooden crate that appeared to be of similar dimensions. This crate was lying on its side and was about three feet high and eight inches deep, but of an indeterminate width.

The van drove away. The guard stopped the recording and looked to Death expectantly.

"Good," Death said. "That's what I was looking for. Now I'm wondering if there's similar video of them being unloaded. And if there is, how I could get my hands on it."

"You could just ask," the guard suggested.

"You have it?" Death asked. "From the lab when they unloaded?"

"Yup."

"Our insurance only covers objects when they're in our possession," Warner explained. "As part of the agreement to let them study the paintings, Miss Myers and her associates were required to take out their own insurance policy to cover damage or loss to either or both paintings while they were in her possession. When we discovered the painting was forged, we put in a claim. They wanted to see the security video, to verify that the painting left our possession and was under the control of the lab when it was discovered missing." He sighed. "Since no one knows when it disappeared, neither carrier wants to assume responsibility. This nightmare could take years to resolve."

"Maybe not. Can we watch the other video?"

The guard already had it cued up and she played it at a nod from Warner. The angle into the van was more acute in this one, and Death could barely make out what was happening. Still, it showed him enough.

"Did you see that?"

"I don't know," Warner said. "What are we looking at?"

The guard obligingly set it to replay and Death pointed out the open back door on the van. "Watch where he takes the second shipping crate from. When they loaded these, remember, they were next to one another and both standing upright. But here, where they're unloading, they're taking the first one, then skipping one and taking the crate beside it. And that crate is lying on its side rather than standing upright."

"Play that again," Warner demanded.

The guard obliged.

"I'll be damned," Warner breathed.

"That painting wasn't stolen from your museum at all," Death said. "They switched them out on the way to the lab."

TWELVE

"Did people do a lot of drugs in the seventies? I'm just asking." Robin Keystone set a cardboard box down on the big table in the supper club's kitchen. Leona had come to pick him and Mercy up and give them a ride back to town. Wren was packing up one last carton and Mercy had gone in search of her coat.

"It was . . ." Leona thought about it, deciding on "a unique time. Can I ask what prompted the question?"

"It's just, this whole place is like a time capsule," Robin said. "A really weird time capsule. Look at some of this stuff." He reached into the box and pulled out a heavy gold medallion. "There's curly little hairs caught in this chain."

"They're chest hairs," Leona said. "Or at least we're gonna hope they're chest hairs. There was a fad for a while of men going around with their shirts open to their navels and wearing heavy gold jewelry. The more chest hair they had, the sexier they were considered."

"So that's a yes on the drugs?"

His great-aunt laughed. "What else do you have there?"

"The Hip Entertaining cookbook," Robin said. "I found it in the kitchen. They seem to have done a lot with gelatin molds."

"That's not so weird," Wren objected.

Robin turned the book around to show her a picture.

"Gah!" Wren reared back. "Oh my God! Is that salmon in gelatin? And it's got eyes! It's looking at me! Make it stop looking at me!"

"That's nothing. You should see the suckling pig."

"I'm not looking and you can't make me."

"They seemed to be big on cooking whole animals and then decorating them with fruit and vegetables and other animals . . . and they really liked mayonnaise. They seemed to think it was elegant."

"Crafts were big too," Leona remembered. "Slightly strange crafts, like making macramé plant holders with jute and wooden beads. And braided rag rugs — those were fun. And I remember one summer we cut up beer cans into rectangles and punched holes around the sides and crocheted them into hats."

Wren and Robin both just stared at her.

"You crocheted beer can hats?" Wren asked.

"Don't judge us." Leona laughed. "We only got three channels on TV and there was no way to record things and watch them later. You could only watch what was actually on. If you wanted to see a movie, you had to go to the movie theater. If you wanted a new book, you were limited to whatever was available at Walmart or the library. There was no Facebook, no Twitter, no YouTube, no video games."

"So what you're saying is you were really bored," Wren said.

"Which is why you did drugs," Robin teased.

"Now listen, you!" Leona retorted.

Robin flipped open the cookbook he'd found. It was the size of a magazine but hardback, with glossy pictures. He turned it to face her.

"What in the world is that thing?" Leona demanded.

"Can't you tell? What does it look like?"

"It looks like the Swedish Chef had a nightmare."

Wren took the book and studied it in horrified fascination. "This does kind of support his drugs theory," she said.

"What is it?"

She turned the book around again so she could point. "It's a pig made out of devilled ham, on a bed of lettuce, in a wallow made of mayonnaise. And it's suckling a bunch of piglets made of Vienna sausages." The pig's eyes were cherry tomatoes and its tail was a curl of carrot. The sausage piglets also had carrot tails but their eyes were slivers of black olives.

They just sat for a long minute and stared at the picture.

"Wow, that's a lot of mayonnaise," Wren said.

"We had good music," Leona offered finally.

Robin took the book back and leafed through it. "Here's a guy in a double-knit polyester leisure suit sitting on a zebra-striped, faux-fur sofa drinking a martini. I can't decide if that's awful or awesome."

Wren stood up and pulled on her coat, then swatted him lightly on top of his head.

"Congratulations," she said. "I think you understand kitsch now."

"And that was that," Death said. He dropped a mound of mashed potatoes on his plate and handed the bowl to Emily, to his left, and accepted the gravy boat from Randy, on his right. Edgar sat between Randy and Wren, who was in her usual seat at the other end of the table.

She looked up. "You sound disappointed."

"I am, a little," Death admitted. "I'd have liked to see it through and figure out who hired the lab techs, if they were hired, or why they did it, if they weren't. But Mr. Applebaum and the museum wanted to bring the police in and turn it over to them, and it was their call."

"Did the video have enough evidence on it to charge them?" Randy asked. "Was it conclusive?"

"Yeah, it should be. The recordings were high-definition at both places. Since we knew what to look for, we were able to zoom in on the crates and see that there were differences in the labels. Plus the nails in the crates weren't in the same places and there were variations in the wood grain. I gave a statement to the officer who came to take the report and he got an arrest warrant for the two lab techs. Mr. Warner has promised to let me know what the techs say when they're questioned. If it goes to trial, of course, I'll have to testify."

"Well, I think you're amazing," Wren said,

smiling at him across the loaded table. "First you solve your case by being all clever and everything, and then you come home and cook dinner."

Death grinned back at her, ducking his head a little bit. He only wished Wren's mother agreed with her. Emily had been perfectly pleasant to him, but he couldn't shake the feeling that she still didn't completely trust him with her daughter.

"So what are you going to do now?" Randy asked.

"I dunno. Help Wren pack, for one thing." Death glanced into the living room. Wren had been emptying shelves and closets and cubbyholes and it looked like the aftermath of a small tornado. "We still haven't heard from the realtor. He was supposed to take our offer on the house to Mrs. Sandburg. But it can't hurt to be ready to move, can it? I have no idea how long it takes to close, though."

"Weren't you buying a house with Madeline?" Randy asked. "How long did it take to close on that one?"

"We were," Death agreed, wishing his brother hadn't brought that up. "I don't really know about the time frame, though. I got deployed right after we looked at it and Grandma helped Madeline handle the paperwork. When I came back from overseas it was a done deal and she was living there."

"Madeline?" Emily asked.

"My ex-wife," Death explained reluctantly. "We were married very young, just before I joined the Marines. It didn't work out."

Randy snorted but kept his comments to himself. Emily shot her husband a knowing glance that did not escape Death's notice.

"And where is she now?" she asked.

"Ah, she lives here in town," Death admitted. "We bought the place because I was supposed to be stationed up at the Air Force base after my tour overseas. She got the house in the divorce and is still there."

"She's dating Eric Farrington," Wren said, her voice bubbling over with amusement.

Edgar turned to look at her and raised one eyebrow. "Voluntarily?"

Wren's dad didn't say much, Death had realized. When he did, he spoke softly. He had a deep, gentle voice that rumbled in his chest and he kept his opinions to himself more often than not.

"Apparently," Wren said with a puckish grin.

"She downgraded hard," Randy offered.

"I think it was a couple of months," Death said, trying to change the subject. "Closing on the house, I mean."

"Probably thirty to sixty days," Edgar said, "depending on the loan process and whether anything turns up when you have the house inspected."

"Wouldn't it be amazing if we could be in the new house by Christmas?" Wren asked.

"That would be great," Death told her gently. "Might be best not to count on it, though."

"Oh, I'm not. And with all the things that still need to be sorted out, I'm going to be equal parts eager and stressed out, regardless." She tipped her head to the side. "I wonder if Mrs. Sandburg decorates Bob's grave for holidays?"

"I wonder if Bob's family spends the holidays wondering where he is and if he's ever coming home again," Emily said. "I wonder if his mother still misses him. And his father. Parents generally care about their children, you know?"

The mood around the table sobered.

"You know," Death said, "I never did make it over to the sheriff's office. I wanted to have a look at that facial reconstruction. I think I'm going to do that tomorrow. Anybody want to come with me?"

"I'd love to," Wren said, "but I have an auction I have to help with."

"I'm in," Randy said.

"Salvy wants to take the boat out again," Edgar said. "It's supposed to be nice tomorrow. Why don't you boys come with us? We'll stop by the department first and then you can pick his brain all day. Anything that's happened in Rives County, he knows about it. Even if it was before his time."

Much later, when everyone had said good night and dispersed for the evening, Emily and Edgar were settling down in their camper out in the driveway.

"So what do you think of Death now?" Edgar asked.

"Hmph." Emily frowned and made a face. "He still hasn't said a word about that baby. He even told me that Randy is his only family. Randy and Wren. I'm not so ready to give him Wren, though."

"Well, we can't exactly just come out and ask him. Not after all this time."

"You mean, like we could have when we first met him?"

Edgar shrugged and ducked his head. "I still think there's got to be more to the story. Everything I've seen of him and everything I've heard about him says he's a good kid."

"Everything except for the part about not paying child support. And never mentioning his son. That doesn't say 'good kid' to me."

"You realize you're basing that opinion on overheard comments made by someone who thinks Eric Farrington is a suitable mate?"

Emily countered quickly. "You realize our daughter is dating someone whose ex-wife thinks Eric Farrington is a suitable mate?"

"People seem to like him," Edgar pointed out mildly. "Chief Reynolds thinks a lot of the boy."

"Mmhmm." Emily frowned, skeptical. "That might just mean he's good at pulling the wool over people's eyes. I might be wrong," she said, "and I hope I am, but I'm very much afraid that Wren has gone and found herself a snake oil salesman."

"Gentlemen, meet Bob." Deputy Orlando Jackson set the bust down on the table in front of them and slapped a file folder down beside it. "Here's everything we know about him. It's too bad Thomas isn't here. He loves this stuff, though I don't think he'll ever forgive Bob for being found before he was born. He's always wanted a random dead body to play with and Bob's the only one we've ever had in the county."

"And hopefully he'll remain the only one," Salvy said. He and Edgar and the Bogart brothers were sitting around a table in a conference room at the sheriff's department. They were on the second floor of the old brick building. The glass in the window that overlooked the courthouse square was wavy with age and the wooden sill was thick and uneven with layer upon layer of old paint. A windstorm the night before had flipped the switch between autumn and winter. It was colder today than it had been yesterday and the oak tree just outside was nearly bare, its few remaining leaves dead and brown. The sky beyond was impossibly blue in the early morning.

Salvy opened the folder and slid it over so that Death, in particular, could see the contents. Death took it as an invitation and leafed through the papers. There were several reports dating to the time the remains were found, pictures of the skeleton in situ and of the surrounding area, and a formal report from the state crime lab.

"Race is only speculation?" he asked. The reconstructed head was that of a white male in his late teens or early twenties. He had a burly appearance, with a strong nose and chin and deep-set eyes. For coloring, they'd gone with gray eyes and dark brown hair that was styled in a soft, medium-length wave reminiscent of the eighties.

"It's a best guess," Salvy said. "The remains were incomplete and damaged. There were things they could tell about him and things they could not."

"He was muscular," Orly said. He pulled out a close-up of the skull that was taken against a light green background. "Probably average height and build, but he worked out. These bumps here and here are where muscles were attached. The fact that the bumps were so big means that the muscles were substantial."

"And where was he found, again?"

"There's a map in there, and an aerial photo taken of that piece of land within a year or two of the time he was found. The location is marked on both."

Death located the two pieces of evidence. The map was folded and when he unfolded it, it covered half the table. Randy used the representation of the dead man as a paperweight to hold one corner and Death laid the photo beside the X on the map.

"I thought he was found closer to the water?"

"It's closer now," Edgar said. "This happened only about ten years after the dam went in. It took a while for the water to back up along the tributaries. That whole area is located along one arm of Tebo Creek, even though the name is sometimes spelled differently."

"It's an old French name," Salvy told them. "The first Europeans in Missouri were French trappers and explorers and missionaries. Then came the Spanish. Those of English descent didn't arrive until around 1804, when Lewis and Clark came through after the Louisiana Purchase."

"It's hard to see from the aerial photo," Death said. The parcel of land was heavily wooded. "Is this a ravine, here? Is that where he was found?"

"It's a creek that cuts through. It carved out a ravine in the valley between these two rises, yes. There was an old house, empty and abandoned, here." Salvy pointed to a spot on the photo where a rusty patch was just visible among the trees. Death leaned in close and studied it, but it was little more than a blur.

"That's the roof?"

"It was, yes. When the lake was coming in, a lot of properties that were going to be inundated, or that were close enough to the projected shoreline that they might be inundated, were purchased through the use of eminent domain. The Corps of Engineers then auctioned them off to buyers willing to tear them down for the lumber. That place sold, but the purchaser died in an automobile accident before he could tear it down and it wound up standing there until it finally fell in."

"You think the dead man was squatting in the abandoned house?" Death asked.

"It's a working theory," Salvy said. "We searched it at the time the body was found. There was no direct evidence that anyone had been squatting there, but there had certainly been trespassers. There were windows broken, empty beer cans and liquor bottles and other trash inside, and graffiti on the walls. However, there was also a road that ran through those woods, past the house. It's the same one that runs to the yacht club on what's now the other side of the lake. It was raised above a culvert crossing the low-lying area where the lake is now, and then it ran over a bridge across the creek between the yacht club and the Viking settlement. By the time Bob's remains were found, the road had been closed for years. But it was still passable when the water level was low. In fact, you can still see the remnants of it during times of drought."

"There sure are a lot of roads that disappear under the lake," Death noted.

"There are a lot of things under the lake," Edgar said. "Whole towns, old homesteads, one-room schoolhouses, churches, the odd graveyard."

"They moved the graves first, though," Orly said.

"The ones they could find," Edgar amended.

"I'm sorry," Randy said, "but I'm not following you all. What's the significance of the road going through?"

"They're thinking Bob might not have gotten in that ravine by himself," Death explained. "They think he might have had some help."

"It's possible," Salvy said, "that Bob was killed or died elsewhere and someone drove up along the road and dumped his body in the woods. If he was, though, we have no way to tell. His skull was intact and there was no sign of a gunshot wound or blunt trauma or anything that would spell murder. If he was shot or stabbed anywhere below the neck, it was done in such a way that it didn't leave any marks on any of the bones that we found. And they found no traces of any poisons in his remains. Which is not to say that poison wasn't used, just that if it was, they can't trace it."

"So how on earth do you ever expect to learn anything about him?" Randy asked.

"Good question." Salvy turned to Death.

"What do you think, genius? Do you have any ideas that will help us identify him? There's still an outstanding reward if you can figure out who he is."

Death thought about it. "Were the Vikings there yet?"

"No, Bob was found before they purchased the land. And it was several years after the yacht club closed. The yacht club land had been sold to a local couple who intended to open a bar and restaurant in it that catered to boaters, but they couldn't get a liquor license and that plan never went anywhere. At the time the body was found, there was nothing at all within about a three mile radius."

"At the time the body was found," Death repeated. "But all the evidence suggested that he'd been there for at least a couple of years, right? Was there anything or anyone in the area earlier who might have seen something?"

Orly made a face. "Nope. Sorry."

Death sighed. "Let me think about it?"

"Take your time," Salvy said. "Bob's not going anywhere."

It being Sunday, and near the end of the season when the weather had a chance of being decent enough for a successful auction, Keystone and Sons had two sales scheduled. The twins took the larger of the two, a working farm being sold as part of the late owner's estate. Leona stayed there to run the cash tent and the sons who were available that day joined them.

That left Wren and Doris with a contingent of the grandsons to handle the smaller sale. A small ice cream parlor in a tiny neighboring town had gone out of business. Wren had spoken to the owners, a middle-aged married couple, when they arranged for the auction, and they'd been shocked and completely at a loss as to why their business failed.

Wren had a pretty good idea, starting with its terrible location on a dangerous curve and ending with massively overpriced ice cream. At this point, her advice couldn't help anything, so she held her peace and simply promised to get what she could back on their investment.

They weren't selling the property, and the whole sale, start to finish, took less than three hours. They did well, bringing in a little more than Wren had estimated, but the couple still seemed unhappy.

"I'm sure you did your best, dear," the woman said when they were finishing up the paperwork.

Wren gave her a brittle smile and made her escape. Her mother had accompanied her to the sale and was waiting when she got back to her truck.

"Did I see you buy something?" Wren asked her.

"Yes, I got this nice little set of sundae dishes and some soda glasses and spoons."

"Oh, those are cute."

"That woman was a dingbat, though." Emily rarely hesitated to speak her mind. "Did she tell you what they're planning to put in there next?"

"They're opening another business?"

"So she said. Are you ready for this?"

"Probably not."

"A gourmet, year-round Christmas candy shop."

"Oh, good grief. On Deadman's Curve?"

"They're going to call it 'The North Pole of the South.' "

Wren needed to go left from the parking lot, but she didn't trust the blind curve so she waited for a break in traffic and turned right instead.

"Where are we going?"

"Just up here somewhere to turn around. So . . ." She steeled herself. "What do you think about Death?"

Her mother gave her a tight smile. "Well,

he's certainly something, isn't he?"

"That's carefully noncommittal."

"I'm not saying there's anything wrong with him. It just seems to me that you're rushing into things. Just how well do you know him anyway?"

"You mean like in the Biblical sense?"

"Wren Elizabeth!"

"Hey now! Don't middle-name at me! I'm an engaged woman. I'm allowed to make grown-up jokes."

"Not around me you're not."

Wren grinned, but was more than half serious when she spoke again. "It wasn't very nice of you to trick him on the phone like that."

"I don't know what you're talking about."

"Yes, you do. I'm talking about answering my phone and pretending to be me when he called the other day."

"I never said I was you."

"You never said you weren't, either."

Emily frowned and "hmphed" and peered out the side window. Wren knew her mother knew she was right. They came to a little gas station on the left-hand side of the road. There was no turn lane, but they were on a straightaway now and the coast was clear so Wren turned into the lot, circled around, and made a right turn back onto the highway, going back the way they'd come.

Emily Morgan rattled her new sundae dishes in her lap. "What do you know about this ex-wife of his?"

"Madeline?" Wren frowned and chose her words carefully. "She's very beautiful. Probably not as bad a human being as she seems to me, but she's shallow and self-centered. And she's realized she screwed up and wants him back. I don't think she understands yet that it isn't going to happen."

"Are you sure?" her mother asked. "That it's not going to happen, I mean."

"I'm sure. Death was a Marine. Semper fi. Loyalty is important to him. He's not going to forget her betrayal. He's a good person. He doesn't hate her, but he's done with her." Wren sighed. "Madeline abandoned him when he was at his lowest and needed her the most. Death's forgiven her for that. I haven't, and I never will."

They rode in silence for several minutes.

"Okay," her mother said. "Now explain to me how she wound up with Eric Farrington."

Wren laughed. "She was trying to make Death jealous. She just latched onto the first willing, vaguely male, marginally human creature that came along. Been trying to pry him loose ever since." She fell silent for a moment, thinking. "You know, I don't think she even knows that we're engaged yet."

Emily looked over at her with eyebrows raised. "He hasn't told his ex-wife that he's getting remarried?"

"No. Well, you see, Randy wanted to do it. And Randy's been working so many hours, I don't think he's had a chance."

"Why should Randy be the one to tell her?"

"Because he despises her. He and I are in agreement about her leaving Death injured and alone, plus he and she never got along before. They have a long, bitter history. When we thought Randy had been killed last summer, Madeline told me it was karma because she didn't like him, so he deserved to die."

"She sounds charming," Emily said drily. "And what did your young man see in her again?"

"A lot of good things that weren't really there," Wren said frankly. "That and boobs." She grinned at her mother. "He was only a teenager when they got married. He's matured a lot since then, in all the best ways."

She flipped on the turn signal and made a left that would take them back into East

Bledsoe Ferry.

"He's a good man," she added. "He's a good man and I love him, and if you'll only give him a chance, I know you'll come to love him too."

Thirteen

Death's phone rang Monday morning at straight-up nine a.m. He glanced at the caller ID before picking it up.

"Hello, Mr. Warner? This is Death Bogart. How can I help you?"

"We're hoping you can take on our case again."

Death raised his eyebrows. "It's not resolved? The lab techs were cleared?"

"Oh, no. They took the painting. They admitted it under questioning. However, they claim to have no idea who hired them, nor what ultimately became of the real portrait. They were approached via text message. The police traced the phone number that sent it, but it was a cheap cell phone — I think, on television, they call it a 'burn phone'? It was only used to contact them and hasn't been used since. They agreed to switch the painting. Their defense is that it's not really a valuable painting anyway and they were being offered a lot of money."

"That doesn't make it right," Death said. He always felt that if someone's scruples could be bought, they weren't worth the price.

"No, of course not. However . . . they agreed to switch it, and on the morning of the transfer they found part of their payment and written instructions in their lockers at Eiler Labs. The forged painting was already in the van. They did as they were told and, after they'd x-rayed the copy and revealed that it was a forgery, they put it back in the van with the real painting still inside also. They went across town to a little pizzeria for lunch and when they came out, the real painting was gone and the rest of the cash was in an envelope in its place."

"So you want me to pick up the investigation again?"

"Yes, if you could see your way clear to. The police will keep looking, of course, but it's not a high priority case for them. So I'd like for you to find out who hired those men to steal that painting. And I'd really, really like for you to get it back."

"I finalized the auction bill and sent it to all the local papers, plus KC and Springfield," Wren said. "The teenagers are going to be out putting up fliers after school today and I told them, because of the amount of collectibles and nostalgia items, to be sure to get them to all the antique malls and flea markets."

"Sounds good," Roy said. He finished setting up a second folding sawhorse, mate to the one Wren had already erected a few feet away. Then the two of them lifted a sheet of plywood to lay across them and create a makeshift table.

A blaringly loud horn sounded through the Ozark Hills Supper Club and they both jumped. After a few seconds, it cut off and Sam came in looking pleased with himself.

"Could you hear that?"

"Yeah," Wren said.

"I may never hear anything else," Roy groused, "but yeah."

"One of the things that increased the death toll when the Beverly Hills club burned was that there wasn't an audible fire alarm. So I got us all air horns. Of course, we're not going to have anything like the crowd that was there that night, but I don't want to take any chances with the crowd we do have."

"Well," Wren said, "speaking as someone who's going to be part of that crowd, I approve of that sentiment."

"Did you see all the Vikings?" Sam asked. "There's something going on next door."

The three of them went out front. It was a bright, frigid morning. The temperature was in the upper thirties and Wren shivered. Her breath fogged the air in front of her face. Dead leaves crunched underfoot and the trees between the club and the village were mostly bare now.

The Vikings' parking lot was full and warriors and farmers and maidens in Iron Age attire milled around, collecting things from the trunks and back seats of their vehicles.

"We should go let them know there's going to be an auction over here on Sunday," Roy said.

The three strolled over to the gathering crowd and several of the Viking reenactors came to meet them. Wren saw Neils Larsen and his son among the crowd. The Larsens saw them too and came over to talk.

"You're still here," the old man said. "I thought you might have gone by now."

Neils was dressed in dark brown homespun breeches and a yellow tunic. He had a heavy blue cloak thrown over it, a simple leather cap on his head, and a long walking stick fashioned from a branch. He leaned on the stick now, swiveled the toe of his boot in the gravel, and looked down at the ground before raising his eyes to meet Roy's.

"I'm sorry I created such a fuss," he said.

"Nothing to be sorry about," Roy replied. "We're just glad to see you doing better."

"We're having an auction this Sunday," Sam said. "There are bound to be a lot of people here, and a lot of vehicles. If you'd like, we'll block off your lot with trestles so no one parks here."

"It should already be full of our cars," Jacob Larsen said. "We're planning a harvest celebration. We'll have to come over and see what you have for sale."

"That place was something when it was open," Neils said. "It was never as crowded as Bender seemed to expect it to be, but sometimes, on a Friday night when there was a good band playing, it was a party. At least until the Beverly Hills club burned. It was common knowledge that this place was patterned after that one, and after the fire the crowds he was getting just stopped. The last few times I was here, the place was so empty it echoed."

"You know, Bender should be down for the harvest," Jacob Larsen said. "Maybe he'll come over and see his old business get sold off again."

"If he does," Neils said drily, "he'll probably try to claim everything that goes on the block. Bender is a bit of a Grabby Gus," he explained to Wren and the Keystones.

"Oh, I met him last Friday," Wren said. "A little old man in an electric scooter, right? He came to the weekly consignment auction. He told me he'd lost a ring here when he was the owner and if we find it he wants it back."

"Sounds like him," Jacob said. "Did you meet his son?"

"No, I didn't notice him."

"Oh. Well, you might not. He just kind of drifts along behind his father. He's easy to miss. He never says anything or does anything unless his dad tells him to."

"I hope you don't mind," Wren said, "but my fiancé and I walked around your settlement after they took you to the hospital, just to make sure there weren't any untended fires or things standing open or anything. We just wanted to make sure everything was okay, since we knew you didn't expect to be leaving like that."

"Oh, that's fine," Neils said. "I appreciate it. You know, I thought that someone had been there. I left the door to my workshop open, and it was closed."

"Yes, that was Death and me." Wren hesitated. "I know I shouldn't have looked. I'm sorry. But I noticed a notebook lying there. Do you write poetry?"

"I attempt it from time to time, yes. That was a little thing I'm working on. Just a short verse in the Viking tradition, following the heroic patterns regarding meter and rhyme and alliteration. Only in English. And somewhat simplified, if I'm being honest."

"You don't write in Old Norse?"

"Not so much. I do speak it a little, and I may translate that piece into it when it's done. But it's a difficult form and I find it easier to work in my native tongue."

"Well, what I saw looked lovely. It was about your daughter, wasn't it?"

Larsen nodded. "I understand my 'ghost' was a little boy playing dress-up?"

"Matthew's very sorry he startled you."

"Nothing to be sorry about," Larsen said, echoing Roy's words. "I suppose we see what we want to see. And I still want to see Ingrid, very much."

"What was she like?"

He smiled. "My little shield maiden," he said. "You know, women weren't allowed to fight or carry weapons in Viking society, legends notwithstanding. But they could defend themselves if someone was so lowly and dishonorable as to attack them, and they could be fierce. She punched a football player in the throat when he got fresh with her. Did you know that? A football player. Twice her size and she dropped him to his knees."

"Good for her. Women weren't warriors?"

"No, not generally. Gender roles were strictly defined, but even so, Viking women had a lot more power and autonomy than their contemporaries in other societies. They couldn't fight or take part in politics, and they essentially belonged to their fathers or husbands, but they handled the family finances. They could own property, and a divorce was fairly easy for them to obtain and could impose a significant financial burden on their former husband." Neils favored Wren with a sweet smile. "Of course, you've already broken Viking law."

"I have? How?"

"You're wearing men's clothing and you've cut your hair."

"Technically, that's not true," Wren countered. "These clothes belong to me. I'm a woman. Therefore, I'm wearing women's clothes. And I didn't cut my hair. I had a long braid and a crazy guy cut it off."

"See now," Neils said, "in Viking society that would have gotten him heavily fined and probably beaten. Possibly killed, if your husband had a bad temper or you goaded him into it. Viking women were notoriously bloodthirsty and tended to be instigators."

The old man dropped his gaze. When he spoke again his eyes were distant and his voice was soft and introspective. "Maybe they just wanted justice. Maybe they just wanted someone to recognize that they were honorable women and to treat them with dignity. You know, they called Ingrid an instigator. All she wanted was for someone to defend her honor. But none of us ever did."

Edgar Morgan wasn't getting any younger. A lifetime spent largely outdoors had left him in good health overall, but arthritis was beginning to take its toll. His fingers grew stiff and sore when the weather turned cold and his right knee ached so that sometimes he could hardly walk.

The staircase up to his future son-in-law's office was long and steep, so he took it slow and leaned on the handrail. He remembered that Death Bogart had suffered some combat injury that compromised his lung capacity, and he'd seen for himself how the young man sometimes struggled quietly after overexerting himself. These stairs must be difficult for him, also.

Edgar wondered if this choice of an office was a failure of forethought or an act of defiance.

The door at the top of the stairs was closed but he could see a blurred figure behind the frosted glass window. He tapped his knuckle on the glass and a voice bade him enter. He went in and found Randy Bogart slouched behind the desk with his cheek propped in his hand, studying an open gift box with a troubled expression.

"Hey, Mr. M! What brings you here?"

"Just stopped by for a visit. Is your brother here?"

"Nah. He went back up to the city. The museum guy called him. The two techs who swapped those paintings don't know who hired them and he wants Death to try to find out and maybe get the real painting back."

Edgar pulled out one of the visitor's chairs and dropped into it. "Well, that's good, right? He seemed to want to finish up the investigation."

"Oh yeah. I wouldn't have been surprised if he'd kept at it on his own. But this way's better. This way he gets paid."

"So what are you up to?"

Randy sighed. "Did you ever want to do something mean? I mean, really want to? But you know it'd be mean and you'd feel bad, even if the person you were doing it to wasn't a nice person and really deserved for you to do mean things to them?"

Edgar laughed. "That sounds like a loaded question. I think you'd better tell me exactly what you're talking about before I answer it."

"Well . . ." Randy sat up straight. "You know that Death and Wren haven't made any kind of formal announcement yet? Wren wanted to tell you and her mom before they told anyone else. The Keystones know and of course I know — I helped Death pick out the ring, so technically I knew before Wren did. Anyway, the point is that a lot of people still don't know they're engaged. One of those people who doesn't know, so far as I know, is Death's ex-wife, Madeline."

"That's a lot of knowing and not knowing you've got going on there. You and Madeline don't get along?"

"Have you ever heard the expression that two people 'cordially despise' one another?" Randy asked.

"Sure."

"Well, Madeline and I despise each other, and there's nothing cordial about it. She wished me dead, did you know that? When she thought I'd been killed, she told Wren that she was happy."

"That would tend to make you not like

someone," Edgar agreed.

"Oh, I didn't like her before that. Death could have taken her to the cleaners when they got divorced. He could have kept their house and everything. My grandmother was a lawyer, and before Death and Madeline got married she got them to sign a prenup that said neither of them could claim anything paid for with the other's earnings. You know how she got Madeline to sign that?"

"How?"

"When they got married, Death was headed to Twentynine Palms, California. That was where he was stationed right after basic training. Grandma pointed out to Madeline that if she became a fashion model or a famous actress while they were in California, Death would be entitled to a share of everything she made. She didn't sign that prenup to protect him. She signed it because she thought she was going to get rich and famous and she wanted to be able to drop him for a rich, famous husband without having to give up anything."

"Why didn't it work out between them, do you know?" Edgar asked.

Randy sighed and shook his head. "Man, I want to tell you. It wasn't Death's fault, I can tell you that. It just feels wrong talking about my brother behind his back."

"I can respect that." Edgar nodded toward the box on the desk. "So you're going to tell Madeline that Death and Wren are engaged? Do they know you're planning to tell her?"

"Yeah, they said I could."

"So what are you going to do?"

Randy grinned. "I got this box and this helium balloon and I made this banner." He pulled a long, white, tissue paper banner out of the box and held it up. He'd written on it with a bright blue marker: *Death and Wren are engaged!*

"I thought I'd tie the banner to the balloon, so that when she opens the box the balloon comes out and the banner unfurls right in front of her face. And I filled the bottom of the box with lemon drops. I was just going to take the box to where she works and leave it on her desk with no note or card."

"Clever. But you think it's too mean?"

"Maybe? I don't know. If she just gets mad, then it would be funny. But what if I make her cry? I mean, I do hate Madeline. But if I deliberately make someone cry, I'd have to hate myself too. And she works in an office, so I'd be humiliating her in public. Plus she'd have to go through her whole work day dealing with it. It would be too mean. I shouldn't do it. I really want to do it, but I shouldn't."

Edgar sat back, laced his fingers together over his stomach, and thought about it.

"She's going to find out eventually anyway," he pointed out mildly.

"Yeah. She is."

"And she might very well find out in public. If you don't tell her, you don't know when or how she'll hear."

"Death will probably call and break it to her gently. That would be the kind thing to do. And Wren has too much class to go poke Madeline in the nose with her engagement ring."

"You think?"

Randy sighed deeply. "Yeah. And that's probably for the best. But it doesn't feel fair to me, dang it! Madeline gloated over me when she suckered my brother into marrying her. Then she treated him bad. Then she celebrated when she thought I died. I want revenge, damn it."

"So maybe you could strike a happy medium," Edgar suggested.

"Like what?"

"Well . . ." The older man's voice was thoughtful. "How she reacts to the news isn't really your responsibility. So if she cries or if she gets mad or even if she's indifferent, that's not because of you. So you can pass the news on without being mean. But the mean part would be to do it in public. If you want to tell her, and even if you want to gloat a little, that's fine. But I would do it so she finds the box when she's in private. Could you leave it on her car, or maybe on her doorstep?"

"I could do that. You think that would be okay?"

"I don't see anything wrong with it."

Randy jumped up and leaned over the desk to offer Edgar his hand. "Mr. Morgan, I like the way you think."

Edgar shook Randy's hand and returned an amused grin. "I think you'd better call me Pop," he said. "All Wren's friends have always called me Pop."

FOURTEEN

"Olivia Trenton is a seventeen-year-old high school junior earning money for college by working part-time for the cleaning firm that contracts with Eiler Labs. She was the one who left the envelopes with the instructions and cash in the lab techs' lockers. They threw away the notes and envelopes, and there's no security camera in the locker rooms, but she came forward when the police went there to ask about it."

Chase Warner kept his voice down. He, Frank Appelbaum, and Death were sitting in the back row of the museum's auditorium, watching dress rehearsals for a series of Christmas-themed one-act plays from the late 1800s.

"Where did she get the envelopes?"

"A 'well-dressed old guy,' in her words, gave them to her and asked her to deliver them. He told her it was a small amount of money the two men had won on a sports pool. She couldn't describe him beyond being well-dressed and old."

"That figures. And I'm going to assume police have checked the pizzeria where the painting was removed from the van and there are no security cameras that cover the parking lot?"

"You're psychic."

One of the performers launched into a musical number and Death waited out the song before he spoke again.

"I've been talking to some of my sources," he said, wondering how Doris would feel about being labeled a "source." "Someone has gone to a great deal of trouble to acquire a painting that doesn't have a lot of monetary value and couldn't be openly sold even if it did. It's most likely the person responsible wanted it for other reasons." He looked at Appelbaum. "Is there anyone in your family who may have coveted the picture and, perhaps, resented the museum having it?"

Appelbaum shrugged. "I've wondered that myself, to be honest. I can't imagine who it would be. If my daughter wanted it, she knows that all she'd have to do is ask. Besides her and my wife, I have no close relatives. I mean, I have a huge extended family, but all of them are second cousins or more distant. I don't even know any of them. They're just names on a family tree that one of our cousins compiles and sends out every year."

"Your cousin does that?"

"Second cousin twice removed or something like that. I don't really understand all the terminology, to be honest. His name is Martin Aldrin and he lives in Minnesota. He's a genealogist. Grandma Mimi — the subject of the Ring Portrait? She came here from Prussia with her two sisters in the 1890s. All three women married and Mimi's sisters both had huge families. Martin has tracked all of their descendants, or at least as many as he can, and he maintains contact with an enormous number of them. He's forever sending out updates on what this or that distant relative is doing."

"You say he sends them out," Death said. "You mean that he sends them to everyone, or just that he sends them to you?"

"Oh, no. Everyone. He has an email list and I think he does something on Facebook, though I'm not really on Facebook, in spite of my daughter's best efforts to get me there."

"Mr. Appelbaum, is there any way I could get a copy of that family tree?"

"Sure. I'll send it to you as soon as I get

237

home. You think one of my relatives stole my great-great-grandma?"

"At the moment, that's the only theory I have."

"How would you ever figure out which one?"

"I don't know. But three times in the past two years there have been other odd, not particularly valuable collectibles that were found to have been replaced with copies. I want to see if I can find anything the four items have in common."

"What were the other three?" Warner asked.

"A collection of seventeenth-century coins from Prussia, a reconstructed thirteenth-century clay pot from a peat bog in Belgium, and a thing called a death crown or angel crown. It was basically a tangle of feathers, in a feather pillow, in the shape of a nest or a crown."

"Well," Appelbaum said, "Mimi was from Prussia, like the coins, and Belgium wasn't that far away. I have no idea about the death crown, though. I've never even heard of such a thing."

"I've been thinking," Wren Morgan said.

"That can be dangerous," Randy said. "What have you been thinking about?"

"Ingrid Larsen and Bob and the bloody dress the kids found in the boathouse."

"You think they're connected?"

"I'm wondering if they might be."

With Death up in the city working on his forged painting case, Wren had conscripted Randy to join her on a metaphorical fishing trip.

"So where are we going?"

Wren was driving them in her truck. With the yacht club auction nearly ready and no other sales on the books until Saturday, the Keystones had given their employees three days off. Wren's parents were visiting family in a neighboring town, but she'd begged off and recruited Randy to go play detective with her.

She'd turned off the main highway and they were following a small county blacktop that wound across the landscape like a black snake. It rolled down out of a cut between two low hills and struck out across a long, low bridge. They crossed above a wide, shallow valley with a stream running through it. Dead brown vegetation climbed both sides of the valley, but the floor was a wasteland of cracked mud dotted with stagnant pools of water and blackened tree trunks.

"This is the upper end of the Thibeaux arm of the lake," Wren said. "Normally it's all water under here. We just really need rain right now."

"Okay, but . . . ?"

"Keep an eye out for J Highway. It should be on your side of the road."

"J?"

"J. It's the other end of the road that the yacht club is on. It used to go all the way through until it got cut off by the lake."

"You want to go see where they found Bob?"

"Couldn't hurt."

"No, couldn't hurt," Randy agreed. "And hey! The sheriff said they never found all of Bob. Maybe we can turn up a stray vertebra or something."

Wren glared at him. "I know you think you're funny, but you're not."

"I am funny. I'm also adorable."

The day was cold and overcast. They crossed a second bridge, this one over a deeper and more robust section of the lake, and a mist rolled up off the water. The sky was gray and the road was gray and the still surface of the lake mirrored the silver clouds. In town, people were rushing around to prepare for Thanksgiving and Christmas, but out here in the middle of nowhere it was peaceful and depressing.

Randy spied a sign for J Highway. "Here

it is, coming up. Slow down."

Wren did, and made the turn. A faded sign advertised a church. They passed it half a mile later, and when it was behind them the surface of the road deteriorated much the way the road in front of the Sandburg house did once it had passed the driveway.

"There must not be anyone living out here," Wren observed. "Nobody's maintaining the road."

"Man, what is it with all these miles and miles of empty countryside?" Randy asked. He was a city boy. "How can there be nothing out here? And if there's nothing here, why is there a road going to it?"

"Well, obviously there was something here once," Wren said. "I looked at this on a map last night. The lake comes up on both sides of us. This road followed a ridge when there were farms and little towns and things here, and now, with the water up, it's on kind of a peninsula. Just the road and a couple hundred feet of woods on both sides. The houses that used to be along here were all bought up before the dam was built. This is all Corps of Engineers' land now." She slowed down.

"How are you going to find where they found Bob, after all these years?"

"I stopped by the courthouse this morning. They have aerial photos from every year for decades. There's a photo on the sheriff department's website with a mark where they found the body, so I compared that to photos since then and found some landmarks that haven't changed. The first thing we're looking for is an overgrown driveway on the left side of the road, just past the fallen remains of an old house."

"Right. That'd be the house Salvy mentioned when we went in to see Bob's reconstructed head. They think that he might have been squatting there before he died."

"Well, he's unlikely to have been squatting there after he died," Wren joked.

"No, since he died he's been squatting at your house. Or what will be your house."

"Ha ha," Wren said, but her attention was distracted. Rising above the road, on a slight embankment, was the remains of what must have once been someone's home.

It was white, or had been. Now it was mostly bare gray wood. The porch still stood, propped up on a foundation made of odd chunks of red sandstone mortared together with yellow cement. It had gingerbread trim and a waist-high railing, and half of a broken porch swing dangled from a single rusty chain. The steps leading up from the road sagged drunkenly. The house behind it had begun to collapse.

To the left of the porch, an entire bay window had fallen into the yard, leaving a gaping wound in the wall. The roof on the right half of the building drooped nearly to the ground, and when Wren drove past the house and turned into its rutted, overgrown driveway, they could see that the entire back half of the building had collapsed into the basement.

"That's kind of depressing," Wren said. "It kind of makes me sad."

"Don't be sad," Randy said. "It's not like this is going to be the last house you see. Like it probably was for Bob." He paused. "I'm not helping any right now, am I?"

"Not so's you'd notice, no."

They got out and met in front of the truck.

"I trust you're not planning to search the house?" Randy said.

"Do you think we should?"

"No!"

Wren tipped her head to the side to regard him. "You seem awfully certain of that."

"I work search and rescue with the fire department," Randy reminded her. "Do you have any idea how many times I've had to rescue people who thought it was a good idea to go poking around an old building like that?"

"Point taken. Anyway, they searched the house back in '85. If there was anything to find, they'd have found it then."

"They searched everything in '85."

"True."

"So what exactly are we doing out here?"

"I just wanted to see for myself. I wanted to see where everything is and how it all relates. There was a dead body around here that got here some time before the autumn of '85. And over at the yacht club, a mysterious girl in a Viking costume appeared in '78. And a blood-soaked Viking costume . . ." She trailed off.

"What?" Randy asked.

"We don't have any idea when the costume was hidden in the boathouse. We ought to be able to at least come up with brackets. Sam or Roy went out and unlocked the boathouse when we first started working on the yacht club . . . We should ask them if there was any sign of it being broken into."

"If we assume it wasn't broken into, and the costume was hidden while the yacht club was in business, our window is from the early '70s to the early '80s," Randy said.

"Right. Close enough. Now, according to the aerial photos I looked at, the lake hadn't completely covered the road yet in '78. It had drowned it at the lowest points and I doubt you could drive across it, but you could probably cross it on foot if you didn't mind getting wet."

"So what's your theory? Or do you have a theory?"

Wren grimaced. " 'Theory' is an awfully strong word," she hedged. "Come on. I want to look at something."

She led the way away from the house and off to their right, in the same direction they'd been going but at a forty-five degree angle away from the road. The weeds through here were shoulder-high and the field was dotted with sumac. That alone retained its foliage, though even its blazing red leaves seemed dulled by the dark afternoon. A hundred yards or so away from the house they came to a small ravine cutting across their path. At the bottom, a small stream trickled and gurgled by.

"There's a path here," Randy said, surprised.

"It's a game trail, I think," Wren said. "Deer and other animals tend to follow the same patterns between grazing lands and water sources and over time they beat down a trail in places where there's not a lot of room to walk. They found Bob right here, at the bottom of this trail."

For a long moment the two paused side-by-side and gazed down into the hollow. Under the trees the hay-like weeds were less prevalent. Lower-profile vegetation had died away into tangled black webs around the trunks of old oaks and elms and maples. Here and there, a lone yellow stalk poked out of the deep leaf mould.

"I don't see any vertebrae," Randy said after a minute.

Wren elbowed him gently in the sternum and slipped down into the gully, stepping lightly until she'd walked the length of a fallen body. Randy followed her. The creek was narrow here, no more than two or three feet across at its widest, and only a few inches deep, and they found a place where they could step across.

"What now?" Randy said. "You don't want to look for more dead guy bits?"

"No, I don't want to look for dead guy bits. I was thinking about what Bob was doing here. I don't mean here in general, like in the woods, but here specifically. If he was hunting or fishing, they should have found something on or near the body to suggest it. Coyotes aren't likely to carry off a gun or a fishing pole. But there wasn't anything. So I thought maybe he was going somewhere."

246

"The yacht club?" Randy asked.

"There wasn't anything else out here."

"The yacht club wasn't still here in '85," Randy pointed out. "Or rather, the building was, but it was closed and locked up. And the Vikings hadn't bought their land yet."

"So if he was headed for the yacht club or coming from the yacht club, he must have died before it went out of business."

They climbed the opposite side of the gully, following the same game trail as it cut between a pair of mature elms. The path was steep, though short, and they had to use branches and small saplings to pull themselves up. The trees ended after just a few feet and they came out on the bank of the lake.

On their right, the road curved in and disappeared under the water. It emerged half a mile away and to their left. They could see, through the mist and the trees, the weathered structures of the Viking village.

"The yacht club and the village are on a cove, remember?" Wren said. "The club is through the trees, pretty much due north of here."

"We need to find out when exactly it closed," Randy said. "And if we could get a list of members, maybe we could show them the picture of Bob. If he hung around the club, maybe some of them know him."

"Well, we'll have a chance this weekend," Wren told him. "Mr. Larsen said that Bender and his son are probably going to be at the village for the Vikings' harvest celebration. We can go over and ask them about it then."

She started to turn away and return to her truck, but Randy caught her arm and nodded at the lake. She followed his gaze.

The Viking longboat had emerged around the point, from beyond the village. The sails were full and the oars were up. The wind carried it, silent, like a ghost, across the silver water until it disappeared into the fog.

"Who's Daddy's little sweetums? Is you Daddy's little sweetums? Oh, you are! Yes, you are!"

Death, in the parking lot of the corner grocery, turned to look at whoever was talking behind him. With just over a week left until Thanksgiving, he had volunteered to start the shopping. He had an ulterior motive, truth be told, which was simply that he was still hoping to impress his future in-laws by being helpful, diligent, cheerful, thrifty, and neat. Or something.

A big guy in motorcycle leathers was leaning into the window of a gold sedan, talking baby-talk to a tiny Chihuahua. The guy glanced around, caught Death watching him, and started guiltily.

Death blinked. "Hagarson?"

The biggest, baddest bail bondsman in Rives County straightened up, shifted his shoulders self-consciously, and said gruffly, "Yo, Bogart. What are you doing here?"

"At the grocery store? Buying groceries. What are you doing?"

"Oh, huh. Yeah. The, uh, the wife sent me down here to get some more kibbles for her pet rat." He nodded at the dog. "Even insisted I bring the spoiled little monster with me so it could pick out a new toy." He rolled his eyes. "Seriously!"

Death laughed. "Sorry, man. That's not gonna fly. I heard the daddy-voice. I saw the kissy face."

Hagarson tipped his head and peered at Death in a calculating manner. "You were hallucinating," he said. "You're short of breath and it's making you lightheaded. You imagined it."

"Nope. Sorry."

Hagarson's shoulders slumped and he sighed. "Well, hell. Listen, Bogart. I've been good to you. Cut me some slack, all right?"

"I suppose I could do that." Death chuckled. "Anyway, I wouldn't want you to sic

249

that attack dog on me. She looks ferocious." The dog was wearing a sparkly pink bow and a crocheted sweater. She noticed Death paying attention to her and bounced around the car's seat yipping happily. He'd seen bigger stuffed animals. "How old is she?"

"Almost four."

"Really? She's not a puppy?"

"Nope. This is as big as she's going to get." Unsnapping a big pocket on the side of his leather vest, Hagarson bent toward the window again, holding it open. The dog hopped in and lay down out of sight. "Her name's LeeLee. Shut up and don't rat us out when we get into the store."

"Wouldn't dream of it."

They strolled toward the front entrance side by side. "Say, listen," Hagarson said. "What are you planning on doing on Thanksgiving?"

Death shrugged. "Eating, I hope."

"No, I mean after dinner."

"Digesting?"

"Ha. Ha. But, seriously, you want in on a little excitement?"

"What kind of excitement?"

"Black Friday!"

"You mean one of those sales where crazy people pack themselves into stores on Thanksgiving night and punch each other out for toys and sheet sets? You can't be serious."

"Dead serious. I think you should come with me."

"Oh, no. There's literally nothing I need badly enough to go arm wrestle old ladies for it. I can't believe you like those things. What's wrong with you?"

"Dude," Hagarson said, "I'm not talking about shopping. I'm talking about hunting."

"Hunting? Hunting what? Bargains?"

"Felons."

"Come again?"

They'd reached the building now. Hagarson dragged Death off to the side before he could enter and lowered his voice. "Every year, on Thanksgiving night, the stores hold these giant sales. Everybody gripes about them and complains that they're ruining the holidays, etc. etc. But every year those places are packed. They always have a selection of big ticket items and special merchandise that isn't available any other time. There are never very many of any given item; they're just there to get people in the door. But if you get there early, and you're patient and lucky, sometimes you can get something really cheap. Something you've always wanted. Or, you know, at least since you saw the ad."

"Okay, but —"

"No, listen. The thing is, these sales are really enticing. Customers pack in, crowd the aisles, clog the parking lot. They're just focused on shopping and sales. It never occurs to them that there will be people like me there, watching."

"You're starting to sound a little creepy, man. Not to put too fine a point on it, but right now the kissy face, daddy-voice thing is actually coming down in your favor."

Hagarson sighed. "I'm talking about fugitives."

"Fugitives?"

"People who have warrants out for their arrest. They spend 364 days a year avoiding the authorities, and then Black Friday comes along and they're like, 'Oh! I've always wanted this video game! Maybe if I get there early, I can find these pajamas in purple!' And so on and so forth."

"So you go there to look for people who have warrants out?"

"Right. You wouldn't believe how many bail jumpers I've caught waiting in line for TVs and remote-controlled cars."

"Do you have a lot of bail jumpers in the wind?"

"Not at the moment. But I've got wanted posters and lists of outstanding warrants from every law enforcement agency in this part of the state."

"So you're just going to go and watch for wanted people. And then what? You're not a cop. You just being a good citizen and helping to apprehend?"

Hagarson frowned at him. "You're awfully shortsighted for a businessman."

"Sorry. I just don't understand."

"I watch for people who have warrants out for their arrest. When I see one, I alert the authorities and they get arrested. And then, of course, I go bail them out! And then they have to pay me. It's a gold mine." Hagarson grinned. "If you want in, I'll share a cut of the proceeds."

Death laughed. "Maybe next year," he said. "This year I'm trying to impress my future in-laws. I don't think running off right after Thanksgiving dinner would help my case any."

"In-laws?" Hagarson asked. "You getting married?"

"Yup. I proposed to my girlfriend and she said yes."

The bail bondsman pounded him on the shoulder. "Well! Congratulations! Who's the lucky lady?"

"I'm the lucky one," Death said. "The lady's name is Wren Morgan."

"Oh." Hagarson's smile dropped and he looked dismayed.

"What?"

"Wren . . . isn't that Emily Morgan's daughter?"

"Yeah. You know her?"

"Yeah. You're trying to impress Emily Morgan?"

"Why?"

"Oh . . . nothing." LeeLee whimpered and Hagarson patted his pocket gently. "Don't worry, snookums. Daddy'll take you to get your num-nums."

Death glowered at him. "Listen. If you want this whole snookums/daddy/kissy-face/num-nums business to get swept under the rug, you'd better tell me whatever you know about Emily Morgan."

For the second time in the conversation, Hagarson's big shoulders drooped. He sighed. "Okay, well, it was a long time ago, but Emily Morgan might have caught me putting Vaseline on people's doorknobs one Halloween. And their car windshields. And I might have TP'd a couple of houses. And she's little, but damn that woman has a scary temper!" He patted Death's shoulder. "All in all, it would probably be best if you just pretend you don't know me."

FIFTEEN

Madeline Braun, formerly Madeline Bogart, came into work Wednesday morning with a bounce in her step and a large gift-wrapped box in her arms. Madeline was a member of the secretarial pool at one of the largest local insurance firms. She was a competent typist and could handle basic accounting, but her main asset, in her own estimation, was her appearance. She played it up at every opportunity. Her hair and makeup were always perfect. She wore her necklines a little lower than the other women and her skirts a little shorter and made it a point to get her nails done weekly.

She had a desk in an office she shared with five other women. Two of her fellow secretaries were married, and one was single but in a long-term relationship. The other two were single and unattached. For Madeline, these five represented the competition. She didn't dislike them, exactly. She just liked to remind them every now and again that when it came to beauty and popularity and sex appeal, she was at the head of the class.

Betty, one of the older, married women, gave her a puzzled look as she entered. "Is it someone's birthday?"

"No, I don't think so. If it is, I don't know about it."

"So what's the present for?"

"You know, I don't know." Madeline beamed. "I found it on my doorstep when I got home last night."

"And you didn't open it?"

"I'm trying to figure out who it's from."

Renee rose and crossed to get a paper out of the printer. "Eric?" she suggested.

"No, Eric didn't know anything about it. I do believe I made him a little jealous when I asked him."

"I can't imagine why." Renee rolled her eyes.

Allie, a young woman with an unfortunate skin problem, raised her eyebrows. She was busy typing away at her computer and spoke without breaking stride. "Do you often get mysterious presents that aren't from your boyfriend?"

"Oh, sure," Madeline said casually. "All the time. I have so many secret admirers."

"If they're secret," Allie said, "how do you

know about them?"

"I can tell. There's just that feeling you get when a man is giving you that hungry, needy look. You know." She looked over at Allie. "Or maybe you don't," she said pointedly.

"Why don't you just open it and see what it is?" Betty asked.

"Oh, all right," Madeline said. "I suppose you're all probably curious too."

"Yeah, can't live without knowing," Allie deadpanned, still not looking up from her typing.

"Well, everyone come over and see what I've got. If it's chocolate I'll share. I can't eat too much because I don't want to risk my complexion." She cut a pointed side glance at Allie. "I know not everyone has to worry about that."

The four other women came over at once, at least pretending to be interested. Madeline read it as jealousy and smiled to herself. After a moment, Allie sighed and rolled over in her chair, not bothering to rise.

"Okay," Madeline said. "I'll just clip the tape and then the lid should come up." She made a production of cutting the tape on all four sides of the gift, then set the scissors aside. "Ready?"

"Oh, for God's sake. Just do it," Allie said.

Madeline gave her a miffed, insincere little smile and pulled the lid off.

A balloon floated out and rose toward the ceiling. There was a thin white banner attached to it, which trailed behind. The six women all tipped their heads to the side so they could read the blue writing scrawled along it: *Death and Wren are engaged!*

Madeline could only stare in shock. "What?"

Allie reached into the box and pulled out a handful of candy. "Oh, look! Lemon drops."

"What?" Madeline repeated.

Betty turned the box lid over. "Here. There's a card," she said. It was just a folded sheet of paper taped to the inside of the box lid. She opened it and read it aloud. *"To Madeline from Randy. P. S. I'm not dead yet."*

Madeline grabbed the banner and hauled the balloon back down into her hands. "What. The. Hell?"

"Well, I don't know, but it kinda sounds like your ex is getting married again," Allie said. She could not possibly have been more amused.

Madeline picked up her scissors and stabbed the balloon, popping it. "Like hell he is!"

"Cecily? This is Death Bogart. I wanted to ask you a couple of follow-up questions about the Volkmer painting."

He could hear her sigh travel across the phone connection. "I don't know anything about it," she said, sounding fed up. "I told the cops, I don't know anything about it. I understand that the lab techs stole it for someone, but it wasn't for me. Where would I even put it? I live in a one-bedroom apartment the size of a postage stamp. My bathroom is a converted closet. And not a walk-in closet either! I eat ramen five days a week. I'm not a criminal mastermind!"

Death chuckled, but quietly so she wouldn't hear him. "I know, okay? I don't think you are. I'm not calling to accuse you of anything, I just want to ask you a question about the forged painting, as an expert and as someone who had a chance to examine it."

She was quiet for a long moment before she answered him. "Fine. What is it?"

"Just how good a forgery was it?"

"What?"

"How good was the copy? If you'd studied it without the x-ray, would you have pegged

259

it for a copy? I'm wondering where one gets a forged painting. What level of skill was involved?"

"Oh." He waited while she thought about it. "It wasn't a very good copy, honestly," she said finally. "I like to think I'd have figured out on my own that it was a forgery, but of course that's easy to say with hindsight. I might have decided there was another explanation for the quality of the painting, though. And if I were admitting things, I'd have to admit that I probably wouldn't have dared to say anything."

"What do you mean?" Death asked. Then, "No, wait. Let's break that down. First, what do you mean, 'another explanation' for the quality. What sort of explanation?"

"At some time around the turn of the century, Volkmer was injured in a knife fight over a prostitute. He got hooked on morphine while he was recovering and it affected the quality of his work. By the time he painted the Ring Portrait he'd gotten his drug addiction under control, but he could have had a relapse."

"And what do you mean about not saying anything?"

"Well," Cecily replied, "I'm not proud to admit this, but I don't know if I'd have had the courage to tell a museum that one of their display pieces was a forgery, even if I'd figured it out."

"Ah," Death said. "I think that's understandable. Okay, one last question. If you were looking for a forgery, and this level of quality — or lack of quality — was acceptable, where would you go?"

"Heck," Cecily said. "I don't know. I don't suppose I'd go to anyone. I'd print a good-quality picture of the painting on a transparency and project it onto a white canvas. Then I'd just paint over it as best I could. Any competent art student could probably do it if they took their time and used a high-resolution print, and maybe a computer analysis to help get the colors right."

Death thanked her and hung up, then sat at his desk and thought about it. The Ring Portrait forgery was a poor copy. The thirteenth-century clay pot that had been stolen was replaced by one that hadn't been put together along the same break lines. The angel crown was replaced with a copy sewn together from acrylic feathers.

In the case of the painting, it seemed to Death that whoever had arranged the substitution was actually counting on them discovering that it was a forgery (though probably not counting on them figuring out when and how it was swapped out). With the pot and the angel crown, the person or persons who'd stolen the original seemed to be relying on the fact that these were obscure items and unlikely to be closely examined.

He still thought the family angle was his best bet, but so far it hadn't paid off. The genealogy information Appelbaum had sent him was contained in a 174-page PDF. That was small print, and Death had been lost in relationships and notations before he even got started. He'd tried searching the document for the name of the donor who'd given the Prussian coin collection to the museum in Maryland and for the names of the owners of the angel crown, but neither had turned up. The pot had been unearthed during an archaeological dig that the museum in Pittsburgh had helped sponsor. There was no name to search for there.

Death pulled his phone over and called the museum in Alabama that had lost the angel crown. He had some difficulty understanding the woman who answered due to the strength of her Southern accent, but eventually he convinced her to give him the phone number of the person who'd owned the wayward curiosity.

That was his next call.

"Hello, Mrs. Eichenwald? I'm sorry for

disturbing you. I got your number from the Little Museum of Appalachian History. I wanted to talk to you about your missing angel crown."

"And what's your angle?" He could hear her skepticism from two thousand miles away.

"My name is Death Bogart. I'm a private investigator. I'm working on a case that's similar to the disappearance of your angel crown, and it's occurred to me that the two thefts might be related."

"Somebody stole somebody else's junk?" she asked.

"Ma'am?"

"Look." Mrs. Eichenwald sounded tired. "That angel crown was nothing but a piece of worthless crap. And I know it was nothing but worthless crap. But dammit, it was my worthless crap."

"Yes. I understand that," Death began. "If I could just ask you —"

"What kind of nonsense did you get stolen?"

"Ma'am?"

"Your thing. Your doodad. Are you daft? I'm trying to ask you what got stolen."

"Oh, right. Sorry, I wasn't following you. I'm trying to track a missing oil painting."

"A painting? That don't make sense.

What's a painting got in common with an angel crown?"

"That's what I'm trying to figure out. Now, the information I have about your angel crown said that the woman whose pillow it was found in was your ancestor, is that right?"

"Many-greats-meemaw. That's right."

"Right. And it says here that she immigrated from Germany in the 1890s?"

"Yup. Came over with her brother and his wife. Married twice. Had a slew of kids. Ran her own business. Made moonshine during the Depression and sold it out of the trunk of her car and lived to be almost a hundred."

"She sounds like a remarkable woman."

"She was mean as a snake and tough as old shoe-leather."

"Like I said, a remarkable woman. And it was definitely Germany that she came here from?"

"Yeah, Germany," the woman said. "Well, it's Germany now. Back when she lived there, it was still part of Prussia."

Death felt a little tingle run up his spine. He had the genealogy PDF open on his desktop computer and touched one finger gently to the short list of names at the top of the document. According to this, the three sisters had come to the US before getting married, but Death was betting that the distinctions had blurred somewhere along the line and the supposed brother that many-greats-meemaw Mean-As-A-Snake had traveled with was in reality one of Mimi Appelbaum's brothers-in-law.

"Okay," he said. "So this is my next question. Mrs. Eichenwald, was your great-grandmother's maiden name Bering? Or Derkin?"

"What? No. It was Warner. Claudia Warner."

"Your uncle missed you," Wren's mother told her. "He asked where you were."

"Really?" Wren was skeptical. "Usually he asks who I am."

Her father, sitting at the table to her right, cut off a chunk of meatloaf and speared it with his fork, but he stopped to speak before putting it in his mouth.

"She prompted him," he said.

"I did not. You hush," Emily told him.

Edgar raised an eyebrow.

"I just mentioned that you were planning to get married and he said, 'Where's she?' "

Edgar swallowed his food and took a drink of coffee. He drank it black, like Death did. "Or he might have said, 'Who's she,' " he muttered.

His wife glared at him. "He did not. Stop. You're not helping."

Death gave Wren a questioning glance.

"Uncle Teddy is . . . unusual," she explained. "He works as a toll-taker and collects bottle caps and in between visits he forgets that I exist."

"That's not true."

"He came to our house for Christmas every year from the time I was born until I left for college and every year he brought all the children presents but me."

"He's just a little bit scatter-brained. Besides, you always got something. One of your cousins would always give you theirs."

"Yeah, because they were teenage boys and he'd bring them teddy bears and fashion dolls. But that isn't the point. The point is, he forgot me. He still forgets me. Every time he sees me he gives me an odd look and asks me who I am."

Emily made a face and helped herself to another roll. "So what did you do today, since you didn't go with us?"

"Randy and I went out and looked at where they found Bob."

"Bob?"

"You know. The body in the rosebushes at the house we're trying to buy."

"We looked for random body parts,"

Randy said helpfully, "but we didn't find any. You need some more mashed potatoes, Pop?"

"Sure. Thanks."

Now it was Randy toward whom Death directed his questioning look. Randy grinned back and offered no explanation.

Emily turned to Death. "What about you, dear? What did you do today?"

Death quickly swallowed his food so he could answer. "I'm still working on the investigation into the forged painting. I went up to the city to question the lab techs who were hired to steal it — I didn't learn anything new from them — and then I made some phone calls. And then I did some shopping for Thanksgiving."

"Did you make any progress on your case?" Wren asked.

Death considered. "Maybe? We know there've been four instances in the past two years where a collectible that wasn't particularly valuable was stolen and replaced with a forgery. The cases have several similarities and I'm certain they're connected." He explained, for the elder Morgans' benefit, about the missing items and the history of the painting.

"I was thinking it was possibly a member of Mr. Appelbaum's extended family that took the painting," he went on. "I have a whole list of relatives that one of his cousins compiled. But I couldn't find any connection between them and the people associated with the other missing objects. I finally called the owner of the missing angel crown, Mrs. Eichenwald, and asked her for her however-many-times-great-grandmother's maiden name. And it was a name I recognized, though not one I was expecting. The lady whose pillow contained the angel crown was named Warner, like the director of the museum that the painting was stolen from. I tried to get ahold of Chase Warner so I could ask him if he's related to those Warners, but he's gone to the opera and won't be available until tomorrow."

"Now let me get this straight," Emily said. "Appelbaum's great-grandmother — I'm not going to try to remember all the greats — Appelbaum's great-grandmother came here from Prussia in the 1890s."

"Right."

"And the angel crown lady also came here from Prussia in the 1890s?"

"Yes, that's right."

"And the museum man, his ancestors came here from Prussia in the 1890s too?"

"Right. And Appelbaum and Warner — the museum Warner, that is — both told me that their families had been friends for decades. So now I'm wondering if they were friends before they came to America. They came from the same country. Maybe they traveled together on the same ship. I don't know. It just feels like I'm getting close to a solution. But I don't have all the pieces yet."

While they were talking, Wren's phone rang in the other room. She got up from the table to answer it and everyone else fell silent, waiting for her to return and openly eavesdropping on her end of the conversation.

"Yes? She did? Okay, great . . . can we come in tomorrow afternoon to discuss it? Okay, wonderful. No, not at all. Thank you for calling to let us know. I appreciate it. We'll see you tomorrow. Thank you again."

She hung up the phone, came up behind Death's chair, and put her arms around him.

"Was that what I think it was?" he asked.

She nodded, still hugging him, and kissed his cheek.

"That was the realtor," she said. "Mrs. Sandburg has accepted our offer on the house."

Sixteen

"There's a ring on your ring finger! Is that an engagement ring? Are you engaged? Oh my God! Are you engaged?"

Cameron Michaels jumped up from his desk in the big main room at the local newspaper and grabbed Wren's wrist so he could look more closely at her ring. Wren grinned at her old friend and one-time sweetheart and wiggled her hand in front of his face. "You see?" she crowed. "The first time I see you, and you immediately noticed. You're the only person who's immediately noticed."

"Of course I noticed. I gave you one of those myself once upon a time. Oh, Wren! That's awesome! I'm so happy for you, I could hug you. Can I hug you?" Cam hugged her, lifting her off her feet. "Where's Death? Can I hug Death? I've always wanted to hug Death."

"He's not here, but when you see him you can hug him. Just this once."

"Great! Can I kiss him?"

She glared at him. "Don't push it, sunshine."

Cam laughed, then looked past her to her companion. "Mrs. M! You're back. Hi!" He leaned down and she reached up to give him a quick hug and a peck on the cheek.

"Hello, Cam. How are you doing, sweetheart?"

"I'm good. I'm really doing well. Not as well as Wren is, obviously . . ."

"Jealous?" Wren teased.

"Absolutely."

"You like Death, then?" Emily asked.

"Well, yeah. What's not to like? He's adorable."

Wren smirked at her mother and Emily rolled her eyes.

"So are you here to do the engagement announcement, then? Let me see your pictures. Who did them?"

"Um, no. What pictures?"

"Your engagement pictures. Haven't you taken engagement pictures?"

"No, we haven't really thought about it yet. Everything's kind of been a whirlwind, to be honest. Cam, we're buying a bigger house! The seller just accepted our offer. We're meeting the realtor to start the paperwork this afternoon."

"Oh, that's exciting. What house? Where?"

"It's the last house out at the end of CC. The Sandburg place."

"No, it's the old Duvall place," her mother said. "The Sandburgs bought it in the early seventies, but it was built by the Duvalls in the nineteen teens, or maybe the twenties."

"Oh, I know that place," Cam said. "The house with the little tower, right? It's gorgeous. Did you know that there's a —"

"Body buried in the rosebushes?" Wren asked. "Yeah, we know. In fact, that's kind of why we're here today."

"I don't understand."

"We're trying to figure out who Bob was."

"Bob?"

"The dead guy in the rosebushes. The Sandburgs call him Bob. He was found in the woods across the lake from the old yacht club out at Cold Creek Harbor." She explained about the location of the body and her speculation that he may have been traveling between the abandoned house and the club. "So now we're trying to find out exactly when the yacht club opened and when it closed."

"You want to check our morgue for stories?"

"Yeah, if we could."

"Sure."

272

Wren and her mother started for the basement, but turned back when they realized Cameron wasn't following. He was sitting at his desk grinning at them.

"Where are you going?" he asked.

"The morgue?"

"Why?" He punched a button on his computer. "It's all on the computer now."

"All of it?"

Cameron shrugged. "Ernie Johnson has no life. It's not very elegant and the articles aren't searchable, but you don't have to dig around in the basement to find things anymore. He scanned in images of the articles and uploaded them into a file system that duplicates the physical file system downstairs."

Wren returned to perch on his desk and Cam snagged the chair from a neighboring desk for Emily. "We're looking for anything about the Ozark Hills Supper Club," Wren told him. "The owner was Claudio Bender."

Cameron pulled up a database and checked the index. "I have the Ozark Hills Supper Club, the Cold Creek Harbor Supper Club, and two Benders, Claudio and Henry."

"Henry is his son, I think," Wren said. "I've never heard the club called the Cold Creek Harbor Supper Club. Maybe that was a name that the people who bought it from Bender were going to use?"

"I'll just give you everything," Cam said, pulling a thumb drive from a drawer. He made short work of copying it all, and, when it finished, removed the thumb drive from the port and handed it to her. "Let me know when you're ready to do an engagement photo shoot. I know a great photographer. It will be amazing."

"Okay, sweetie," Wren said. "Thank you. And thank you for this, too." She waved the thumb drive.

"No problem," Cam said. "Just remember to warn Death about the hug, okay?"

At nine o'clock sharp Death phoned Warner's private line at the museum. The older man picked up on the second ring.

"Hello?"

"Mr. Warner? This is Death Bogart. There's something I need to ask you about."

"Shoot."

Death took a sip of his coffee, leaned back in his chair, and kicked his feet up on his desk. "You remember I told you about the stolen angel crown that I thought might be somehow connected to your missing painting?"

"Sure. The superstitious feather pillow

thing. What about it?"

"I tracked down some information on the woman whose pillow it came out of. I was thinking it might have been one of Mr. Appelbaum's ancestors."

"Yeah. It wasn't?"

"She doesn't seem to have been. Mr. Warner, her name was Warner."

Warner made a bemused noise over the phone. "Really?"

"Her maiden name, yeah. Claudia Warner. Does that ring a bell?"

"Not right off the bat. You know," Warner said, "it is a pretty common name."

"Yeah. I know. But she came to America from Prussia in the 1890s."

"Okay, now that's just weird. Do you know anything else about her?"

Death shrugged, reminding himself even as he did that Warner couldn't see him through the telephone. "She married twice. I believe her second husband's name was Eichenwald. She had a large family. She sold moonshine out of her car trunk during the Depression and, according to one of her descendants, she was mean as a snake."

Warner laughed. He sounded incredulous. "I'll be damned. I wonder if you could be talking about Aunt Cici?"

"Aunt Cici?"

"Something of a family legend. She was part of the group that immigrated here together at the end of the nineteenth century."

"Your family and Mr. Appelbaum's family?" Death guessed.

"Yeah. We told you our families go way back. There were three families, actually, that all came over together and pretty much stuck together once they got here."

"Three families?"

"Yeah. The Warners, the Appelbaums, and the Benders."

Death put his feet on the floor and sat up slowly.

"In fact," Warner said, "Cici married one of the Benders. She left him after she caught him cheating on her. Well, actually she tried to emasculate him with a meat cleaver, but her brother wrestled it away from her and then she left him."

"Are there still descendants of the Bender family around, do you know?"

"You know, I don't. If there are, they're not part of my circle anymore. Have you asked Frank Appelbaum?"

"No, not yet."

"Well, let me call him. I think one of Aunt Cici's sons married into the Appelbaum family, come to think of it, so he might know something about them that I don't."

■ ■ ■ ■

"Mice have been at this box of T-shirts," Robin Keystone said. He held up a virulent green shirt riddled with holes and caked with molded rodent droppings.

Wren made a face. "Where were those?"

"Under the eaves up in the top of the boathouse. This is the last of the stuff from up there. Gramps wants to lock the boathouse up tonight so no one can get inside."

"Yeah. The last thing we need is someone falling in the lake. Hey, that reminds me, I wanted to ask the twins what it looked like when they unlocked it in the first place."

"It looked locked. What do you think it looked like?"

"We were just wondering if anyone could have broken in after the club closed down and the boathouse was locked."

"You mean other than by swimming under the dock doors?" Robin asked.

Wren gaped at him. Robin smirked.

"Some of the time you're smart," he said.

"Randy didn't think of that either," she defended herself.

"So what do you want to do with these disgusting T-shirts?"

"Burn them?"

Robin laughed and took the box over to dump it into the nearest big trash can. "There are a few of these the mice didn't get to," he said, fishing one shirt back out. "The fabric is still rotting, though. And it was kind of hideous to begin with anyway." He held it up. The front had a design of martini glasses against a background of palm trees, with oversized bubbles rising from them and the words *Ozark Hills Supper Club* in an elaborate font.

Wren frowned at it. "Were there a lot of shirts like that up in the loft?"

"Six or seven boxes," Robin said. "This was the only one the mice got to. My theory is that they got into this box first and ugly shirt poisoning killed them all off before they could take over the building. That or I understand the Vikings keep barn cats. One or the other. Why? What are you thinking?"

"I was wondering why someone would choose to hide their bloody Viking costume up in the top of the boathouse. What if they knew there were other clothes up there?"

"That makes sense, I guess," Robin said. "There weren't any pants, though. Only shirts and jackets. Do Vikings wear pants under their dresses?"

"I don't know. I suppose we could go ask them."

Wren picked up her jacket from the counter of the coat check booth by the door and she and Robin wandered outside.

Friday afternoon was cool but bright and shiny. Sunlight sparkled off the ripples on the lake and the sky was deep blue with only a few fluffy white clouds drifting across it. At the yacht club, they'd filled half the rooms with neat rows of furniture and large appliances. The garish room at the front was lined with trestle tables and they'd set out the small items on them. They'd reserved the entryway for Leona and Doris and their cash operation, and Sam's middle son, Dylan, and his wife would set up their barbecue grill and food truck in the parking lot, right outside the door.

With the auction as ready as they could make it, the Keystone company members were milling around out front, chatting and watching carloads of Vikings arrive at the parking lot next door. The school kids Leona had picked up from various bus stops and brought to hand off to their parents were running up and down the sidewalk, burning off the day's pent-up energy.

Sam and Roy came out and locked the club behind them, then Roy waved for everyone to gather around.

"Okay, folks, looks like we're ready ahead

of schedule. Good job, everybody. I just want to go over the fire evacuation plan one more time."

"You know," Robin said, "you guys have spent so much time worrying about a fire and planning for a fire that I'm kinda gonna be disappointed if there isn't a fire."

"I could arrange a fire," Matthew offered. Leona gave him a look and he bit his lip and faded into the background.

"If the comedy act is finished," Sam said drily, "everyone take one of these sheets." He passed around a stack of papers. "This is a blueprint of the club with all exits marked. All doors will be unlocked and any that open in will be propped open. Yes, it will be cold if the weather is cold. Pray for a warm snap."

"I have flashlights for everyone," Roy said, waving one over his head. "They all have fresh batteries, but when I hand them out Sunday morning I want you each to test yours and make sure it works. Sam and I will be out tomorrow to mark exit routes on the walls and carpets with reflective tape. We've assigned people in each room and hallway to keep an eye on things. Look at the paper and if you see your name, come find me Sunday morning to get a bullhorn. No, Matthew, you cannot have a bullhorn."

"Obviously," Sam said, "we don't anticipate trouble. Not a fire, nor anything else out of the ordinary. But a building designed very much like this building cost a great many people their lives because no one anticipated trouble. We're not going to let that happen here." He looked around. "Okay, so for the first weekend since last spring, we have a Friday night with no sale scheduled on Saturday. Everyone go enjoy yourself and we'll see you all here bright and early Sunday morning."

As Wren walked to her truck, her gaze drifted over to the gathering next door. There were about a dozen vehicles in the lot and fifteen or twenty people had emerged from them. She picked out Neils Larsen again, with a woman she decided was probably his wife. He saw Wren watching him and waved, and she took it as an invitation to go over and say hello.

"Mr. Larsen, hi! It's good to see you. It looks like you guys are planning quite a weekend."

"Hi!" His smile faltered. "I'm sorry, dear. I know we met a few days ago but I can't remember your name."

"That's okay. It's Wren. I'm Wren Morgan. I work with the Keystone auction company."

"Right. Yes. That I knew. Oh, this is my wife."

The older woman gave her a warm smile and offered her hand. "Call me Maggie."

"Maggie. Pleased to meet you. Looks like you've got a lot of people out here for the festival?"

Neils answered her. "There should be a good crowd here. There'll be more for the feast on Sunday. This is just the core group today. We like to spend the whole weekend, sleep here. Make the most of it." He nodded toward the vehicles leaving the club parking lot. "I hope you're not leaving on our account?"

"Oh, no. We've just finished for the time being. We're done with our preparations, but we'll be back early Sunday morning to conduct the sale. That's apt to draw a huge crowd," she reminded him.

"Great. Maybe we can recruit some of them to join our village." Neils took a long wooden horn from the trunk of his car and handed it to his wife, then reached back in for a stringed instrument of a type Wren had never seen before.

"Is that — I'm sorry — is that like a guitar? Or some kind of harp?"

The instrument in question was a long board with rounded ends. There was a large hole at one end and strings running across a bridge from end to end. It was almost like a rectangular guitar without a neck or a sound box.

"You're close," Larsen said. "It's a lyre. It can be strummed like a guitar, plucked like a harp, or played with a bow like a violin."

"Is it an authentic Viking instrument?" she asked. "And the horn," she added, nodding toward his wife.

"The lyre is a pretty widespread instrument from the period. We find evidence of them all over the Old World. The horn is called a lur. It was definitely a Viking instrument. There was one in the Oseberg ship burial."

Maggie put the horn to her lips and played a few notes.

"It sounds like an oboe," Wren said.

"It's similar," she agreed. "And, after all, they're both woodwinds. Though there's more wood to my lur than to your average modern oboe."

"So you play the lur," Wren said, "and do you" — she turned to Neils — "play the lyre?"

"Oh, my dear. I play everything. I'm a skald, you know?"

"No, not really. Is that like a minstrel?"

"Pretty much, yeah. In Viking society there

were two types of minstrels, if you will. Jesters were looked down on. Reviled, even."

"Like mimes?"

"Worse. It wasn't illegal to kill a jester."

"Wow! Talk about your harsh critics. It was against the law to kill a skald, I hope?"

"Oh, yes. Unlike jesters, skalds were highly respected poets and musicians. They performed at important ceremonies and before the courts of kings and warlords."

"That sounds fascinating. I'd love to hear you both perform sometime."

"What are you doing tomorrow night?"

"Gosh. I don't know. I'd have to talk to my fiancé and see if he's made any plans."

"Well, if he hasn't, come on out. Bring him with you. We'd love to have you."

"We don't have any costumes to wear," Wren said.

"That's okay. We'll just pretend we've kidnapped you from the twenty-first century."

Seventeen

"I can't go in there."

Eric Farrington froze in the coffee shop doorway like a deer in the headlights.

Madeline, following close behind, ran into him. She was carrying her toddler son, Benji, and he was getting heavy. She poked Eric in the ribs with her finger. "What are you talking about? Of course you can. Move."

"No. I, uh, I got a, um, I got an appointment."

"What kind of appointment?"

"A dog. I mean a man. A dog man. A man about a dog. I gotta see a man about a dog."

"Oh for heaven's sake. If you have to go to the bathroom, just go to the bathroom."

"No, a dog. I'm gonna get a dog."

"Don't be ridiculous. Dogs hate you. They bark at you and growl at you and pee on your leg. Seriously, Eric. You need to move now. I haven't had my coffee yet and I am in no mood for this."

She put her shoulder into his ribs and he stumbled, finally, into the coffee shop. Madeline ducked in behind him and looked for a seat. Three tables from the door, in the row of booths along the window, there sat an older man of massive proportions. Their awkward entry had caught his attention and he regarded them mildly.

Eric was staring at him and swallowing repeatedly, like he was trying not to throw up.

The man nodded and spoke calmly, his voice deep and resonant.

"Eric."

Eric cringed, and when he replied his own voice had climbed half an octave.

"Hello, Mr. Morgan, sir."

Mr. Morgan raised one eyebrow, but otherwise his expression betrayed nothing. "I trust you're not doing any more bow hunting."

"No, sir! No bows! I'm not . . . I don't . . . I gotta go to work." Eric broke suddenly, turned, and ran back out the way he'd come, nearly bowling over Madeline in the process.

"Brilliant," she muttered bitterly. "Now I'm going to have to buy my own coffee." She turned to the older man. "Do I want to know what that was all about?"

He took a sip of his coffee, watching her from under half-lowered lids. "Probably not," he said.

She regarded him thoughtfully. "Mr. Morgan," she said. "Are you any relation to Wren Morgan?"

"Some." He allowed himself a faint smile. "She's my daughter."

"Oh!" Madeline smiled and helped herself to a seat on the other side of his table. "So is it true that she and Death are engaged now?"

"That's what they tell me."

Benji looked around and chirped, "Deese?"

Madeline shushed him. She sighed and plastered a concerned look on her face. "I just hope she realizes what she's letting herself in for."

Mr. Morgan raised his eyebrows. "Oh?"

"Death is my ex-husband," she confided. "And he's a good guy, sure. But he just has so many problems . . ."

Wren filled the left-hand sink with soapy water and lowered half a dozen already-clean pans into it. She washed them gently, rinsed them in clear, hot water in the right-hand sink, and set them in the drainer to air-dry. She had the oven turned on, but very low, and it was filled with pans she'd already put through this procedure. She took them out one by one, made certain they were entirely dry, and wrapped them in newspaper before setting them in the big open carton in the middle of the kitchen table.

Her mother came in and stood and watched her for several seconds.

"What are you doing, exactly?"

"I'm packing all my pots and pans," she said, thinking it was an odd question. Surely it was obvious what she was doing. "I wanted to make sure they were clean and dry, so they wouldn't rust or anything between now and when I unpack them in the new house."

"Mmm. I see. Don't you think you're rushing things just a tiny little bit?"

"I'm just trying to get a jump on it. I haven't moved anywhere since I moved here, and with all my stuff, plus Death's apartment to move, it's going to take a lot of work."

"Won't you have Death to help you?" her mother asked. "Or does he only cook?"

"He'll help," Wren said. "I don't want him to do too much, though. I told you about his lungs, remember?"

"I remember. It's not at all convenient, having an invisible injury that keeps him from doing physical labor."

Wren glared at her mother.

"I'm just saying . . ." Emily opened a nearby cupboard. "Where are all your dishes? They're not sitting around on the floor in the living room any more."

"I know. I got tired of tripping over them and I was afraid I was going to break something."

"You could have put them back in the cupboard."

"But then it would have felt like I hadn't accomplished anything."

"So where are they?"

"I went ahead and packed them up, and all the knickknacks and doodads and such, and stored them out in the garage until we're ready to move. That wide shelf along the back of the garage didn't have anything on it but junk. I mean actual junk, like boxes things came in that I bought years ago and saved the boxes in case I had to return them but I never did. So I threw them away and put the cases of dishes and such out there. It's just about the same height as the back of a truck, so all I'll have to do is back up and it'll be easy to load."

"Brilliant," Emily said. She didn't sound

particularly sincere. "And now you're going to put all your pots and pans out there too?"

"That's the idea."

"Ah. I see."

"Would you like some coffee?" Wren asked. "I've got some ugly plastic cups that I bought at an auction once when no one would bid on them. I figure we can use them until we move and then just donate them to the thrift shop. I also found a huge package with about a hundred paper plates left over from Fourth of July three or four years ago. Now's as good a time to use them up as any. It's not fancy, but I don't think it'll kill us to rough it just a little for a few weeks."

"No, probably not," her mother agreed. "Although it is a little sad."

"What is?"

"Setting such a poor table for your first holiday dinner with your future husband."

Wren sat down suddenly and her face fell.

"Oh, no! I completely forgot about Thanksgiving!"

When Death had furnished his little apartment, he'd only been worried about utility. It was an efficiency apartment, one room with a kitchenette in the corner and a tiny bathroom, and he'd been satisfied with a twin bed, a second-hand sofa, and a desk and chair. Since Randy had come to stay with him, they'd added a second bed and a couple of armchairs and that was that. It wasn't fancy, but it worked fine most of the time.

The drawback was that when one of them had to wake up early, both of them woke up early.

Randy was covering a half-shift for another paramedic who'd promised to make his daughter's basketball game, so he set his alarm for six a.m. After he'd left, Death lay awake for another hour or so, but his mind was working overtime and he finally gave up, threw on a robe, and went in to his desk. He opened the blinds to let the morning sun in, started a pot of coffee, booted up his computer, and pulled out his notebook.

He had an idea what was going on with the stolen painting and the other missing items, but at this point it was just a hunch and he had no idea how he was going to prove it even if he was right. He opened the file with Frank Appelbaum's family tree, went to the top where the diagrams outlined the original immigrants from 1893, and laid a blank sheet of paper on his desk. Sooner or later he was going to have to explain this to someone. It would help to have it all clear in his own mind.

The document only tracked the Applebaums, but there were references to two other families, or parts of families, that had left Prussia for America with the Applebaums at the end of the nineteenth century. The three families had left, according to the notes provided by Frank's second cousin twice removed, for economic reasons. Life in Prussia had promised scarce jobs and scant fortunes, and the Warner siblings' father had already come over decades before, when they were small, and made a name for himself as a tinker on the westward trails.

Miriam Appelbaum, aka Mimi Blossom, the subject of the Ring Portrait, was already a young widow with a child. She joined her two sisters in the move. They traveled on a ship called the Nordstern with two brothers with the last name Bender, Chance Warner's great-great-grandparents, and his great-great-grandfather's sister. This sister was Claudia Warner, known in family legend as Crazy Aunt Cici and remembered still for her resourcefulness, quick temper, and occasional homicidal tendencies.

Cici had married the eldest Bender brother, Henry, who had made a fortune in the railroad industry. She bore him six children before she caught him cheating on her and went after him with a meat cleaver. Only three of the children survived to adulthood, two daughters and one son, Henry Jr., who eventually married Miriam Appelbaum's niece, Rose Derkin.

Henry Jr. and Rose Bender had one child, a son. They named him Claudio, presumably in honor of his ferocious grandmother. He, in turn, also had a single son. His name was Henry.

Death was 99.9 percent certain that this was the same Claudio Bender who had, in the early 1970s, built the Ozark Hills Supper Club.

This was not where he'd expected the case to lead, but it made a certain sort of sense if you looked at it in the right light. Bender was wealthy. He'd grown up that way, and seemed to be used to people catering to his every whim as a result. Dr. Bailey, the professor Death had talked to in Columbia, said that Bender was infatuated with his own history and loved anything that was related to his past. According to Wren, Neils Larsen had described him as "grabby."

Death surmised that if Bender wanted something he couldn't have, his first instinct would probably be to copy it. After all, what was the Ozark Hills Supper Club but a copy of a popular nightclub? At some point, Death reasoned, Bender had found an opportunity to swap his copy for the real thing. He'd gotten away with it the first time he tried, and so he'd kept it up. The swaps he'd pulled off, at least for a time, were of things that didn't draw a lot of attention. No one had noticed the fakes, even though they weren't very good copies, simply because no one had looked closely.

Made bold by his success, he'd gotten ambitious with the Volkmer portrait. If Death could prove his theory, that was the heist that would be Bender's downfall. The circumstantial evidence was there. Bender owned a large share in Eiler Labs, whose employees had facilitated the swap.

And Death was willing to bet that Bender had gone even further to get access to the Ring Portrait. Funding for the film class project that had led to the painting being removed from the museum had come from the Nordstern Foundation — a charity that bore the same name as the ship that had carried Bender's ancestors to America.

But Claudio Bender was a wealthy man. Fair or not, that gave him a certain amount of power and an advantage in the court of public opinion. If Death was going to accuse him of being a thief, he was going to need more than a hunch to go on.

Death sighed, shuffled his papers together, and decided to walk over to the coffee shop and pick up some donuts to take to Wren's house.

". . . And someone told me that Wren's going to sell her house so they can buy a bigger house together? I mean, that just doesn't seem fair to me. She's putting her whole house into it and what's he got? He doesn't have a house, that's for sure. He let me keep that. He was living in his car when he and Wren first met. Did she tell you that? He said he wanted to be sure that Benji would have a safe place to grow up in." Madeline laughed unpleasantly. "Really? Who does that? Benji isn't even his kid. I think we all know what he's really thinking."

Madeline was pretty, Edgar would give her that, and she probably had a capacity for charm. She had invited herself to join him, got a waitress to bring over a high chair for her baby, and ordered a cinnamon roll and a cup of coffee that Edgar suspected he was going to wind up paying for. He supposed he didn't mind. It was proving to be an enlightening morning. She was telling him more than she realized.

It was Edgar who had asked for a sippy

cup of juice for her little boy and had them bring him some dry cereal. It didn't seem to have occurred to Madeline that the toddler might see her eating and want to eat too. Edgar had poured the cereal out on the tray of the high chair for him and the little guy was concentrating on picking the pieces up and shoving them in his mouth. Every time his mother said the name "Death," the toddler's head came up and he looked around hopefully. When he suddenly pounded his fists on the tray, kicked his feet, and said "Deese! Deese!", Edgar knew before even looking that his future son-in-law was outside the window.

He followed Benji's gaze and found Death at the end of the sidewalk, looking at them in, if Edgar was reading him right, surprise and dismay. His vehicle was nowhere in sight. His face was flushed and even at this distance Edgar could see that he was breathing heavily, as if he'd run a marathon.

Madeline turned to look at him and her eyes narrowed. "Walked here," she said with a frown. "He's such an idiot. You know, he has a perfectly good handicapped parking pass. He could drive over here and park right by the door and no one could say a thing, but do you think he uses it?"

Death gave them a slight nod and walked

toward the entrance. Edgar drained his coffee and sat back, curious to see how this was going to play out.

The bell over the door jangled. Death came in and headed for them. One of the waitresses cut him off.

"Hey, darlin'! No Wren this morning?"

"No, I'm just on my way over there. Can I get a dozen donuts to go?"

"Sure thing."

She left to get his donuts and he came over to the booth where Edgar and Madeline were sitting. Benji was bouncing in his high chair and he immediately held up his arms to be picked up. Death obliged and the child wrapped himself around the former Marine, lay his head on his shoulder, and sighed.

Death turned to the adults. "Hey. What's up?"

"Just getting some breakfast," Edgar said. "What are you up to?"

"I was going to head over to Wren's house. I thought I'd take some donuts."

"You walked?"

"Yeah. It's just across the square."

"Why don't you ride back with me?" Edgar said. "Someone can take you over to get your car later if you need it."

"If it wouldn't be an imposition, sure.

Thanks."

"Oh." Madeline sat up and looked from one of them to the other. "We're going to need a ride home."

Death peered at her. "Where's his car seat?"

"I, uh . . ."

Death's face darkened. "Dammit, Madeline! If you're driving him around with no car seat —"

"I'm not, okay? Jeez. That was one time."

"It only takes one time. I will turn you in. So help me God, I will."

"I'm not, all right? We rode here with Eric, but he freaked out and ditched us. I don't know why. The car seat is in the back of his car."

"Did he say where he was going?"

"He just suddenly up and said he had to go to work."

Death nodded sharply and juggled Benji so he could get his phone out. He touched a couple of buttons and waited a moment to speak.

"Hey, Chief? Yeah, it's me. Listen, do you know where Eric Farrington has gotten to? . . . He is? . . . Uh huh . . . No, he just ditched Madeline and Benji at the coffee shop and the baby's car seat is in his car. Can you make him come pick them up and take them home? Okay, thanks. Okay, bye."

He hung up. "Eric will be here in a couple of minutes."

"Okay. Great."

Death pulled a chair over and sat down and an awkward silence ensued. The waitress brought his donuts and he paid for them, and then she waved two more bills at Edgar and Madeline.

"Who gets the bad news?"

"Oh," Madeline said, "Eric was supposed to be treating us. I didn't even think. I don't have my purse."

Death reached for it with a resigned air but Edgar took it first. "I've got it," he said.

"Thank you so much," Madeline simpered. "You're such a sweetie. I can certainly see where Wren got her kind disposition."

Death rolled his eyes and bounced the baby on his knee.

When Eric Farrington showed up again, he sat in the parking lot in his car and honked the horn. They left the coffee shop in a group. Death insisted on buckling Benji into his car seat personally. Madeline climbed into the front, and Edgar went and stood by the driver's door and made small talk while Eric stuttered out replies and tried not to hyperventilate.

Death Bogart said goodbye to the child

who was not his son and closed the door. Edgar tapped one finger on the driver's window, which Eric had rolled up almost all the way. Eric looked up at him fearfully and Edgar met his eye.

"You drive carefully with that baby in the car."

"Yes, sir! I am, sir! I will, sir! Goodbye, sir!"

Edgar stepped back and Eric put the car in gear and eased away. Edgar and Death came together behind it and watched them leave.

"I caught Eric poaching one time," Edgar explained. "Or trying to poach. With a bow and arrow. He put an arrow in my truck tire. I yelled a little bit."

He led the way to his truck. He'd unhooked the camper and left it in his daughter's yard, but he was used to having it attached so he'd still parked at the edge of the lot, where there was more room to maneuver. When they were standing on opposite sides of the vehicle, ready to get in, Death stopped and just looked at him through the cab.

"Mr. Morgan," he said, "I want to say something."

"Okay."

"I want you to like me. You and your wife

both. I really do. And it's nerve-wracking because I don't know what you expect of me, or what you want. And I know Madeline, and I can only image what she might have told you. But ultimately, the only thing that I can be is me. And I know where I stand with Wren. That's what matters to me more than anything."

Edgar just nodded and got in behind the wheel. After a moment, Death joined him.

"Cute little boy," Edgar said after a moment. "How old is he?"

"About fourteen months?"

"Do you see him often?"

"I babysit every chance I get. I'd take him, if she'd let me have him."

Edgar just nodded and didn't say anything more about it.

East Bledsoe Ferry was a small town and the drive to Wren's house didn't take long. When they arrived they went in and found Wren and her mother at the kitchen table drinking coffee and unwrapping pots and pans from the newspaper they'd been packed in.

Edgar went to the stove and poured a cup of coffee. Emily was red in the face and Wren looked miffed.

"I just think you're rushing this," Emily said. "Getting married is a big step and buying a house together is a big step and I don't see any reason you can't wait a little bit and make sure you know what you're doing."

"It's okay, Mom," Edgar said. "Death's a good boy." He slid the coffee he'd just poured over to the younger man and poured another cup for himself. Death looked stunned. He opened his mouth and closed it again without saying anything.

"Well . . ." Emily hesitated. "If you're sure?"

"I'm sure." Edgar went around the table to an empty chair, dropping his big hand on Death's shoulder in passing. He settled himself at the table, took a sip from his cup, and set it down.

"I'd like to have a look at that house before you close on it, if you don't mind," he said.

"I . . . uh . . . yeah." It took Death a minute to find his voice. "Yeah, that'd be great. I'd love to have your opinion."

"Wren and I will come too," Emily decided. "We can bring a tape measure and measure the windows. And I want to see this grave in the rosebushes. I've seen it before, but I wasn't really paying attention at the time." She looked at Death. "You'd better start calling us Mom and Pop."

EIGHTEEN

"So do you want to hear something a little weird?" Death asked.

With her mother's help, Wren had un-packed the pots and pans they'd need to cook Thanksgiving dinner. She made a note to go out later and dig out enough nice dishes and glassware to set a respectable table. Edgar's endorsement had completely allayed Emily's reservations about Death and she was cheerfully helping them make plans. At her suggestion, they were going to start packing spare linens and out-of-season clothing next. At the moment, though, they'd run out of boxes, so they took the coffee and donuts into the living room and made themselves comfortable.

"I'm always interested in weird things," Wren said. "Whatcha got?"

"I think I've figured out who's behind the missing painting. You'll never guess who it is."

"Someone I've heard of?"

"Yup."

Wren thought about it. "Well, it couldn't be the guy who owned it, or the man who owns the museum."

"Why not?" her mother asked. "Couldn't one of them want the insurance money?"

"Maybe, but that wouldn't be weird. Death said its weird." Wren sat silent for a moment, then shook her head. "I give up. Tell me."

Death grinned. "Does the name Claudio Bender ring a bell?"

"The yacht club guy? I mean, the supper club guy?"

"The same."

"Who?" Edgar asked.

"Claudio Bender," Wren said. "He's the man who built the Ozark Hills Supper Club, where we're doing an auction tomorrow. But why would he steal a painting?"

"It's a long story. He's related to the woman in the painting and he has a tendency to obsess over his own family history." Death went through everything he knew about Bender and his family ties and outlined his reasoning.

"It makes sense," Wren said when he'd finished. Her mother nodded but her dad frowned.

"How you gonna prove it?" he asked.

"That I don't know." Death looked around. "Any ideas?"

"What sort of proof do you need?" Emily asked.

Death shrugged. "Most of the cases I work on that involve theft involve employee theft or industrial espionage. In either case, it's an ongoing problem. I usually solve the matter by catching the thief in the act. But that's not an option in this case."

"Is it like court cases you hear about?" Wren asked. "You need either physical evidence or an eyewitness testimony, or something like that?"

"Something like that," he agreed. "If I knew where Bender was keeping the things he steals, I could try to get enough evidence for the police to get a search warrant. But I have no idea. From what little I've found out about him so far, he has five or six houses and at least a couple high-dollar apartments, not all of them in the United States."

"So what does that leave?" Edgar asked.

Death shifted in his chair. "There is one other way to convict someone, but it's notoriously difficult. You can use circum-stantial evidence, but it has to be pretty well overwhelming. That's the only route I can see open, though. I'm just going to have to learn everything I can about Bender. I've already tied him to the portrait and to the lab where the switch was made. I suspect he's behind the foundation that was responsible for funding the documentary, too."

"What documentary?" Emily asked.

"The reason the painting left the museum in the first place was so it could be studied as part of a documentary on art during westward expansion," Wren explained. She turned to Death. "Isn't information about charitable foundations public?"

"It should be, yes. I just need to get on the computer and start pulling up files."

"Would the articles about the yacht club help any?" Emily asked.

Now it was Death's turn to be confused. "What articles?"

"I was thinking about where they found Bob's body, and it seemed to me he could have been going to or from the yacht club," Wren explained. "We went to the paper and Cameron copied a bunch of articles about it for us so we could look through the pictures to see if we saw him."

"Any luck?"

"No. Mom and Randy and I have been poring over the files, but no one stands out. There might be something you could use about Bender, though, to help you with your background research."

"Great. I'll have a look at it."

"Speaking of the yacht club," Wren said, "after I finished up there last night I went over and talked to Mr. Larsen again. There are a bunch of the Viking village people down this weekend —"

Death laughed. "Viking village people? Did they sing for you?"

"Okay, very funny."

"S-A-C-K!" Death sang. "It's fun to go out and S-A-C-K!"

"I'm marrying a comedian," Wren sighed.

"Sorry." He grinned, not looking at all contrite. "What did the Viking village people say?"

"They're having a harvest festival tomorrow. Tonight they're going to get together around the fire and sing" — Death smirked — "and tell stories, and we're invited to join them if we don't have other plans."

"Do we have other plans?"

"I don't know. Do we? Do you want to go?"

"Sure. Sounds fun. Do we have to dress up?"

"Mr. Larsen said no." Wren turned to her parents. "Mom, Dad, do you want to come?"

They looked at one another. Edgar shrugged and Emily nodded.

"Why not?" she said. "But first, I want to see this house you're buying."

"Can I ask you a question, sir?" Death said.

"Pop," Edgar reminded him gently. "Call me Pop. If you want to."

Death smiled to himself. "Can I ask you a question, Pop?" The two men had walked down a long path that led through the woods behind the Sandburg house and came out on the shore of Truman Lake.

"Sure. Shoot."

"How long were you a conservation agent?"

"Almost fifty years. I started in April of '65, when I was eighteen."

"Did you like it?"

"A-yup." The big man settled himself on a fallen log, scooting over to make room so Death could join him. It had been a dry autumn, and several feet of mud stretched between them and the blue expanse of the lake. The day was still, and the smooth surface of the water reflected back the sky and the now nearly bare trees on the shore.

"You remember when the lake came in?"

"Sure."

"Wren looked at some old aerial photographs. She says the old road that ran under the lake by the yacht club was still visible in '78."

"And it still is, when the lake is down. Salvy and I went out that way in his boat the other day, the day before you and Randy joined us. You could walk across it if you really wanted to." Edgar gave the younger man a shrewd, sideways look. "You think Bob is connected to that bloody Viking costume, don't you?"

"You find a dead body in the woods and bloody clothes hidden less than a mile away, it sure seems to me like it could be connected. And Ingrid Larsen's father thought he saw her in the woods in a Viking costume the weekend she disappeared. If she was somehow connected to Bob's death, it could explain her disappearance. Either she ran for some reason, or . . ."

"Or Bob wasn't the only victim."

"Is it possible her body could still be out there in the woods somewhere?" Death asked.

"After Bob turned up in '85, the police went over the woods with a fine-toothed comb. They figured he must have been carrying something durable that would help them identify him — a gun, a watch, a wallet. Never found a thing. Also never found another body." Edgar shifted on the log. "That doesn't mean there's not one, but if there is, it's most likely under the lake where it'll never be found."

Half a dozen geese flew in, coasted low across the water while honking raucously, and wheeled off around a spit of land and out of sight.

"We should put a real bench down here," Death said. "This log gets uncomfortable."

"Why would Ingrid Larsen have even been around here?" Edgar persisted. "I understood she disappeared from a Renaissance faire in Cleveland. And she couldn't have been looking for her father. She had no way of knowing he was down here."

"Maybe she didn't come on her own," Death said. "Maybe someone brought her here. And maybe I'm just overly suspicious and reading too much into coincidences. But it wasn't Cleveland, it was Cincinnati. And Cincinnati is right across the river from Southgate, Kentucky."

"And what's in Southgate, Kentucky?"

"Nothing now. But in the early seventies there was a popular nightclub there. It was called the Beverly Hills Supper Club."

"When I was a girl my momma had these hollyhocks. They were her favorite flower.

She had them planted in a big mass in the corner of the yard and in summer, when they were in bloom, we'd pull the blooms off and put little round hat pins in the stem for a head and make dollies of them. And they were exactly that color. So when other people look at my walls and see chapped babies' butts and dried stomach medicine, I look at them and I see my momma's flowers."

"Gosh, that's sweet," Wren said. "Now I feel bad about wanting to paint."

"Don't be silly," Myrna Sandburg said. "It's gonna be your house. Paint it whatever color you like. I don't care! I'm just explaining myself because people always see my living room and look at me like I'm insane. I told you my son built me a little house in his yard? You know what color he painted it inside? White! He actually painted it white!" She grinned. "But I found me a paint chip this exact color and let me tell you, that boy's in for a surprise."

Wren and her mother were sitting with Myrna in her dining room, chatting. Myrna had been doing some packing of her own. The walls were bare and the built-in china cabinet stood empty. Emily had a list of measurements on a notepad in front of her and was calculating how much fabric it was going to take for curtains.

They heard the men's voices first, a quiet conversation too soft for them to make out the words. Shadows passed the north window and then footsteps crossed the porch. There came a knock on the door.

Myrna leaned back in her chair and shouted through the living room, "Death Bogart, is that you?"

"Yes, ma'am."

"Well, what are you doing knocking on your own front door? Get that cute little hiney in here and keep us company!"

The door opened and Death came in, blushing and bashful, with Edgar chuckling behind him. They joined the ladies at the table.

"Randy's been trying to call you," Wren told Death. "He's on his way here to see us. He's acting really weird."

"That's not an act. Weird how?"

"Excited and secretive. He asked me if we saw him, but he won't say who 'him' is. He said no one's stealing his thunder this time. What's he talking about?"

"Heaven only knows."

Myrna got up and poured the men each a cup of coffee.

"Myrna's been telling us about her mother's flowers," Wren said. "We should plant

312

some hollyhocks in the yard." She looked toward the living room dubiously. "They come in other colors, right?"

"Lots of colors," her mother assured her. "Some morning glories and four o'clocks would look nice climbing the porch posts, too."

"And irises. I love irises." Wren beamed at Death sentimentally. "Death gave me irises the first time we had dinner together."

"I got them out of a ditch," he remembered. "Because I was flat broke but I wanted to give you flowers."

"That was so sweet." Wren sighed. "It's too bad they got shot."

Death winced and glanced furtively at his future in-laws. "Maybe we shouldn't be telling this story."

"Car," Myrna said, apparently at random.

The other four looked at her and she nodded toward the front of the house.

"There's a car coming. You'll start to notice them yourself after you live here for a while. Not a lot of traffic out this way. If you hear a car, it's probably coming here."

Now that she was paying attention, Wren could make out the sound of an engine approaching. Death rose and strolled over to the dining room window. It looked north, toward the highway that led back to East

313

Bledsoe Ferry. He pulled the curtain aside and leaned over an antique sideboard to peer out.

"It's Randy," he said. "He's just pulling into the driveway now."

"It's good that he found the place," Myrna said. "He hasn't been here before."

"No, but I described where the house was when I told him we were looking at it, and he's in the volunteer fire department so he spends a lot of time studying maps."

"And he knows Death's Jeep," Wren added.

Randy pounded across the porch and rapped urgently at the door. Myrna looked at Death.

"You wanna let him in, sweetie? Since you're already up and all?"

"Yes, ma'am."

Death opened the door and Randy bounced in, manic with excitement. He was a walking exclamation mark. "Where's Wren? And her mom? Is her mom here too?"

"Yes. Chill. They're in the other room." Death led his brother into the dining room and Randy immediately focused on Wren.

"Did you see him?" he demanded again.

"See who?" she asked.

Randy turned his attention to her mother.

"Did you see him?"

"Sweetheart, none of us know what you're talking about."

He stood up very straight and tall and beamed at them.

"Sit down," his brother told him. "You're making everybody nervous. Take a seat and tell us what's going on."

Randy, still grinning, seated himself at the table and leaned forward, hands clasped on the polished surface. He looked around at everyone, one by one.

"I found Bob," he said.

"Found him?" Myrna asked. "He better still be in that grave out there."

Randy glanced at her, caught off guard. "Uh, yes, ma'am. I'm sure he is. I mean, I think I found a picture of him when he was alive."

"What?" Wren demanded. "Where?"

"On that thumb drive that Cameron Michaels gave you. I made a copy of the files and took it to work with me today. We had a pretty slow day so I had a chance to go over it, and there he was."

"That's impossible," Wren said. "Mom and I studied every picture in that file."

Randy held up a finger. "Which file?"

Wren frowned. "The Ozark Hills Supper Club file. And the Cold Harbor Supper

Club file, which turned out to be just one article where the writer got the name wrong. But the thing is, we looked at every single picture. We even used a magnifying glass for group pictures. He wasn't there."

"No, he wasn't." Randy was grinning, drawing it out.

"So where was he?" Death demanded. "Come on, man. Show us. Put up or shut up."

His little brother laughed and pulled out his phone. "I copied the article. It was in the file marked 'Henry Bender.' " He read it aloud. *"May 22, 1973. Fifteen-year-old Henry Bender today became the youngest pilot ever to land a plane at the East Bledsoe Ferry Municipal Airport. The talented youngster, who first soloed at the age of thirteen, flew his father's private jet from Cincinnati to East Bledsoe Ferry so his father could check on the progress of the nightclub he's building on the lakeshore. The Ozark Hills Supper Club, when it is completed, is expected to draw visitors from across the country. It will feature boating, dancing, gourmet dining, and performances by popular celebrities, and will make East Bledsoe Ferry a new hotspot for the fashionable set. When that happens, we will surely see a lot more of this young man."*

Wren and Death left their seats to lean

over Randy's shoulders as he swiped the screen. The print article slid aside and a picture came up of two young men standing next to a small aircraft.

The younger boy was obviously Henry Bender. There was a second picture of him, a headshot, next to the first one. It was his companion who had caught Randy's attention.

He was a brawny young man, not too tall, with a round face and straight blond hair in a cut that reminded Wren of Hutch from *Star- sky & Hutch.* He wore tight jeans that flared out at the ankle in a pale color that looked light gray in the grainy old black-and-white photo. His shirt was a tunic, tight across his chest and on his upper arms but loose below his waist and over his hands. He was, she thought, very seventies in his appearance.

"It could be him," Death agreed. "It would mean forensics got the coloring wrong. This guy's more blond. And the hairstyle is off and the nose isn't quite right. But it could be him. Wow. This could very well be him."

"Is there a name?" Wren asked.

"Scroll down," Randy said. "Look at the caption."

"You scroll down," Death said. "You're

317

holding the phone."

"You scroll down. You're the one who wants to see it."

"Don't you want to see it?"

"I already did."

Death rolled his eyes and reached over Randy's shoulder to scroll down. *"Fifteen-year-old pilot Henry Bender of Southgate, Kentucky, seen here with longtime friend Trevor Burt, 18, of Cincinnati."*

There was a sort of finality in Death's voice as he read it off. Wren tipped her head to look at him and saw him exchanging a glance with her father. Death raised one eyebrow.

Edgar nodded.

NINETEEN

"Hello? Jackson? Hey, listen, is the sheriff there? He's not? He's where?"

Wren tugged on Death's sleeve. "Where is he?"

He took the phone away from his mouth and put his hand over the speaker. "He got delayed on his way back from lunch. He had to arrest the Snyder kid for disturbing the peace again?"

"Oh, yeah. He always gets drunk and tries to start arguments about baseball." Wren made a face. "Like Matt knows anything about baseball," she mocked. It never ceased to amaze Death how she knew everything about everyone in this small town.

Death turned his attention back to the phone. "Okay, listen, I might have something for you."

"Be still my beating heart," Deputy Jackson replied wryly.

"Well, hey. If you're not interested, I can call the city guys. I mean, it's your case, but I'm sure they'd love to take the credit if this solves it."

"If they have as much experience with your stupid ideas as I do, they're not going to be jumping for joy either."

"I was the one who found that picture," Randy called from across the room.

They were back at Wren's, where they'd retreated to discuss the situation. The day had grown overcast and an early twilight was starting to fall, turning the world a dreary blue gray.

Death nodded at his brother and spoke into the phone. "Actually, this one is Randy's stupid idea."

"That's not an improvement," Jackson sighed. "Okay, what you got?"

"We may have a name for Bob. You know? The body —"

"In your rosebushes? I know. Where did he come up with it?"

Death kept it simple. "He was looking through some old newspaper stories from the early 1970s and he found a picture of a guy who looks like the reconstruction."

"So this is just a shot in the dark?"

"Maybe, maybe not. Can you see if you can find anything about him?"

"I suppose. Give me the name and anything else you have."

"The name is Trevor Burt and he was eighteen years old and living in Cincinnati in May of 1973."

"All right. I'll let you know if I find anything."

Emily and Edgar were sitting in the two easy chairs on one side of Wren's coffee table. Randy sprawled loosely across the love seat and Death helped himself to the end of the sofa. Wren came over to join him and for a long minute they just sat there, each lost in their own thoughts.

"Are we going to say anything about this to the Larsens tonight?" Wren asked finally.

"What's to say?" Death countered. "At this point, we don't know anything they don't already know themselves."

"You have to say something," Emily objected. "Ingrid was their daughter. They have a right to know."

"But all we have is speculation," Death said gently. "A theory, and not a very complete theory at that."

"What exactly do you think happened?" Edgar asked.

Death sighed and shrugged. Wren kicked her shoes off and curled up next to him on the couch.

"It was the summer of 1978," she said. "Ingrid was seventeen and traveling with a Renaissance festival dressed as a Viking maid. In late July they set up in Cincinnati. If Henry Bender was fifteen in '73, he was twenty by '78. He lived with his father across the river in Southgate, Kentucky."

"We know Bender Sr. is obsessed with anything relating to his personal history," Death said. "We know he can be persuaded to donate money to the Museum of Art and Archaeology if the projects catch his interest, and I suspect he arranged for the theft of several things from various other collections related to northern Europe's past. If his son shares that interest, it's a given that Henry would have gone to the Renaissance faire when it turned up in his home town."

"Except that he wasn't there that weekend," Wren said. "At least, according to his father he wasn't."

"What are you talking about?"

"Claudio Bender was at the consignment auction last week. I thought I told you that."

"Rude little old man on a scooter, right?"

"Right. I mean, when you first see him you think, 'oh, what a sweet little old man,' but then he starts talking and you realize he's not."

Death raised his eyebrows. "You asked

him about his son's whereabouts the weekend Ingrid Larsen disappeared?"

"Not exactly."

"Exactly what?"

She shifted a little. She felt warm and soft and *right* nestled close against his side. "I just asked him if he remembered when Dr. Larsen thought he saw a ghost. Claudio told me they sent his son to search the shore but he couldn't find any trace that anyone had even been there. Which means Henry was at the supper club."

"That . . . might very well fit," Death said, not bothering to elaborate just then.

"I've got a question for you," Edgar said. "If Randy's right and the body in the roses is Trevor, why hasn't Henry said anything about it all these years? That picture has been up on flyers all over town for decades. And even if he didn't see the picture, didn't he miss his old friend? Didn't he worry at all when they found a body? If your buddy went missing and then a skeleton turned up, wouldn't you at least wonder?"

"Guilty conscience?" Death guessed. "He knows something. If that body is Trevor Burt, he almost has to. Hell, maybe he put him there. We need him to tell us what happened. If he did it, we need a confession. Speculation is only going to take us so far."

"The Larsens seemed to think that Henry and his father will be at their feast tomorrow. Maybe we can just ask him," Wren suggested.

"Do you think there's any chance he'll answer?"

"Do you?"

Death sighed. "I've never met him. I have no idea what he might or might not do. If he's there tonight, or tomorrow night, I'll try to get him alone and show him the reconstruction. See how he reacts. But if he refuses to tell me what he knows, I have no idea how we could force him to."

Randy shifted sleepily on the love seat. "You could always go full Scooby," he said.

"Go full what?"

"Scooby." Randy opened one eye to look at his brother. "Fake a ghost and scare him into talking. I'll dress up as Bob with a sheet on my head and go, 'Woo! Woo! Why did you leave me lying all alone in the cold dark woods? Woo! Woo!'"

Death just looked at him for a long minute. Wren was giggling against his ribs. Emily was laughing and Edgar had a grin on his face.

"You think it would work?" Randy asked

"I think it would work. No?"

"Okay," Death said. "One, you're too tall.

Two, you're too lanky. Three, that is the stupidest idea I've ever heard."

"Well, you don't have to be rude about it."

"I know I don't have to. That's just one of the perks you get for having me as a brother."

Randy blew him a raspberry.

Death gave Wren a one-armed squeeze and pulled himself up off the couch. "Shall we go meet the Vikings?" he asked.

"What about the Benders?" Wren wanted to know.

"If they're there when we get there, we'll play it by ear."

If Wren had heard the music without knowing where it was coming from, she'd have imagined she was listening to an oboe, a flute, and a piccolo. Maggie's lur carried the main melody, while the pipes alternately complemented it and provided a counterpoint. Two young girls were playing the pipes. They wore matching dresses and overdresses. Their hair was braided on top of their heads and their long, hooded cloaks made Wren think of Little Red Riding Hood, except that they were blue. Little Blue Riding Hoods. Neils sat off to one side, watching, with his lyre propped on his knee and a flagon in his right hand.

A fire blazed in the fire pit and Wren and Death and Randy and her parents sat on rough-hewn benches at the edge of the circle of firelight, surrounded by men and women in the costumes of eighth-century northern Europe. It was a cold night, but not unpleasant given the fire and the press of bodies. The smoke from the fire carried old music up to a star-spattered sky and there wasn't a modern light in sight.

The music reached a low, melancholy passage and Neils set his mead down, stood, and strummed a chord on his lyre. He stepped forward, still playing. The women altered their music to complement his, lowering the volume to provide a background for his voice as he chanted:

"Softest, sweetest, fleeting
Songbird, long I sought thee.
Weeping, haunted, wanting,
Woeful, hope full waning.
Lost beloved dove now,
Love above all lingers.
In imagination,
Ingrid. Iridescent."

"Be careful of the honey mead," Jacob Larsen said, leaning over Wren's right shoulder to hand Death a mug. "It's stronger than you expect. Wren, are you sure I can't get you some?"

She smiled up at him as the music ended. "Thank you, but no. I have to work early in the morning."

"What do you do," a man to her left asked, "that you have to go to work on a Sunday?"

"Wren's an auctioneer," Jacob explained. "She and her company are the ones who'll be selling the old supper club tomorrow."

"Really?" The stranger, an older man with long white hair and a full beard, leaned to his side to give her a penetrating look. "Now that I might have to come see. I haven't been inside that place in thirty-odd years."

Death ducked his head forward to look past her at the man. "Were you a member of the supper club?" he asked.

"Not a member, exactly," he said. "Bender invited me because he was involved in a research project I worked on back in the early eighties. I work for the Brandburg House. It's —"

"A museum in Pittsburgh," Death said.

"Yeah." The man was surprised. "You've heard of us?"

"I have. And recently. You specialize in the influence of Germanic and northern Euro-

327

pean heritage on American history."

"That's right." The man leaned around Wren and offered Death his hand. "Andrew Markham."

"Death Bogart. Pleased to meet you."

"Are you another academic?"

Death grinned, the firelight catching the planes of his face and finding red highlights in his close-cropped hair. "No. I'm a private investigator, actually. I'm going to take a wild guess here. That project you worked on . . . was it an archaeological dig in a bog in Belgium?"

Markham leaned back. "Wow. You're good. Are you sure you're not a psychic? How did you figure that one out?"

"Just a hunch. You've recently discovered that one of your artifacts is a forgery. A reconstructed clay pot. It came from that dig, didn't it?"

"Ah, hell," another of the Vikings said. "Did you let him get away with one, Marky?"

Markham shrugged and looked embarrassed. "What was I supposed to do? Hold his hand every minute?"

"Wait," Death said. "You know who took it?"

"Oh, I think we all know who took it," the heckler said.

"It's not like I can prove it," Markham said. He turned his attention back to Death. "Let me just put it this way. The Benders are supposed to come to the festival tomorrow. If they show up at your girlfriend's auction, don't let them wander around on their own."

"How long have you known that the Benders — both the Benders do this?"

"The old man more so, I think. Henry's more worried about getting caught."

"Right. So how long have you known?"

"Gosh." Markham looked around at his fellow Vikings as if taking a survey. "Decades?"

"We try not to ever leave him unattended anywhere there's something he might take a fancy to," Neils Larsen said from the other side of the fire. "He still tries to swipe things, but you can call him on it and take them back."

"What do you say to him?" Wren asked. She'd admitted to herself a long time ago that she'd make a terrible cop. She had a feeling that if she saw someone steal something, she'd be too embarrassed for them to be able to react.

"You pretend like you think he's done it by mistake," Jacob Larsen said. "Oh, Mr. Bender, you've slipped that vase into your pocket by mistake again. Oh, Mr. Bender, I'm afraid you've gotten them switched up. This is your copy and the one you put in the box is our original."

"But you've never done anything about it?"

"You've got to understand, my dear," Neils Larsen said. "Claudio Bender is a major donor to the university. He's given hundreds of thousands of dollars to support our museums and educational projects. And most of the things he tries to take aren't particularly valuable. Not in dollar terms. It's just never been worth it to alienate him for the sake of making a point. Although I'm guessing he's finally overstepped his bounds." Neils looked at Death. "What did he steal that you're tracking?"

"I can't prove that it was him," Death said. "Not yet. But I suspect he was behind switching an oil painting for a forgery."

"A painting? Really? Doesn't seem his style. Why would he want it?"

"The woman in the painting was a great-great aunt," Death explained. "Maybe three greats. Anyway, she was an opera singer. The painting is of her dressed as a character in the Ring Cycle."

"Ah." Larsen nodded. "Okay. That sounds about right then."

Randy was sitting on Death's right, between him and Wren's mother. He leaned over now and hissed at his brother. "Show them the picture!"

Death hesitated, but two or three of the reenactors were looking at him questioningly. He took a quick breath.

"Ah, one other thing." He chose his words carefully. "In the fall of 1985, a man's remains were found about a mile from here, on the other side of the lake. You might have heard about it?"

He looked around the fire carefully, but no one looked enlightened.

"What did he die of?" a woman asked across the flames.

"They don't know. They've never been able to identify him or determine a cause of death."

"Probably a native burial, don't you think?" Markham said. "Or an old grave from the pioneer days? They tended to bury their dead at home, you know."

"No, this was recent. Sometime in the ten years before he was found, they think. Wren and I have gotten interested in the case because he wound up buried on private property. We're in the process of buying the house his grave is attached to, and we thought it would be nice if we could find out who he is and what happened to him. The sheriff's department had a facial reconstruction done from the skull. Can I show you a picture of it? We thought, since he was found close to the supper club, maybe he was a member or was connected to someone who was."

"You got it with you?" Markham asked. He seemed interested.

Death took out his phone and brought up the photo from the sheriff's department website.

"Sorry for the anachronism," Wren said sheepishly.

"I think we can make an exception for a dead body," Neils said.

Death passed his phone around, tracking it from hand to hand and watching the faces of the Vikings as they looked at it. It was hard to tell, in the shifting firelight, but he saw nothing to suggest recognition from anyone there.

It came back to him without anyone offering a name for the corpse. Neils stood and took up his mead.

"Whoever he is, may he rest in peace," he said, lifting his cup.

The others around the fire followed suit and they drank in silence.

■ ■ ■ ■

Like Wren, Randy had to work the next day and had refrained from the honey mead. He drove them back to Wren's house through the dark countryside in his brother's Jeep. The senior Morgans went into the house to get ready for bed and Randy waited behind the wheel while Death kissed his future bride good night on her front porch.

Death was relaxed and looked sleepy when he returned and climbed in the passenger seat, but he was far from drunk. He'd been a Marine a long time, and while he never made a habit of binge drinking, he'd drunk much more than honey mead on several occasions.

He leaned his head back and closed his eyes. "So what did you think?" he asked.

"About what? The Vikings?"

"Yeah."

"Huh. I thought there'd be more weapons and armor. And horned helmets," Randy said.

"Yeah, Jacob tells me there's a lot more to Vikings than what people tend to imagine. And apparently the horned helmets aren't really a thing. There are, like, two representations of horned helmets in all of the material they've found. The one actual helmet is too flimsy to be real armor and the other one is a carving of some kind. The experts can't agree about them, but most seem to think they were ceremonial and maybe represented some deity or something. They sure didn't wear them into battle. And did you know that Vikings didn't call themselves Vikings? Viking was a verb. They would go viking. It meant going on raids."

"Not Vikings. No horned helmets. No dragon on the prow of the longboat. These guys are just killing all my dreams of being an old-school marauder." Randy sighed elaborately. "It was kind of cool, though. And you know you're right about Bender now." He slowed down and took a left turn onto the street that made up the east side of the square. "None of them recognized Bob, though."

"No. I need to get hold of Jackson in the morning and see if he learned anything about Trevor Burt."

"Or maybe not," Randy countered.

"Huh?"

"Maybe you don't need to get hold of Jackson in the morning."

"Why not?"

" 'Cause it looks like he's waiting for you now."

Death opened his eyes and sat up as they pulled up beside Jackson's cruiser. Randy turned off the engine and the deputy jumped out to meet them, shivering and blowing on his hands.

"Where have you been? No, don't tell me. I don't want to know. Is it warm in your office? We should go up to your office."

Death raised an eyebrow. "Cold?"

"Of course not. Why would I be cold? I've only been sitting here waiting for you for almost two hours. How come you weren't answering your phone?"

"Your phone never rang," Randy said to Death.

"Oh, yeah." He flinched a little guiltily. "We were out at the Viking village. I didn't want to be rude with the twenty-first-century technology, so I put it on airplane mode." He unlocked his door and let Jackson go in first. "You don't have heat in your car?"

"I'm not gonna run the engine and burn gas when I'm just sitting around. I'm responsible about spending county money."

Death gave him a side look as they climbed the stairs.

Orlando Jackson sighed. "Okay, and the

thermostat might be out. It overheats if I sit at idle."

They went in Death's office and Jackson dropped into a chair. Randy went through to the apartment for a glass of milk and Death turned up the thermostat before circling his desk and taking his own seat.

"What did you find out about Bob?" Randy demanded, returning. "Is it Trevor Burt? It is, isn't it?"

Jackson held up one finger and hesitated a second before speaking. "It . . . might be. We're looking into it. It's a distinct possibility. Proving it could be tricky, though. So far we haven't found any relatives and Burt was never reported missing. There's no DNA, no dental records, nothing."

"So what did you find out about him?" Death asked.

"He disappeared from Cincinnati the summer of 1978. Dropped off the face of the earth. Since then he hasn't had a driver's license, held a job, filed taxes, or applied for any kind of public assistance. Cincinnati police have been looking for him since early September of that year. Nothing."

"If no one had filed a missing person's report, why were the police looking for him?" Death's eyes narrowed. "What was he wanted for?"

"Failure to appear," Jackson said. "Trevor Burt skipped bail on a sexual assault charge."

TWENTY

"Are you an important man?"

"Yes, I am. I'm probably the most important man you'll ever have the privilege to meet. Now go away. I don't like children."

"Oh, don't worry." Matthew Keystone grinned, undeterred. "There aren't any children here. I'm Matthew and this is my cousin Mercy. We're here to be your escort."

Claudio Bender made a noise deep in his throat and tried to drive his red mobility scooter past the young Keystones, but there wasn't room in the crowded club building. His son, Henry, tall and pale and silent, followed him with drooping shoulders and downcast eyes.

"I thought you said you were important," Matthew said.

"I did say that. I am important. Go away."

"But if you're important, you need an escort. Important people can't just go wandering around like normal people.

Nobody would know you're important then."

Death stood off to the side with Edgar and the sheriff and watched. Around them the auction was in full swing. Wren was in a room off to his left, selling "genuine 1970s kitsch." Roy was auctioning off furniture down the hall to his right, and Sam was outside answering questions about the property, which was set to go on the block later that afternoon.

"Leona sicced the kids on him," Salvy said.

Death grinned. "They're the best shoplifting deterrent I've ever seen."

"I have an escort," Bender was saying to Matthew. "That's what my son is for."

Mercy tipped her head to look up at the tall man. "He's not an escort," she objected. "He's your son. He should have an escort too. Isn't he important?"

Henry cut his eyes toward his father and Death had the distinct feeling that he was waiting for the answer. Claudio just waved his hands in front of him as if to brush off the question. "Bah. You're annoying me. Go away."

"You don't mean that," Mercy said cheerfully. "Here, would you like for one of us to push your chair?"

"No. I don't need you to push my chair. It's motorized. Go away."

"We could get Bitty Sam to ride on your lap," Matthew offered. "He'd love that."

"I know you said you don't like children," Mercy chirped. "But you'd love Bitty Sam. Everybody loves Bitty Sam. And that would make you happy."

Salvy shifted away from the wall. "As entertaining as this is . . ." He walked over to the group. "Excuse me, Mr. Bender?"

Henry didn't react. Claudio turned immediately. "Yes! Thank heavens. Will you remove these children?"

The sheriff held up a big finger and pointed it at the older man. "Not you," he said. He turned to Henry. "You. Henry Bender, yes?"

Henry looked up and what little color there was in his face drained away.

"Yes?"

"I'm Sheriff Salvadore. May I speak with you outside for a moment?"

Claudio spun his scooter around and peered up at the sheriff querulously. "What do you want to speak to him about?"

"That's between me and your son. If you could just excuse us, sir?"

Henry went along obediently, holding his hands in front of him as if they were in invisible handcuffs. He was breathing fast and shallow and his eyes had a glazed-over look.

Claudio followed after.

"I will not excuse you. Do you know who I am? Do you have a warrant? I'll have your badge for this."

Since the sale was taking place inside the building and it was too early for most people to be leaving, the entryway was empty save for Leona and Doris and a trickle of late arrivals. The double doors were propped open, admitting a splash of brilliant sunshine and a wash of cold air. Salvy stopped just inside it and guided Henry to a seat against the wall. Death and Edgar had tagged along but hung back now and watched the sheriff work.

"Mr. Bender, your son is not under arrest," he said. "I merely want to ask him a few questions to help me with a case I'm working on. If you don't mind."

"I do mind. We're not even from your jurisdiction. What could he possibly know about your case?"

"That's what I'm trying to find out." Salvy turned back to Henry. "An old newspaper story concerning you has recently come to light. About you piloting a private jet here when you were fifteen. In the picture that accompanied the story, you're standing next to a man named Trevor Burt, who's described as a 'longtime friend.' Can you tell me where Mr. Burt is now?"

Henry stared at him, speechless.

"He doesn't know," his father said impatiently. "Henry! Tell the man you don't know."

"No, I'm sorry. I don't know. I don't know anything."

"Can you tell me the last time you saw him?"

"He doesn't remember."

"Mr. Bender," Salvy said, turning to the older man. "Will you please allow your son to speak for himself?"

"He. Doesn't. Remember." Claudio turned his head and sniffed. "I don't know why you're even looking for Burt."

"He's wanted in Cincinnati. He failed to appear on an assault charge."

Claudio snorted inelegantly. "Ha. That was almost forty years ago. The statute of limitations has long since expired."

"Actually, it hasn't. You see, when someone skips bail or goes into hiding to avoid a charge, the clock freezes on the statute of limitations until such time as they're found."

"Well, it hardly matters. That has nothing to do with my son."

"Maybe it does and maybe it doesn't." Salvy returned his focus to Henry. "In the fall of 1985, a body was found in the woods not far from here. I have here a facial reconstruction that was done on the skull —"

Henry jerked away physically and put his hands over his face. "I don't want to see it. I don't know anything. I don't know anything."

Claudio shot out of his scooter and stood ramrod straight, quivering with anger, in front of Salvy. He still didn't look him in the eye — the sheriff stood six-foot-four — but what he lacked in height he made up for in anger. "This has nothing to do with us," he said. "We did not come out here to be interrogated by the local fuzz like common scofflaws. Henry! Wait for me in the car."

Henry looked uncertainly between his father and the sheriff.

"Is my son under arrest?" Claudio demanded.

"No," Salvy admitted reluctantly.

"Go to the car, Henry. Do as you're told."

Henry rose and headed for the exit. At the threshold he stopped and turned back, giving Salvy a desperate, searching look.

"I don't know who she was," he said. "I'm

sorry. I've never seen her. I'm sorry." And then he was gone.

Claudio resumed his seat and his scooter whirred to life. "If you have any further questions, you can address them to my lawyer," he said and drove off after his son.

"Well," Salvy said when he was gone. "That was something."

"Did he really call you the fuzz?" Death asked.

"He did. And in the same sentence with 'scofflaw,' no less."

"What now?" Edgar asked.

"Well, I think it's pretty clear that Henry knows something," Salvy said.

"I'm pretty sure I know what it is, too," Death said. "But me knowing it doesn't help without proof, or an admission on Henry Bender's part — that's the only thing I can think of that might give us a chance of finding out what happened to Ingrid Larsen."

"He'd talk if you could push him on it," Edgar said. "You'd have to get him away from his father or shock him into blurting it out."

Salvy sighed. "I'm open to ideas. Gentlemen?"

Death cocked his head to the side. He could hear Wren's voice over a loudspeaker from the depths of the building, not clear enough to make out the words but just definite enough to reassure him she was there.

"Even crazy ideas?" he asked.

"How crazy?"

"Well, it was Randy's . . ."

Sunday night was cold and clear. Trees rustled as Wren passed in the darkness. Dew glittered in the light from her cell phone and a light mist rose out of the hollow. Wings shushed softly overhead and an owl spoke in passing.

The pocket on her dress was anachronistic, but she needed a place to carry her phone. The night, under the trees, was pitch black and eerie, especially when she passed the place on the trail where Bob — or Trevor — had lain dead for so many seasons. At the edge of the woods she paused to rearrange her garments, and then she stepped out onto the lakeshore.

A waxing gibbous moon rose over the water and cast its reflection toward her in wind-driven ripples. On the opposite shore, way off in the distance, she could see a handful of yard lights like a scattering of low-lying stars. They were still waiting for rain, and the remains of the old highway had risen above the surface of the lake. It made a ragged, narrow black spear tracing across the silver water.

Wren wore a long white shift and a dark blue overdress. A braided blonde wig hid her red hair. A veil on a flowered circlet topped off the costume. Randy had suggested bloodstains made of red ink or colored syrup. Death had vetoed that, and instead had sprayed her lightly, just in patches, with light blue fluorescent paint.

Across the water she could see flames rising from the Vikings' bonfire and hear ancient music and voices raised in song.

Her cell phone shivered in her pocket. She took it out and read the text message from Death: *Benders are here. Go when ready.*

Stowing it again, she took a deep breath and walked along the dead, frozen grass to the point where the road began.

It was cold. Wren wore sweats beneath her costume and kept her hands inside her sleeves. There was ice on the worn surface of the road and a thin glaze of it floating in shards on top of the lake. The berm surrounding the roadway had eroded badly and the road itself was almost gone in places. She paced it carefully, watching where she placed each step. The lake opened out on either side, surrounding her and isolating her.

She felt like she was walking on water. She felt that if she looked down, she'd sink.

Near the middle she came to a place where the path across the water was barely wider than the width of her shoe. Black wavelets floating with slush lapped at the edges and reached for her feet, and the lake around her seemed bottomless. Stars reflected off the waves.

The entire distance, from one shore to the other, was slightly less than the length of a football field. She was about two thirds of the way when her vantage point shifted and she could see the longboat, tied up at the primitive dock. A path led from the boat to the village and a dark figure was walking along that path, head down.

If all was going according to plan, that figure should be Henry Bender, walking toward the boat to retrieve a cloak. One of the young girls who'd been playing the pipes the night before — who also happened to be Jacob Larsen's daughter — was supposed to ask Henry to get it for her.

When asked about the body in the woods, Henry had told Salvy that he didn't know who "she" was. For whatever reason, he obviously thought they'd found Ingrid. The idea behind Wren playing ghost was simply to shock him into admitting to whatever part he'd played in the events of that long-ago day.

Wren hurried her step, getting closer. Wanting to see Henry's face when he turned and saw her. She watched him climb aboard the long-boat, a moving shadow in the night. He stooped, came up with a drape of dark fabric over his arm, and moved to return to the gathering.

She knew the instant he spotted her. He froze, one foot in the boat and one on the dock, and his face was whiter than her skirts. She came closer, but not too close. Not enough for him to see her as she really was. Light from the fluorescent paint shimmered along her arm and up the side of her skirts and danced along her blonde braids.

Henry made a sound deep in his throat, like a wounded animal moaning in distress.

"Oh, no," he whispered. "No. Oh, please, God. No. Oh, no."

Wren made her voice as thin and ghostly as she could. "Henry!" she called. "Henry, why?"

Given his habit of hiding his face and his willingness to flee from the sheriff, she was expecting him to collapse, or to break and run.

Henry threw the girl's cloak aside and drew a long sword.

Wren froze. "Uh oh."

He staggered toward her, waving the weapon in front of himself unsteadily. "Undead spirit, still you haunt me. I'm sorry. I'm sorry! But you have to stay dead!"

Wren turned and fled back the way she'd come. With an anguished bellow, Henry charged after her.

The dark sliver of roadway was slick and treacherous beneath her feet. She stumbled and skittered over the frozen potholes, hoping against hope that she wouldn't turn an ankle or fall in the icy lake. She was young and healthy and athletic, and Henry was middle-aged and out of shape, but he ran with a madness upon him.

He was less than ten yards behind her. She could hear his footsteps pounding on the wet asphalt and his ragged, heaving breaths.

Shouting trailed after them. There had been quite a few people watching their encounter, hidden in the boathouse and within the shadow of the dark trees. Both of the Bogart brothers were there, and Neils and Jacob Larsen and Salvy and Orlando Jackson.

They were all giving chase now, but none were close enough to intervene in this bizarre and deadly footrace.

Wren reached the opposite shore and left the roadway, heading for the shelter of the woods. Her foot slipped on the wet grass and she went down to one knee.

Henry's sword sliced past, just missing her head, and plunged into the ground beside her hand. Wren swore and dragged herself up, gathered her skirts, and dove down the game trail and into the ravine where Trevor Burt had died.

It was dark under the trees. As dark as if someone had spilled India ink over the world. The phosphorescent paint on her costume shimmered, looking more ghostly than ever, like random streaks of glowing ectoplasm. Henry saw them and ran toward her, then tripped and fell hard.

Wren splashed across the creek, put herself behind a tree, and called out to him.

"Henry! What did you do? You know my secrets. What did you do?"

"It wasn't my fault!" He was sobbing. She could hear it in his voice, and when a stray moonbeam found its way through the branches, his face shone with tears. "You should have kept your mouth shut. You should have minded your own business. It wasn't my fault."

He tracked her to the tree she was hiding behind. She could hear the others drawing closer, the sheriff shouting for him to halt and drop his weapon. Henry wasn't listening. Perhaps he wasn't even really there, in the present, but rather was back on that July day in 1978.

Wren backed away, trying to put distance between them, and her foot caught on a vine. She fell back hard and suddenly Henry was right there, standing over her, raising his sword in both hands with the tip of the blade pointed straight down. If he brought his arms down, he'd stab her through the heart.

"I'm sorry, but you have to stay dead," he said.

"Oh, God," Wren breathed. She knew now why wild rabbits would freeze in the face of danger. Staring up at her own mortality, she couldn't move.

The winter-bare branches rustled above her head, and then Death was there. He'd found her, but he'd come in at an angle that put him too far away to stop Henry. He simply threw himself on top of Wren, putting his own body between her and the deadly blade. As soon as he did, the paralysis of fear gave way to panic. Wren fought him, desperate to roll him out of the way. He was holding her down, as determined to save her as she was to protect him.

She had a sense of movement in the darkness, a swish of weaponry cutting through the trees, and then there came the ring of metal on metal.

Another figure had joined them on the creekbank. The night hid its identity, but whoever it was was also armed with a sword and was swinging it at Henry Bender with the abandonment of fury.

The newcomer attacked Henry, slashing at him again and again. Bender countered the attacks, but the force of the blows drove him back. There was shouting all around them now. Wren could hear Salvy and Orlando Jackson ordering the combatants to stop, and Randy, with an air of desperation, calling out for his brother and for her.

As the battle moved a little ways away, Wren relaxed and cradled Death in her arms. He must have run all the way, and he was gasping for air.

"Who is that?" she whispered.

He lifted his shoulders a little.

"You bastard!" The second fighter was a man, but his voice was a low growl, so thick with fury that Wren couldn't immediately identify it. "You lowly, sniveling, cowardly little bastard. What did you do to my sister, you son of a bitch?"

"It's Jacob Larsen," Wren said, surprised.

"Jacob! Don't kill him! He has to tell us what he knows."

Jacob swung his blade again and again Henry countered the move.

"My sister's blood is crying out for vengeance!"

There was a quick, sharp flash of blue-white light and an electric buzzing sound. Henry froze suddenly and started to shake. Violent shivers ran through him from head to toe. He dropped his sword, fell to the ground, and lay there twitching.

Jacob lowered his own weapon in shock. "Thor?" he breathed. "Did he get struck by lightning?"

Orlando Jackson stepped around the nearest tree. "Not exactly. I tasered his ass."

". . . And then I caught Death and Wren making out in the woods."

"Henry was chasing me with a sword," Wren protested. "Death saved my life!"

"Maybe," Randy said. "But I'm the one telling this story and in my version, I caught you making out in the woods."

Wren's dad had turned up in Salvy's boat. Apparently he'd been waiting just around the point in case they needed him. He was ferrying them back across the lake to the Viking settlement, and Randy was catching him up on what had happened while they were out of his sight.

Edgar pulled up to the Viking's dock and Randy jumped out and tied up the boat. He helped Wren out and they both tried to help Death, even though he scowled at them and slapped at their hands.

Henry was moving on his own again, though still a little shaky from the Taser. He was cuffed, with his hands behind his back, and Salvy and Orly lifted him bodily to the solid wooden dock. Edgar and Jacob joined them and they moved toward the shore.

"It's damned cold out here," Salvy said. "Let's take this party up to the fire."

When they entered the circle of firelight, everyone there stood to meet them except for Claudio Bender. He was sitting in a clear space, in an elaborate, wheeled wooden chair that was decorated like a throne. The officers lowered Henry to a seat on the nearest bench. He had his eyes closed tight and was mumbling under his breath.

Wren went to kneel in front of him, Death at her side.

"I'm not Ingrid. Okay? You can look at me. It's all right. My name is Wren. I'm not Ingrid. I'm just wearing a costume."

"Sheriff, this is an outrage," Claudio seethed. "My lawyers —"

"Right now your son is in custody for assault with a deadly weapon," the sheriff said. "I've read him his rights under the Miranda act, but I haven't formally charged him yet. If you'd rather wait until it's official, I'm sure I can come up with a lot more counts to add to the tally." Salvy cut a look at Claudio. "If I get a search warrant for your properties, how many stolen items will I find?"

Claudio huffed indignantly. "Do you *know* who I am?"

"Someone whose arrest would make front page news?" Death guessed. He grinned. "Your cousin wants his painting back, by the way. The girl you told to put the envelopes in the lab techs' lockers can identify your son."

The old man deflated. "You're raving mad," he whispered, sinking back into his seat.

"Maybe. Just shut up now." Death turned back to Henry. "Do you want to tell us what happened?"

Henry moved his mouth but no sound came out. In that instant he looked older than his father.

"How about this," Death suggested. "How about I tell you what I know and you can fill in the blanks for me. Will that work?"

Henry hesitated, then nodded reluctantly.

"Okay," Death said. "I figure it went like this . . ."

Twenty-One

"It was the summer of 1978," Death said, "and you were twenty years old. You'd been going to a prestigious private university, but you got caught trying to smuggle a rare book out of the special collections room at the library. They didn't prosecute but you got expelled." One of Neils Larsen's colleagues had known this part of the story. "You also got kicked out of your fraternity and barred for life." He regarded the shivering man with sympathy. "That must have been difficult for you."

Henry laughed bitterly. When he finally spoke, his voice was thin and whispery. "At the time, I thought it was the end of my life."

"You still had a good chance at getting accepted at another college, but you needed to make up your lost course credits, so you moved back home and enrolled in summer classes at the University of Cincinnati. In late July, your father came down here to meet with a group of University of Missouri faculty members about a potential archaeological dig in Belgium. But you had classes, so you stayed back in Southgate. Right?"

Henry nodded. A log popped on the fire. The crowd around them was silent, hanging on his every word. Wren, sitting next to him, smelled like shampoo and spray paint.

"But it wasn't all bad," Death continued. "That last weekend a traveling Renaissance festival came to town. It must have sounded like fun. You went on Saturday. Did Trevor go with you?"

"Yes." The word was barely audible.

"Did you dress up for it?"

Henry nodded again.

"As a Viking, right? But you had something extra as part of your costume. Something you weren't supposed to have."

"It was only eleventh century," Henry said, voice hoarse. "Barely even in the Viking era. They weren't even certain it was authentic. One of the professors thought it was a sixteenth-century reproduction."

"What was it?" This was the one thing Death hadn't been able to figure out.

"A dagger. Just a dagger. Probably part of a dowry."

"A dagger. Right. A dagger that belonged

in the Museum of Art and Archaeology at the University of Missouri. Yes?"

Henry studied the backs of his hands. "I know."

"So you're walking around the faire, you and Trevor — he had problems of his own, didn't he?"

"Yeah. A woman said . . . something."

"She said he tried to rape her."

"Yeah. She said that. I wasn't there."

"But you bailed him out."

"He was my friend."

Death exchanged a glance with Salvy. "Weren't you worried then that he'd jump bail and leave you out that money?"

Henry shrugged. "I have lots of money."

"But only one friend?"

He hesitated for a long minute, then nodded once, reluctantly. "Yeah."

"So you went to the faire. And there was a girl there. A pretty girl?"

Henry stared into the fire but his eyes were distant and Death knew that, whatever he was seeing, it wasn't the flames. "Yes," he whispered. "She was. She really was."

"And she was dressed as a Viking too. So you went over to talk to her. Maybe try to impress her a little? Were you wearing the dagger where she could see it? Or did you show it to her?"

"I showed it to her," Henry said. "God help us all. I showed her the damned thing."

"And that's where it all fell apart. Because Ingrid Larsen had spent the previous year doing volunteer work with the Museum of Art and Archaeology. And she loved everything about Vikings, too. I'll bet she knew every single Viking artifact in that museum."

"She helped restore the handle," Henry said. "She recognized it right away. And she knew who I was."

"Did she threaten to expose you?"

"She was so angry. She acted like I'd stolen it from her. It was all we could do to keep her from screaming it out right there in the middle of the faire."

"So you decided to ask your father for advice."

Henry nodded again, a jerky, reluctant motion

"How did you convince her to come with you to Missouri?"

He fiddled with the hem of his cloak. "Trevor helped," he said. "Trevor made her. I gave him money so he could run away and start a new life somewhere and he said he'd help me first."

"Did he threaten her?" Salvy asked.

"Yes. With the dagger. We walked out of the gate together and got in my car and drove to the airport. I didn't ever mean to hurt her," he said. "I only wanted to ask my dad what to do. I thought maybe we could say she stole it. We talked about that in the plane. People would have believed it if we said it. It would've been just her word against the two of us. And I'm Henry Bender and she was just a girl."

"Really?" Death quietly reached over and put a hand on Wren's knee, grounding her in case she started feeling stabby. He didn't *think* she was carrying a weapon, but with Wren he could never be sure.

"And I thought maybe we could promise not to say anything. Let her return the dagger, but talk to the museum director and arrange it so she didn't get in trouble. And then maybe she'd be grateful and —" Henry broke off.

"And she'd like you?" Wren asked, her voice dry.

"Yeah . . ."

"Okay," Death said. "So you flew down here in your dad's private jet. What did you do when you got to the airport?"

"Trevor went and got a car. I don't know where he got it. I waited with her. I found out later the car was stolen, but I didn't know that at the time."

"Right. And then the three of you headed

for the yacht club — sorry! Supper club. In a stolen car?"

Henry nodded.

Death looked around, taking in the rest of his audience for the first time. "The most direct route here from the airport was over the highway from the north," he explained. He turned his attention back to Henry. "It must have been a shock finding out you couldn't go that way anymore. But the water, it wasn't completely over the road yet, was it? Too high to drive, maybe. But you could still walk it."

"Trevor wanted me to drive right through it. I was afraid we'd float off the road and turn over and drown."

"You parked in the driveway of an abandoned house and left Ingrid with Trevor while you walked over to ask your father what to do about the girl you kidnapped."

"I didn't kidnap her," he objected. "I just brought her here without asking her first. And it was Trevor's idea. He offered to watch her."

"I'll bet he did."

"And it didn't occur to you that it might be a bad idea to leave a young girl alone with a rapist?" Wren demanded.

"He hadn't been convicted," Henry said. "I didn't think he'd do anything. I didn't expect to be gone that long."

"And then what happened?" Death asked. "How long were you at the club? Were you out on the boat with your father and Mr. Larsen when Mr. Larsen saw Ingrid on the shore?"

"They were just getting ready to go out when I got there. Father said to come with them. He didn't have time to talk to me right then."

"Obviously," Claudio said, "I would have made time if I'd understood what the issue was."

"So you're out on the boat and Mr. Larsen sees someone in a Viking costume. Then what happened?"

"Then my idiot son practically passed out," Claudio said. "It was apparent to me that this had something to do with him, so I sent him ashore to go take care of it."

"And what did you do?" Death asked Henry.

Henry shrugged. "I went back to the car."

"Did you cut through the trees or follow the road?"

The younger Bender frowned at him, perplexed. "I followed the road. Why would I go into the woods? There are bugs in the woods. And snakes and bobcats and things."

"Right. Okay, so you went back to the car.

And what did you find?"

Henry turned his attention back into the fire, gazing into it like a seer gazes into a crystal ball. "Nothing. They were gone. Only the dagger. And so much blood . . ."

"Did you look for her?" Neils Larsen asked, voice hard. "Did you follow them?"

"No! I didn't want to find her. I didn't want to see her like that."

Claudio spoke again. "We figured, if she was alive, she'd turn up. If he'd killed her, there was no point looking. It was nothing to do with us, after all."

"Nothing to do with you? Nothing to do with you?" Jacob Larsen spun and reached for his sword again, and it took Edgar and Jackson both to hold him back. "It had everything to do with you. You and your son were responsible for this, you miserable, crawling, filthy lowlife."

Death waited a beat, giving everyone a moment to calm down. "And you never heard from Trevor again?" he asked.

"No. I told you. I'd given him money to start a new life."

"Right. Was Ingrid there when you gave that to him?"

Henry shrugged. "Well, yes. It was when we were on the plane."

"And we're talking about cash, right?"

"Sure."

Death nodded once, decisively, and looked to Salvy. "You got that picture, Sheriff?"

Salvy took a folded sheet of paper from his breast pocket and passed it to Death. Death held it up in front of Henry, who looked away.

"Look at this," Death said. "This is a facial reconstruction of the body they found in the woods." He let a hint of the old gunnery sergeant creep into his voice. "Look at it."

Henry raised his head slowly and opened his eyes. He stared and blinked.

"But that . . . that's . . ."

"Not Ingrid. No. It's Trevor, isn't it?"

"Yes. I mean, it could — I mean . . . I don't understand."

"Trevor Burt wasn't the first man who'd thought Ingrid Larsen would be an easy mark. She was assaulted at a party the winter before and got away by punching the football player in the throat. Trevor didn't kill her. She got the dagger away from him, and she stabbed him with it in self-defense."

"Why didn't she come to me," Neils asked, anguished. "I was her father. I was right there."

"I don't think she ever saw you on the boat," Death said. "You didn't see her

365

clearly enough to recognize her, after all. You didn't even think it might be her until you found out she was missing. And she was probably in shock. Traumatized. When she'd punched the football player, everyone blamed her for it. She'd knifed Trevor. She must have been expecting everyone to blame her again. She ran to the lakeshore and there was Henry Bender, on a boat, asking his father to help him frame her for theft."

"But what happened to her?" Maggie Larsen demanded. "Where is she now? Are you saying she's still alive?"

Death hesitated and took a deep breath, choosing his words carefully. He couldn't even imagine how it must feel to be in the Larsens' shoes right now. "I don't know," he said. "I can tell you what I think happened. I think she stabbed Trevor in self defense and ran, but when she saw Henry and his father she panicked and hid, probably until nightfall. She sneaked into the loft of the boathouse, for shelter maybe? And while she was up there she found some boxes of T-shirts, so she changed clothes and hid the bloody costume. Would she have had shorts or something on under the dress?"

"Yes," her mother said. "She wasn't supposed to, but the faire organizers made an exception for her. She was insecure after what had happened with the football player. She wore blue jean shorts with a heavy belt. It gave her peace of mind."

Death nodded thoughtfully. "Okay, so she changed clothes and snuck away. She'd have gone back the way she came because it was the only road she knew. Only, unlike Henry, she'd have gone through the woods and tried to stay hidden. When she went across the creek, she must have found Trevor's body. He'd chased her when she ran, but he only got that far before passing out from blood loss. He was probably long dead by then. She knew he had money, and she was desperate. She thought she was going to be accused of murder. She didn't dare go home again. So she took the cash and disappeared."

"Disappeared where?" Jacob asked.

"That I can't tell you," Death said regretfully. "And I don't know of any way to trace her after all this time. The best advice I can give you now is to make this story known. Put it on your website, call the newspapers, have everyone you know share it on Facebook. See if you can get it televised. If she's still out there, maybe she'll hear it and contact you."

■ ■ ■ ■

"I feel like an idiot," Wren said. She was back at Arnhold and back in costume, fluorescent paint and all. She'd just been running around in the woods, reenacting the chase scene for a news crew from one of the local Springfield channels.

Randy made an elaborate show of zipping his lips and throwing away the key.

"You better really throw that key away, buster," she warned him good-naturedly.

"It's for a good cause, honey," Death said. "One of the news guys told me they expect this segment to get picked up nationally. It really is the best chance we have of helping the Larsens find Ingrid."

Neils and Maggie Larsen, with Jacob and his wife and daughters, were sitting beside the fire in their Viking costumes being interviewed by the reporter. Salvy had joined them. The eighth-century village was filled with anachronistic cameras and lighting fixtures, and a white van with the station logo on the side was just visible in the parking lot, through the trees.

"Wouldn't it be wonderful if we could find her before Thanksgiving so she could spend the holiday with her family?" Wren asked.

"You mean tomorrow?" Death asked.

"Don't be silly. Thanksgiving isn't . . ." Wren froze. "Oh my God! It is tomorrow! I haven't even done any shopping yet."

"Don't worry. I went last Wednesday. I think I've got everything covered. If I've missed anything, we can stop and pick it up on the way home."

"Are you crazy? Have you ever been in a grocery store the night before Thanksgiving?"

"That bad?"

"Yeah!"

"Okay. We'll send Randy then."

A young production assistant came over and interrupted them. "Mr. Bogart? They'd like you to join them now, if you would."

"Which Mr. Bogart?" Randy asked. "The handsome one or my brother?"

The PA just smiled at him and shook her head and Death got up and followed her around the fire pit, drying the palms of his hands on his jeans as he walked.

Wren looked around. "Where did Cam go?"

Cameron Michaels had been the first one interviewed, to give the news team the background story about Ingrid's disappearance and the ghost story that had grown from it. Now he was nowhere in sight.

"He wouldn't leave," she added. "Surely?"

"He was checking out one of the cameramen," Randy said. "Maybe they slipped off somewhere together."

"No. The cameraman's right over there."

"Huh. I don't know, then."

The person calling the shots (Wren wasn't sure if she was called a director or something else) signaled for the cameras to roll and the reporter introduced Death. Wren and Randy fell silent, watching the interview. The newsman asked Death a few questions about himself and how he became a private investigator and reminded viewers that this wasn't the first time Death Bogart had made the news in his new profession. Then he got down to Ingrid Larsen's missing person case.

"There are so many different aspects to this case. How in the world did you figure it all out?"

"You know, I don't really know," Death said. "I guess it's like a jigsaw puzzle. Once you get a good look at the shape of the pieces you can get a feel for where they go. The more pieces that slip into place, the better idea you get of what the picture looks like. And the more you can see of the picture, the easier it is to make the pieces fit."

"And you believe she ran away because she was afraid she would be accused of murder?"

"That's our theory, yes."

"But she wouldn't be prosecuted for that if she returned now, is that right?" The reporter directed that question back at Salvy.

The sheriff shifted on the hard bench and leaned forward. "That's correct. We do believe that she killed Burt in self-defense. Even if we felt otherwise, though, we have Henry Bender's testimony that she was kidnapped from the faire in Cincinnati and brought here against her will. And we know that she was left alone with Trevor Burt, who had already run to avoid facing a rape charge. There were no witnesses to what happened and the physical evidence is inconclusive. It would be impossible to prosecute her and have any chance of proving beyond a shadow of a doubt that it was anything but self-defense. And frankly, prosecuting someone without a compelling case is nothing but a waste of taxpayers' money."

"So what you're saying," the reporter said, "is that if Ingrid is out there somewhere listening, it's safe for her to contact her family?"

"It is," Salvy said. "And I told her as much this morning."

"Wait. He what?" Wren said.

Death and the Larsens were staring at the sheriff in disbelief. Salvy just grinned his most mischievous grin. The reporter turned to the camera.

"What the Larsens and Death Bogart don't know is that the woman who was born Ingrid Larsen saw a news story about this on the internet Monday night. She called the sheriff's office yesterday and arranged to turn herself in. She arrived late last night and shared her story with the sheriff, and with us, before we came out here today."

After a dramatic pause, the reporter resumed the tale while everyone gaped at him. "After stumbling across Burt's body in the woods, Ingrid Larsen took the cash she'd seen Henry Bender give him and ran away, afraid of the consequences if she were found. She obtained a birth certificate for a child who was killed in a tornado in the mid-sixties, assumed that name, and built a life for herself in Minnesota. She went to college, got a teaching certificate, and taught high school history for nearly thirty years. She's married, with one daughter, two sons, and three grandchildren."

The reporter then returned his attention

to the Larsens. "Do you want to see her? She thought you might not, after what happened."

Neils was overcome, tears streaming down his face, unable to speak. Maggie nearly tackled the newsman, grasping his lapels in her fists and glaring up into his face.

"Of course we want to see her! She's my baby! Where is she?"

He smiled at her and turned her shoulders so she was facing the Mead Hall. One of the assistants standing near Wren and Randy clicked a button on a walkie-talkie. The door swung open and Cameron came out, holding the door for a thin, fair-haired woman in a white shift, blue overdress, and long brown cloak.

Ingrid looked a lot like a younger version of her mom. She wasn't a large woman, but she walked with her spine straight and her head held high. A sound technician was pacing beside her, holding a microphone over her head just out of camera range.

A few feet from where her family waited she stopped, swallowing hard.

"Hi," she said. Her voice was shaking and the word came out as little more than a whisper.

Neils moved suddenly, like a statue come to life. He crossed to her in three steps and pulled her into his arms for a fierce hug. Maggie ran after him and wrapped her arms around both of them, and Jacob circled them and joined the group, kissing the top of his sister's head.

Death shot Wren a delighted, little-boy look. She grinned back and wiped a tear from the corner of her eye.

"You know, they could pull back all the cameras and stuff and give them a little privacy," she said.

"I don't think they even care," Randy said.

"I'm sorry," Ingrid was sobbing. "I know you were worried. I didn't know what else to do. I'm so sorry!"

"It's okay," Neils said. "There, there. It's okay. It wasn't your fault. None of this was ever your fault. It was Trevor Burt and those miserable Benders. They're the only ones responsible for this."

"And they'd have gotten away with it, too," Randy told Wren, "if it weren't for us meddling kids."

EPILOGUE

"I like that outfit," Randy said. "Get Death a Viking warrior costume and you guys can wear them for your engagement pictures."

"That's a terrible idea," Death said.

"Oh, no. Oh, no. You went full Scooby. You don't get to make fun of my ideas any more."

"I'm your big brother," Death told him. "I will *always* make fun of your ideas."

They were back at Wren's house. Thanksgiving had snuck up on them while they were occupied with other things. Wren and her parents were in the kitchen, all three of them cooking, and Death and Randy were in the living room searching through already-packed boxes for things Wren and her mother had forgotten to unpack when they were preparing for this meal.

"Here's a salt shaker," Randy said. "But it's a clown. And creepy. Why does your fiancée have a creepy clown salt shaker?"

"I don't know. And I'm afraid to ask."

Wren stuck her head through the doorway. "I need a skillet! Find me a skillet! I forgot to get a skillet for the gravy."

"No, I've got a skillet here," her mother said.

"Oh. Never mind!"

Death had spent the night on the sofa so he'd be there early and Randy had come over as soon as he got off shift. Death had helped Emily slide the turkey into the oven at four a.m., and there were four kinds of pie cooling on the kitchen windowsills and homemade candy in bowls and pans on the coffee table.

Edgar came into the room. "You finding any dishes or shall we eat it right off the table?"

"How fancy do we want to be?" Death asked. "I've got dinner plates, and bread plates but they don't match, and I haven't found enough bowls for everyone. Randy's got the silverware, though, and there are glasses. Again, they don't match though."

"We're not going to eat the plates," Edgar said. "Bring what you've got and let's get this show on the road."

Death and Randy set the table and the others busied themselves ferrying food in from the kitchen.

"What's going to happen to the Benders?" Emily asked while they worked.

"The Benders are weird," Wren said emphatically. "Claudio bought the supper club back at the auction. Did you know that? We didn't know it the day of the sale, but the guy who had the winning bid was an agent for Bender. And then, on Tuesday, he suddenly just up and signed it over to the Vikings. He said it was so they could use the extra land for educational purposes. I gather he told one of the reenactors — but not Mr. Larsen. The Larsens aren't on speaking terms with the Benders. I think Claudio said that he wanted to write the money off on his taxes."

Emily stirred her gravy, then turned to look into the dining room. "Do you think he did it because he felt guilty?"

Death laughed. "I think he did it because Frank Appelbaum made him. Claudio had Appelbaum's great-great-grandmother's painting, remember. The Ring Portrait? He returned it, reluctantly. He's claiming it was only a prank and that he was just testing the museum's security. Appelbaum and Warner reached an agreement with him not to prosecute him for stealing it. Or rather, for arranging to have it stolen. I don't know the specifics, but I told them the whole story about Ingrid, and Bender turned the supper club over to the Vikings the next day."

"Well, good for them if they made him do it, then," Emily said.

"What about Bob?" Randy asked. "Are you going to leave him buried in your rosebushes?"

"I don't know," Wren said, cutting a sideways glance at Death. "Are we? You know, I'm kind of sad that Bob turned out to be a creep."

"Well, he died a pretty awful death," Death pointed out. "Probably a better fate for a creep than a nice guy."

"Yeah. But now we have a creep in our roses."

"Does he have family?" Edgar asked.

"Not that we can find. No one who wants to claim him, anyway."

"Then I'd leave him where he is. He's not hurting anyone there, and it makes for an interesting story. Besides, if you have him dug up and moved somewhere, it'd be hard on the roses."

"That's a point," Wren agreed. "I hadn't thought of that. They really are beautiful flowers."

"So what are you going to do now that your case is solved?" Edgar asked Death.

"Find another one. But right now I have a

move to make happen and a wedding to help plan."

They seated themselves around the table, just the five of them, and all hesitated uncertainly.

"We've never been a very religious family," Emily said. "If one of you would like to say grace, though, that would be fine."

"Maybe we could each just say what we're thankful for," Wren suggested.

"Would it be too shallow of me to say I'm thankful for pie?" Randy asked.

"Yes," Death told him. "Come on, Baranduin. Try a little harder."

"Okay, fine. I'm thankful that my brother, Death Dunadin, has a name that's just as weird as mine." Death glared at him. Randy grinned, then sobered, picked up his tea, and held it up for a toast. "And, if we're going to be serious for a minute, I think that Death and Wren and I can all be thankful just to be alive."

"After the year we've had," Wren said, "ain't that the truth?"

They clinked their glasses.

"I'm thankful for my truck," Edgar said.

"You're supposed to be thankful for your family," Emily admonished him.

"Everybody always says they're thankful for their family," Edgar objected. "I want to be thankful for my truck."

"Well, I'm thankful for my grandchildren." Emily smiled.

"You have grandchildren, Mrs. M?" Randy asked.

"Not yet," she said, with a pointed look at Death and Wren. "I'm being thankful in advance."

"Right," Wren muttered. "No pressure."

"What about you, Wren?" Randy prompted.

"I'm thankful for the Marine Corps never leaving anyone behind," she said. "And I'm thankful for Madeline making horrible choices. And I'm thankful we found Randy when we did. And I'm thankful for our pretty new house." She looked around and faltered and her eyes filled with tears.

"What's wrong, sweetheart?" Death asked gently.

"Oh, it's nothing. It's just . . . I'm happy we're moving. I really am. Only I just realized this is the last Thanksgiving I'll spend here."

"You can be happy and sad at the same time," Death told her. "It's okay."

"I know." Wren gave him a watery smile. "What about you? What are you thankful for?"

"Edgar's truck," he said. "And this family.

You know, the last time Randy and I had a family to sit down to Thanksgiving dinner with — not friends, but a family we were actually a part of — it was way back in my senior year of high school. The next year I was stationed overseas, and by the time I got out our parents and grandparents and great-grandmother had all passed away. This time last year, I thought Randy was dead. And I was homeless and penniless and living in my car. I look around and see how much my life has changed and it amazes me every day. I never thought it could be this good again."

Wren jumped up, circled the table, and hugged him.

"Now, now," her father said. "No hanky-panky at the dinner table."

"Mrs. M did say she wanted grandkids," Randy pointed out.

"After the wedding," Emily said. "Nothing ruins a white dress like the bride's water breaking." She slid the turkey over to Death. "Here, dear. Do you want to carve?"

"I would be honored." Death stood, looked around the table, and hesitated.

"What is it?" Wren asked.

He shrugged. "I suppose all the knives are packed?"

ABOUT THE AUTHOR

Loretta Ross is a writer and historian who lives and works in rural Missouri. She is an alumna of Cottey College and holds a BA in archaeology from the University of Missouri–Columbia. She has loved mysteries since she first learned to read. *Death & the Viking's Daughter* is the fourth novel in her Auction Block Mystery series.